LIFE AFTER DEATH

LIFE AFTER DEATH

Dorothea Wallis

The Book Guild Ltd
Sussex, England

BARNSLEY METROPOLITAN BOROUGH COUNCIL	
380590032858 1	
Askews	
AF	£16.95
1857765907	M

First published in Great Britain in 2001 by
The Book Guild Ltd
25 High Street,
Lewes, Sussex
BN7 2LU

Copyright © Dorothea Wallis 2001

The right of Dorothea Wallis to be identified as the author of this work has been asserted by her in accordance with the Copyright, Designs and Patents Act 1988.

All rights reserved. No part of this publication may be reproduced, transmitted, or stored in a retrieval system, in any form or by any means, without permission in writing from the publisher, nor be otherwise circulated in any form of binding or cover other than that in which it is published and without a similar condition being imposed on the subsequent purchaser.

All characters and institutions in this publication are fictitious and any resemblance to real people, alive or dead, is purely coincidental.

Typesetting in Baskerville by
SetSystems Ltd, Saffron Walden, Essex

Printed in Great Britain by
Antony Rowe Ltd, Chippenham, Wiltshire

A catalogue record for this book is available from
The British Library

ISBN 1 85776 590 7

I thank my husband, John,
for all his help
and Sasha McGlashan
for her encouragement.

PART 1

Chapter 1

Therese was standing in her small living room, motionless but with every muscle and sense alert to a precious silence that no move or sound from her must break. No heavenly choir could have been as desirable as that silence. But then it also opened a vista of endless anxieties. They were the price she was presumably willing to pay for that immediate and overriding satisfaction that the present silence meant to her. Yes, she would give anything, perhaps had already given everything for that. It seemed the one and only thing she needed; the one thing her body and spirit had clamoured for so long, and eventually so desperately, that she had been driven to gain it. She had had no more choice in the matter. She had been driven by those 'presences' within her, of whom she never knew who or what they were. They were not her and yet must be hers. She and they seemed apart, yet somehow belonging to each other. Every attempt to evade them increased their power to rend her heart and mind. It seemed to her that this silence should mean the achievement of what they had wanted. They had felt like a small crowd behind her, whose plight she had no longer been able to ignore.

She had had to act; she had had to silence Horace in order to silence their constant cries for attention and protest because everything he demanded of her meant denial of them. She had been in the middle between the man who had never doubted his exclusive claim on her and that shadowy but ever more pressing band of demanding spirits inside her. He had no idea of their existence, let alone their power. These two unceasing, conflicting claims on her had made life an endurance test. It had taken her years to question whether she could stand this indefinitely. She had taken it for granted as a fact of life. It had made her thin and edgy, always trying just to catch up, trying to keep up with someone striding ahead and complaining of her lagging behind, who didn't realise that there were other claims constantly pulling her back. He had never turned round to see if there were some reason why she could not keep up with him. It had not occurred to him. His mind was fixed on where, he said, they were aiming for.

There was less and less choice. She could no longer keep up with his expectations or even follow behind. She was bound to the inner claimants who pulled her in the opposite direction. In theory she could have just stopped, or even moved in the opposite direction. But she could not while his perpetual demand held her as by taut, unbreakable wires. Now the wires had gone slack. Her body relaxed so her own tautness was gone. Where was she? She took a deep breath. The air was hers. She rejoiced. She wanted to express her gratitude as if in the silence she had come into an empty space, her own space, for the first time. She had at last come to take it up. She wanted to raise an imaginary glass, in gratitude, to the spirit that had kept this space for her. She seemed to be coming to take up an, as yet unknown, inheritance.

She sat down feeling as if there were an extraordinary amount of space around her. The walls of the small room might have become transparent so they let into her mind the infinite space beyond. The little room was her particular point in the space that stretched into an infinite distance. She did not wish for a magic carpet by which to leave her place on the ground. She would hate to be snatched up and away because being still in this space she could appreciate it. Before, when she was always straining to keep up with Horace ahead, she felt shut out from space and any view. Now the silence seemed a promise of open space imbued with life. Neither was there any sound now from those elusive yet insistent inner presences that before had made sure she never forgot them. They had made her silence Horace apparently so that they could be better heard and have her attention. Now there was dead silence. No one was pressing, haranguing or exhorting her; neither outside nor inside. She wondered whether theirs was an expectant silence. She then had an uneasy feeling that they expected something dreadful to happen in consequence of what had been done.

She believed they were holding their breath in apprehension. Had her relief been a snare and delusion? She was often rash in her reactions; jubilant or despairing when to be pleased or disappointed would be more appropriate. But she refused to be intimidated. She moved around as if to assert her freedom that the new sense of space gave her. She raised her head, making her long hair fall back, in a gesture of confidence to face the doubts.

The anxiety in the pit of her stomach was always ready to take over and had to be banished. Perhaps it had become a habit that had to be broken, rather than being a true signal of trouble. It was like an oversensitive instrument that was activated at the slightest touch. The mere thought of something that had once been a cause for anxiety roused it, as the word 'walk' can rouse a dog even when it appears to be asleep. She tried to persuade herself that there was no place for anxiety. There was some mistake; as it might be necessary to convince the dog that there was no chance of a walk; he must have dreamt it.

Horace was gone. Had those shadowy presences inside her also gone? When she had tried to escape them they had not let her get away. They had interfered, sometimes in a diabolical way; not as a voice of conscience but as demands to which she could not attend while she must keep up with Horace. She thought of looking to see if Horace was still in the adjoining room. It was the last thing she wanted to do. The one thing she wanted was not to go after him; the great relief was to be by herself.

She had the idea of sealing the room to her right, where he had been, by putting sticky tape all round the door, as you did when you fumigated a room in which someone had died of a deadly infectious disease. Then she would open the opposite door on her left, where she felt that those who had been pressing inside her might be waiting ready to burst in and celebrate her new freedom to be with them. She imagined their happily embracing each other. But whom would she be embracing? Could they be embraced, like people? She never saw them in her mind like real people. She could not see them standing on their own legs. They were more like something rooted in her, though also having distinct personalities.

She opened that door, wishing to release these beings from banishment. She was not altogether surprised when no one rushed in. Just as well perhaps that they could not enter the room now because they needed to be known as within her. Their power and mysterious greyness brought to her mind the phrase 'éminences grises'. She did not know to whom or what that applied but it seemed to fit them, except that it suggested something more dignified than the unruly, clamorous band often shoving and pushing inside her.

Yet she still had the idea that something had to be outside to be real. She would have loved to have them coming into the room to share her happiness. They had seemed to be always behind her, out of full view and more or less in the dark. She sat down dispirited now, feeling alone in an empty house where a little while ago she had relished the empty space, full of the air of freedom. It was confusing. Was she always deluding herself with imaginings that, like beautiful soap bubbles, burst and were gone without trace? The little drop that remained on the ground was so unlike the lovely bubble that it was worse than nothing. Was that all that was real?

She could weep, she felt so bereft. There was the terrifying idea that what made life good, what gave life roundness and luminosity had no substance. She felt heartbroken and recognised the pain as one of touching an old wound, that made her want to weep and weep. Was it the dreadful experience of a child, for whom it had been almost unbearable to find that the world was not – what? Something that it had set its heart on, something in which its heart was. That was it; that was why she was weeping so bitterly now. Again she had the sense of a part of herself, not yet articulate, who bore the full intensity of the pain and who let her know that she had touched the truth. The terror was a true terror – not a crazy, groundless anxiety – of a world that has no place for your heart. In that world what you knew as 'the heart' would be just a feeling that dispersed like hot air and in which the ideas to which it gave rise burst like shimmering soap bubbles. Thank God the profound pain of her heart was living proof of its reality. The heartache was the saving grace.

Alone in the room with these powerful feelings and thoughts swirling around her like mist on a high mountain, she was in danger of losing her foothold. She was terrified and knew that she must stand firm in herself. Since the room had become hostile rather than hospitable, she simply had to stand still in herself. She must not be swept off her feet, however great the forces around her.

In the past she used to seek shelter from the forces threatening to overwhelm her in little ordinary things that persuaded her of stability and were comforting, like a nice meal or a light novel. That way she kept the superhuman, turbulent inner forces at bay, as when one shelters from the storm raging outside in a warmly lit, domestic interior. But this would not do now. She shrank from the possibility as if the devil were waiting in those tempting things. The devil waited happily in a good book as much as in a bad one. She must avoid these temptations like poison. She must stay still in herself as never before.

Others had gained power over her because she avoided being in herself. She had always been homeless because she had left the home which was herself. She had despised her proper home – herself – had been ashamed of being seen there, although drawing on its resources. She found, with a sigh of relief, that for a moment she could be still and be in herself. She seemed to have come to rest for the first time. There was no outside claim on her.

Chapter 2

When she first knew Horace he was already a keen trail finder. He was a geography student. Comparing old and new maps and finding out how the old landmarks had vanished and been replaced by the new was his special interest. When Therese first knew him she was pleased when he invited her to sit next to him at his desk, on which were laid out the maps of particular interest at the moment. Later she always remembered finding it a surprisingly small area of Shropshire countryside by which he was fascinated. She had asked him whether he came from that part of the country and when he said his family lived in Derbyshire when they were in England, she asked if they came from Shropshire originally. Absent-mindedly he just said 'No, no connection with the place but just look!' and excitedly he made her examine the differences and few similarities between the contemporary and an early nineteenth century map of the same place. She was no geographer but had some idea of guessing from a map whether an area looked interesting one way or another. Appreciating his keenness to show her what he found exciting, she was ready to see any interesting feature.

She liked him. Glad to be asked to sit next to him at the desk, she was willing to take the most hopeful view of the patch on the map that seemed to have less than average claims to fame. She felt as if she were faced with a geography exam question: 'List and describe features of interest seen in the area 5H 874 147'; a patch on the given map that looked extraordinarily featureless; almost as blank as her mind when she stared at it. But it was amazing how as barren an area as that had points of interest sprouting in it like plants if only you looked long enough. She might have taken a very long time to discover them but under Horace's eagle eye they leapt into sight.

It might have been the fecundity of his imagination that gave so much interest to the relative blank before them. The few lines on the paper perhaps activated his mind like the ink blots people are asked to interpret in a psychological test. But as she listened to what he was saying he convinced her that she was not being taken on a flight of fancy but on a walk by a guide who knew so much about this apparently nondescript area that it turned out to be full of interest. She was impressed.

Sitting on his right, her attention wandered from the map before them to Horace's face. He was so engrossed in what he was seeing and saying, he failed to notice that her eyes were on his face rather than following the pencil in his hand, pointing to places on the map. She loved his eager face then. He had clear-cut features in a lean, long face, and thick, fair hair. Sometimes he wore rimless spectacles that suited him. There was a simplicity about his total absorption that made her smile as she watched him. His unawareness of anything but the maps, the absence of even a suspicion that she might not be exclusively interested in them, was then a source of affectionate amusement. She remembered wondering what it would feel like putting her fingers through his thick hair; it was tempting. She enjoyed these little forays from the paths to which she was supposed to keep; lanes that she was to look for on the old map and fail to find on the newer. Sometimes she no longer heard his explanation.

When Horace turned to the girl to whom he was talking he didn't see her because he was still seeing in his mind the things he was talking about, but eventually a slight, unnerving sense crept in that she was looking at him and not at what he was seeing. This broke the cocoon of his absorption in his subject and made him see her. It was the first time and was a shock. It made him lose the mental connection between the nineteenth century and contemporary maps before him and he felt lost. He was about to be annoyed with her for interrupting his train of thought, when a particular look on her face, the expression of that 'affectionate amusement', undermined the annoyance. He was bewildered and suddenly had nothing to say. He found himself muttering that perhaps he had gone on too long; he hoped she was not bored. He did not really believe that anyone could be bored by what was so obviously interesting. So, as he glanced back at the map, he eagerly picked up the thread of his excursion and was off again.

She was amused by his unawareness of time too. She wondered, as yet with interest rather than impatience, for how many hours he would carry on like this. That first time she didn't mind how long she stayed. She didn't feel slighted by his lack of any thought of her comfort or discomfort after hours of his conducted tours on the maps. She said once that it would be nice to see some of what he had shown her on the map in reality. She wondered if he ever went out there into the countryside, where there would be much to distract him from the map. Would the wind blowing, the birds singing, the smells of plants or of cow dung, with their advantage of being alive, make the maps fall dead to the ground or at least make them lose their vital interest to Horace?

He had welcomed her suggestion, evidence of her interest, though of course any intelligent person shown what he had shown her would be interested. She was amused rather than disappointed by the fact that, unlike other men, he evidently had no thought of any personal element in her proposal. This kind of innocence seemed endearing to her. It was refreshing to be freed from the usual calculations about how much was meant by either side and what in the end a joint outing to the country would amount to. Was it bound to end in bed that day or another day?

Before she left that evening, when he looked as enlivened by their long expedition on the maps as she felt tired, he said to her enthusiastically, 'If you would like to do this in the field, see on the ground where we've been on the map today, it would be good to do it while the facts are fresh in our minds.' He looked so eager to get started that for a moment she thought he meant 'right now'. Her eyes grew bigger with alarm. He surely wasn't mad enough to suggest setting off that night! She must have become a bit mad herself after several hours of attempted concentration on this passion of his! She nodded in agreement. 'Good,' he said happily. It would not take him long to find out the public transport possibilities as his little old Fiat was temporarily out of action. There would be some local buses. It would be good to cover as much ground as possible while they were in the area.

There was no doubt in Therese's mind that he would get in touch, as there would have been with other people. She felt already engaged as a sort of assistant in his enterprise, that it alone mattered. But again she found this a relaxing change from other people's concentration on her.

He rang two days later to say that he had worked everything out but thought it would be a good idea to have a brief meeting before they set out so she would be fully informed about the particular area on which he thought they should concentrate. She said she was quite happy to trust his plans but he insisted that he would prefer to have the chance of explaining them. Slightly irritated, she said that she didn't really have time to spare in the two days before he wanted to go. Rather than postpone the expedition, he reluctantly renounced the meeting which his standard of preparation demanded. Having got her way, she could be impressed by his thoroughness and forget her irritation. It had not served as a warning. Later she wondered at her blindness to what had stared her in the face.

He had been very satisfied with the result of their research at the end of a strenuous day, mostly in very unfavourable weather. He was by no means always able to find corroboration for his theories on the ground. Often a visit to the given area of interest did not provide sufficient evidence to confirm his hypothesis about the social or economic as well as natural changes that had brought about the changes on the map. That day, he said, they had been lucky. When they sat in the pub with a drink and minimal food before them, he reiterated all the landmarks which provided plausible evidence for his speculations. She was too tired to give any considered judgement, nor did it really matter to her whether all the pieces of the jigsaw in his mind fitted together as they should. As long as he thought they did, that was good enough. Anyway, she wasn't nearly knowledgeable enough to be able to judge.

He was tired enough not to worry about whether she fully followed his account or not. He hadn't realised till now that he was tired. That made him think that she might be tired, which had never occurred to him before. He had been talking in her direction but now he looked at her, as he said uncertainly, 'Perhaps you are tired?'

She laughed. 'Am I tired? I should say I am! You must have the constitution of a horse, the way you can carry on!' but the image in her mind was of a camel. She saw him able to trek huge distances across arid areas because in his hump he carried a great store of interest, which seemed to be of his own making since she saw no sign of anything interesting outside. Today he had dispensed a bit of it to her to keep her going. Without it she would not have lasted as long as she had.

He didn't know what to do with her answer. Normally he would just go on to the next thought that flashed into his mind; he was used to being carried on by a thought always leading ahead. Now in his tiredness he was left with her answer to his unusually personal question. He felt uncomfortable and didn't know how to behave, like someone at a cocktail party who had hardly ever been to one. He quickly glanced at her questioningly and didn't know where to look when his eyes had left her. He stared at the bare table but didn't really see it and felt fidgety. He hated this position. That was why he had given up student social activities, saying they were a waste of time.

He should stick to his work. He couldn't cope with people. He felt angry at being caught out now. They were in a small, rather mean-looking pub with no other people at the tables to distract attention. He felt vaguely guilty; if he were to blame for her tiredness, what was he to do now to make amends? He felt as if he had got a bombshell as an answer to his tentative question. He felt as helpless as if she had suddenly fainted and he had no knowledge of first aid.

They must get out and back to base as quickly as possible. His absent-minded look made Therese think he had not heard what she had said. Having looked at his watch, he said sternly that unfortunately the connection between bus and train that he had worked out in advance in fact didn't exist. He stuck to the bare, grim facts as one does to a minimal footbridge made of one or two planks. If he let his eyes stray to either side, where there would be concern for her, he feared falling off the bridge into deep, dark water where he could not swim.

There was a bus to the station but no train for a while; it went to collect a few late workers from the town and had nothing to do with trains. They didn't speak in the bus. She hoped she might be able to sleep in the train. She nearly dropped off even in the discomfort of a narrow bus seat next to someone on whose shoulder she dared not rest. It was clear that she would not be welcome. He seemed to have become hard and stern since their drink when he had talked animatedly. He would no longer talk about the day's experience or anything else. Had she not shown enough interest or said anything that upset him? She was too tired to find any answer and silently followed when they trekked to the dreary leftover station that was no longer manned. It seemed a relic from a past age and the notice stating the evident fact that there was no longer a booking office, not to mention anything else, seemed to suggest 'You are lucky that this still counts as a station'.

The weather wasn't good enough for them to sit for more than half an hour on the platform bench. What had been a waiting room hardly qualified as such now. The small room had become a rubbish dump where presumably local youths had thrown their cans after they had had a go at pulling out the room's fixtures. They had hardly been a challenge to their strength. Plastic fittings broke easily but not neatly. There was a good part of a bench fixed to the wall with a metal bracket which they hadn't been able to shift. When Horace said that a walk round the little town would be better than waiting here, she quickly suggested that he should go on his own, seeing a chance for herself to stretch out on this bench and shut her eyes. As long as he came back in good time to wake her, she wasn't worried about being found there by anyone else. They might think that she was a drunk collapsed and sleeping it off but she didn't mind that. She sounded confident and Horace told himself that it was most unlikely that anyone would come here. He was tempted by the prospect of being released from the intense discomfort he had felt since their snack supper.

He accepted her suggestion almost enthusiastically. She was too tired to be bothered by that. The prospect of being able to lie on that bench was enough. God, I'd no idea that field work was that exhausting! I shouldn't have changed to geography for my subsidiary, she said to herself. She had decided that that would be easier to cope with than history, given her lack of preparation, but now felt that mastering facts in the comfort of a room would be preferable to field work like this. She wondered, could it be just his way? as she lay on her back and quickly fell asleep.

He was left with her exclamation 'a constitution like a horse'. The personal remark had struck him. He felt immobilised in a position from which no thought could rescue him, which was unusual for him. He could not protect himself against such remarks because although a repeated experience, they were always unpredictable. He suddenly found himself struck and banished into the dark from his light world of interesting thoughts. An iron door might have been shut on him. A remark that he could not have anticipated had the power to condemn him into this position. He had been made to feel impossible.

He knew that he could not cope with other people as others did with ease. He was not without social skills. He had no need to enlist in the communications course which several in his year had been advised to do, even graduates like himself. He had enough technique to get by as long as he kept clear of 'the personal side of life'. Contacts with people must be made carefully, rather like dealing with products labelled 'Avoid contact with skin. Keep away from eyes'. They were all right if handled carefully. He had learnt at school, at a cost, about his ineptitude at 'playing the game', which was worse than not being any good at games.

The very term 'personal relations' sent a shudder through him. He wanted only to get out of this danger area as fast as possible. Nor could intellectual curiosity lead him to look where he was running away from; he seemed to know this was not for him. It was 'just one of those things' – a phrase that at other times he despised.

Here it sidestepped conveniently the fact of being cut off from an area of life he believed to be impossible for him. It had always been like this, as far as he could remember, and it always would be as far as he was concerned. The iron door that clanged shut on him was as much made of his iron determination as by anything else. Others, on the outside, might hurt their hands banging their fists on it, rather than he on the inside, asking for it to be opened.

Therese had yet to learn this. To her he was just very tired when, at the end of their return journey, they separated at the station; she going to her digs and he to his university hostel. Not altogether a bad thing, in her view, that even a man with the constitution of a horse or a camel had his limits; he could be exhausted. But then it could not be tiredness that kept him as distant and uncommunicative as she found him at subsequent meetings, in contrast to the man who had poured out information enthusiastically whenever she had seen him before.

The first time they met after their expedition she naturally met him with a friendliness that came from their joint trip. But she met no response. She felt for a moment that she had made a mistake, as when one smiles at a person in the street, seen as someone one knows, who turns out to be a stranger. There was no such simple explanation here. It was puzzling; on the next occasion it was dismaying, and on the next she felt hurt and annoyed with him. She had done nothing to justify such behaviour, she had to assure herself, because he made her feel almost guilty.

Trying to be understanding, she eventually asked herself, was he worried about his work? He was the kind who could suddenly get depressed about it just because he was so exhilarated about it the rest of the time. 'He may not realise the connection,' she said to her friend Angela. 'His excitement about all these little landmarks or signs of the past that he finds when we're out there in the country is so great that perhaps he goes over the top and then suffers from a reaction. He's like a child finding treasure. I suppose that's just it, a perpetual treasure hunt! A nice idea if you like that sort of thing,' she added doubtfully, because now that she recalled the experience she didn't feel keen to repeat it. She wouldn't accept Angela's suggestion that she could enlighten Horace about the danger of excessive enthusiasm tipping over into depression. She doubted that he would be interested in her thought. He was too absorbed in his own.

She did not take her own thoughts very seriously. They were like flashes whose brightness was exciting for a moment. She did not trouble to investigate what had been lit up momentarily. She lacked any suspicion that if she looked, she might find something of value.

Angela said, 'Anyway, I shouldn't worry about him,' because she wasn't keen on Horace, who from his lanky height always seemed to be looking into the distance through his specs so he never saw you in front of him, or below him if you were small as she was.

Therese gave her a searching look. Was she saying that she didn't like Horace? She wasn't sure that she 'liked' him. She was intrigued by him. Certainly no one could accuse him of leading her up the garden path. She was led on by her curiosity. When she was with him she seemed to observe him with the kind of amused interest with which you observe some strange species. But she did not always want to do this.

She was busy the next week. It was all she could do to cope with her work and sometimes to go out with the others in her little group. She gave little thought to Horace. But at odd times their paths crossed. She wondered at him still looking pale and rather drawn. Hard work, she said to herself.

Chapter 3

Now these times seemed to have been innocent. She felt almost admiring of this young woman – herself as a student – when she looked at that time as if she were looking at old photographs. She admired the cool, confident attitude to Horace she seemed to have had in those days. It seemed so much better than all that followed. She admired that girl for apparently being strong. But just as she was about to regret the loss of her strength, she saw the picture quite differently. Why didn't that girl see? She was blind or dense not to see this man was mad! All very well to be intrigued by a strange species but not so good if the species is a murderer. Now, now! She pulled herself up. Who was the murderer? All right, she mustn't accuse him; after all, she was here to tell the tale, though she really couldn't tell what that was.

Then she disapproved of her past self and wanted to tell her that she had let her down. 'You weren't really interested in people, were you? You were always keen to go on to the next thing, skimming the surface of everything, not wanting to be held by anything or anybody. Did you think that was freedom?'

'I think I did,' she answered, 'in contrast to what went before.'

There had been no problem for her of getting away from home because she had never had one; only the household of her father's two sisters. They were so much older than he that they seemed more like his aunts than hers, when he was already a relatively old father; or would have been, had he lived for more than her first year. Her parents were killed together in an air crash. The aunts took their charge, the task with which fate had presented them, dead seriously. They used to talk about not betraying the trust that their brother and fate had put in them. They never ceased to honour it with utmost conscientiousness, which meant that every little move – like whether she should go to a particular children's party or whether she could go swimming – became a matter for grave consideration. It sapped her, while they seemed to thrive on it. However strong was her desire to be like other children and do what they did, the aunt's constant debates and discussions defeated her.

She saw herself wanting to run about with other children and finding she had big sandbags attached to her feet. However keen you were to run, you were forced to give up; it wasn't possible. The aunts did not stop her. Oh no, they always said they wanted her to enjoy herself but they had to make sure that whatever she did was good for her. They would be failing their responsibility if they did not keep this always at the forefront of their minds. If they stuck to this, they and she would be safe. They also stuck her down like a butterfly pinned in a glass case. If they had resented what fate and their brother had imposed on them, they had their revenge. They killed with kindness, or at least care.

Humans were tougher than the beautiful, fragile butterflies who would have been finished. She survived, but the heaviness of those years came back to her vividly. She saw and felt herself the very opposite of a butterfly, too heavy even to walk, let alone run. This chronic heaviness was linked in her mind with the rooms that seemed always carefully curtained. There was a corresponding deprivation of light and air inside her without which there could be no spontaneous life. She recalled the dreadful monotony, and feeling as if she were surrounded by fine sand which could only be shifted with an effort and prevented her from ever moving freely.

Eventually she managed to struggle out of it, to disinter and rediscover her body in ordinary, but to her extraordinary, space and air.

One aunt had had a stroke and had had to go into a nursing home which accepted that her sister, from whom she had never been separated, should accompany her. It was providential that this happened when Therese had reached the age of going to college. She had no impetus for anything, had lost the very experience of impetus, but with the school's encouragement and by a process of elimination of what she did not want to do, she had gained a place at university.

There was no sudden release as of a bird set free in the air. She became ill at the beginning of her first university term. She had been dragging herself about, trying to follow the movement of others around her and to perform as was expected of her, when she became more and more bewildered and wretched. An obscure immunological complaint was diagnosed, which gave her the time she needed to gain even a minimum sense of herself in a relatively normal environment. It was agreed that rather than returning to college halfway through the first year, she would start afresh the following academic year. There was a suggestion that she might do voluntary service or earn her way round as much of the world as she could. People didn't realise that for her to manage living in the ordinary world was equivalent to making one's way round the world for others.

By the time she came back to college she relished what she thought of as freedom: moving as and where she liked, taking up whatever happened to appeal to her – activities, books, people. She found a social manner that made her appear easy with people. It was enjoyable to feel able – like a recently hatched bird – to fly and alight wherever she fancied.

Now, looking back, she blamed her past self for flitting about and for becoming intrigued by that tall, work-enthusiast whose total unawareness of his odd self had actually endeared him to her. She realised that she had enjoyed being the more aware one. She had felt at an advantage throughout those first years. She had remained the amused observer rather than being immersed and tossed about as others were in a relationship. She could not have been more involved with Horace because most of him was absorbed in his work, except perhaps by sharing his passion for that. She did not really care for his work although she eventually took geography as one of her subsidiary subjects.

She now saw with a shock that, like a cripple who can only move in a special carriage, Horace was unable to move without his work. She had assumed she was marrying an able-bodied man. No one had told her that he couldn't walk and that this vehicle of work was also an invalid carriage. He was psychologically crippled. She was reminded of herself when she could not run like other children though there was nothing wrong with her legs; the sadness and heaviness inside disabled her. Why was such disability not acknowledged like the physical?

Why did no one tell her about Horace? She felt cheated as if someone had deliberately withheld from her the truth about this man. 'They' should have warned her that what was talked about as an enviable combination of ability and enthusiasm for his work hid a serious disability. Would 'they' have assumed she knew? She didn't. She felt like confronting them but could not think who 'they' were. Perhaps people who knew her and Horace in those early days would laugh at her and say, 'You must have been blind not to see. You have only yourself to blame.'

As Therese sat in her room lost in these thoughts, a voice far down inside her had something different to say. It came from a great depth and said what she neither expected nor wished to hear, so she did not register what it said. It told her that she had known better what she was doing than she thought. Far from not knowing the man she had married, she had chosen him precisely for what and how he was; because what she called his disability matched her own. She could no more have had a full relationship than he. The peculiarly limited relationship she had with him had been her measure. There was an unimaginably fine, internal instrument in everyone, directing their steps and infallibly matching their internal and external positions in life. That internal voice was barely heard; the glimpse of precious truth was not registered. It was easier to remain on the level of aggrieved feeling and be a victim.

After the college years she had lost her amused smile and had forgotten about it. But even when life with Horace was more and more of a strain, she had not seen that there was anything wrong with him. She had never doubted that she was the failure. She felt as if there had been a conspiracy to convince her that she was nothing that anyone could respect. She permanently bore the blame for letting down herself and everyone else. In her view Horace was always ahead in life and expecting her to follow him, which she was forever trying and failing to do. The never-ending, impossible demand made her loathe Horace. It made her want to attack him in a desperate fury.

As if she were waking from a dream, she realised that she had actually attacked him. While normally you woke up from a dream to realise with relief or disappointment that it was 'just a dream', she experienced the opposite now. What she had been thinking and feeling was not just a day-dream but was actually true. She remembered what she had actually done. She stared at herself, at the true picture of herself going at Horace with the sharpest kitchen knife. She saw his face staring at her in utter amazement. She saw him transfixed in his incomprehension of the woman he thought he knew; whom he was used to regarding as a shadowy presence always just behind him. Now she was suddenly face to face with him but with a terrifyingly distorted face. It seemed to have grown monstrously till it was so large and close that it overcame him. He had felt a sharp, shocking, totally unknown and yet instantly known as ultimate, pain in the centre of himself, that grew, like the face in front of him, to engulf him. It ended in darkness.

She stared at the images in her mind. She had come back to see what had actually happened. Where had she been? Back to college, where she could smile in that safe, observing way. She envied her detached state then. Had going back there taken a long time, to make her forget what had happened here and now? She had lost her sense of time. She had no idea how long she had been sitting in this room. It was worrying not knowing whether hours or days had passed. Since what? She felt like someone having a dizzy spell who loses his sense of direction. Her sense of time had gone as frighteningly as that of space. She could not tell what was distant and what near. In that state she could only stay still because she dared not venture a step without some sense of distance. 'Stay still!' was the inner command.

She convinced herself that she had never left this room while she had returned in thought to where and when she first knew Horace. She had been as little aware of sitting here in this room as she was in a dream at night of lying in bed asleep. You only know when you wake up. She knew that she had not been asleep. Amnesia? It was one of those words with which she was familiar without really knowing their meaning. It rang a bell. When someone had a shocking experience he would forget all about it and this meant forgetting everything else as well. She firmly brought herself back to here and now – feeling with her hands the chair she was sitting on. It was good and firm wood, not plastic. She hated plastic chairs. Horace had insisted on having one in his study; he said that he felt more at home in that than any other because it was like the college chairs. She had always hated the sound and feel of those and the way they were stacked.

She was alone. Again it was a relief to be alone. Her sense of time was returning. She remembered the bliss she had felt earlier at being alone, followed by disappointment at no one being there, when she was at last able to turn to the inner presences who had been begging for her attention. They had always been there when she could not attend to them because she had to follow Horace. They were always in relative darkness behind her when she had to face in the opposite direction, where Horace was striding ahead. Their constant, legitimate claim on her was like that of children who were not to be neglected. Had they been the children whom Horace and she did not have? She felt that he would not even have seen outwardly visible children. They would not have been real to him; not as real as what he had in his head and wanted to verify on the ground in order to confirm his maps. He would still have expected her to follow and disregard any other claim on her.

She felt expected to come where he was, apparently demanding her but having no use for her as herself. She wondered whether he knew what or who another person was. He not only showed no interest but no awareness of there being a person to be known. What was a person to him?

She got up, feeling she had been glued to the chair for hours, and moved about aimlessly. She stopped abruptly. Something went from her heart down her body and made her feel shivery and cold. She knew in her body what she could not yet bear to know in her mind. It had given her an alarm signal. She wanted to turn away from where she was about to arrive in her return to the present. Anywhere was better than what lay ahead.

Chapter 4

She had come into this room supposedly to meet those who had been clamouring for her. Now she found herself clamouring for them. She had always thought of them as 'small people' compared to herself in the large, outer world. But now *she* felt the small creature looking up at a situation, the scale and nature of which it could not begin to grasp let alone deal with. She might have been a little child, barely the height of a table leg, as she was supposed to face a situation in the next room with implications going far beyond it. Feeling reduced to their size, she might be closer to the inner small people. She desperately needed their help.

Therese felt terrified and was shaking. She felt sweat pouring out of her temples. It seemed pressed out by an awful contracting of everything inside her. Without words, she seemed to cry 'Help me!' She would entrust herself to those inner people as if they must know better. She credited them with a wisdom that belonged to creatures in the darkness which 'the big people' in the light world lacked. It had to be a super-human or sub-human wisdom which alone could help her.

Therese knew that in the room to which she must return was a huge devouring fire about to seize her. She then found those for whose help she had cried, between herself and the fire. They convinced her that she must return to that room. They gave her the impetus to make the move she could not make by herself. She seemed only to lay her fingers on the door handle for the door to open. There was no fire. She was moved to enter and stand with her head bowed before where Horace lay.

Having led her here, they did not desert her. They seemed to hold her up. Their size had no more relation to their strength than the size of a pill to its power. In her utter weakness she vaguely marvelled at their strength enabling her to look at Horace. He was dead and she had killed him. Now she was witness to the fact. It was a fact without judgement. Perhaps the fire, which the dark, helpful beings had put out, was judgement. But here was truth, not judgement. They were in the service of the truth.

They had miraculously helped her to come back here from where she had escaped. Now she saw Horace as having, like a huge snake, nearly strangled her. She could feel the terrible coil clasping her from head to foot until she had finally killed him. It was necessary to register and understand the hardly believable fact that what she had felt compelled to do meant she had killed a man. She needed to wake up fully to see that one acceptable side of the coin had this other unacceptable one. That the two were one and the same thing took time to enter her consciousness fully. She had killed a man, Horace, whose wife she had been. That title 'wife' was always something external to her, put on her by others; as if the Queen's royalty depended on the crown placed on her head instead of residing in her.

She felt as if she had been helped to climb over the greatest mountain in the world to come and face the man she had killed, now before her. She stood firm, knowing that she had had to do this. Human beings were given this terrible power to make and to take life. We help make another human being, and not only let die many of the wonderful gifts brought into the world by that being, but even kill without counting the cost.

She looked down on Horace with neither pity nor hate. What had happened seemed an inevitable part of their relationship. Words had been useless with Horace. He seemed to hear them less than an animal which does not use them. He would not hear her cries, 'I cannot keep up! I cannot!' That she would follow was to him a matter of course. He was always looking into the distance and striding on so he did not see her falling behind, any more than he heard her. She could not simply stop and stay behind, or go her own way, because she had never had a way of her own. She had become an adjunct of Horace. She could only cease to be so by killing him. There was a kind of peace in seeing this necessity and knowing herself a small part of a truth whose immensity was fearful.

This state of being an adjunct of Horace had crept up on her. At the start being an adjunct had been convenient. It was easy to follow Horace, as she had done on that first expedition, which they had made at her suggestion. She could still remember that there were two weeks of silence from him after that, till she found herself next to him in a stream of people leaving a lecture hall. He was holding a sheaf of notes and maps in his hand and talked animatedly to her of the lecture just ended. After all these years, she remembered that the young lecturer had been controversial to the point of being provocative, without being able to remember what he had talked about. The vivid memory was of Horace's lit-up face as he could not contain his spontaneous response. It was a stroke of luck for him to find himself next to Therese. He seized the opportunity and quickly launched into his alternative theory. Therese was back in the same position: looking up to him, enjoying his complete absorption in his subject. The mixture of her detachment and his involvement had a special meaning for her. It made her forget the irritation she had felt with his morose behaviour since their last outing.

He had been left in a sore unease after their last expedition. It was a familiar state for him; feeling guilty and defensive, with an underlying conviction of being hopeless. The only thing to do in that situation, as he saw it, was to turn away and blindly get on with your business, deaf to whatever there might be to hear inside or outside.

Horace's alternative geographical theory that he had eagerly expounded to Therese sounded all right to her but, she said, 'It needed verifying on the ground, I suppose.' It was a way of saying that these facts that poured out of him were above her head and she could give no opinion without the evidence on the ground.

Horace saw her remark as a practical proposition. 'You've got a point there,' and turning to her, asked straightaway, 'Would you like to come and see?' He drew the map from amongst his papers even as they were still walking along in a stream of people. 'It's a fairly accessible area.' As almost nothing was inaccessible in his enthusiastic view, this might mean anything. His keenness also obliterated the memory of past difficulties.

Therese felt that her face had worn that expression of amused, benevolent interest for several years. She had gone on playing the same part: assenting to his enthusiasm – he needed no encouragement – and being carried along in 'his vehicle'. It meant going his way and never her own. She could not have put up with the wearisome geographical expeditions if they had not fulfilled some other function for her than the research, which left her cold. Having so much interest himself, he barely noticed her indifference.

She had been prevented from finding her own interests and potential. The aunts had not only restricted her experience but sapped her energy. As a child and adolescent she had been weighed down rather than enlivened by all her natural capacities and energy because they had had to be repressed. Her first start in life beyond the prison walls of her childhood led to her collapse when she was to start her college career. She wasn't fit to stand on her own feet, let alone run her own life. After a year off, she felt glad of a second start but still had little idea of anything she particularly wanted to do. Since awareness of what she wanted would only have increased her frustration in the past, she had never developed any keen interest. She was to herself like a complex musical instrument that she had never been allowed to play, so she had no idea of its potential.

At college it had seemed all right just to be in the world, apparently freely. It was an interesting novelty and college life with superficial friendships in small groups was pleasant. The extra interest of her relationship with Horace gave her a certain kudos. She had not expected their friendship to last but when college life ended, it was something to continue with. She would otherwise have felt utterly at sea. At the end of three university years she had nowhere to go back to, nor could she see anywhere to go forward to. Her relationship to Horace, however limited and uncertain, was the only life to hold on to.

Apart from the vicarious enjoyment of Horace's enthusiasm for his work, there was a painful place of vulnerability within her that she felt corresponding to something in him. It was a point of contact where there was a charge of sympathy that linked them. Horace was unaware of this. At first his unawareness, like his unselfconscious enthusiasm, made him rather boyish and gave her a sense of superiority. Later, what had been endearing became intolerable and the common point of hurtness became one of torture.

During the last college year when there were regular discussions of plans and prospects for jobs and further academic work, Therese was interested in other people's interests and tried to match them, like colours chosen by others, to herself. She held them against herself to see if they suited her. When someone asked her, 'What are you going to do, Therese?' she shrugged her shoulders and said, 'I haven't made up my mind' or 'I can't decide', as if she had a choice in mind when she had none.

She felt keenly that there was something wrong in her lack of direction. It made her shy away from any discussion of possible plans, even with Horace. He, sensing her unease, took it as a signal to do the same. He would anyway always be wary of touching any personal subject. He could not talk about Therese any more than about himself. He could discuss plans of people with whom he had no connection as an academic matter. Were he never going to see Therese again after they left college, he might have enquired in a polite way what she was going to do or even where she was going to live.

Chapter 5

They had not set out to live together. Neither of them would have been able to make such a decision openly. They were in perfect harmony in their inability to make any explicit statement about their relationship or commitment to it. They were perfectly matched in their aversion to talking about what was personal. Such a match could be a trap. Disparity, even discord and friction, might disturb a deadly calm and lead to new life.

At first it was just more sensible to find a place with two rooms, kitchen and bath than to look for separate rooms or share with others. It seemed better to share with the devil you know than a strange one. Horace saw it as a reasonable arrangement. Therese felt a flicker of pleasure at the idea of sharing a place with Horace which would not be run by anyone else; a new experience for her. She had not learned how to cook or housekeep but thought Horace was unlikely to notice very much. She had no clear idea of the home he came from. Most of his childhood from an early age seemed to have been spent at boarding school because his parents lived and worked abroad. He had given her no impression of 'home'; rather spoke of places in which he had stayed during holidays but to which school was preferable.

When they had got established in their flat, Therese preferred playing around in their kitchen to writing letters of application for jobs which she did not really want. Those for which she did apply did not materialise and she continued to be available for accompanying Horace on fieldwork, typing his reports and eventually his thesis. It was incomprehensible and irritating to him that even when she had been on an expedition with him, she still appeared not to understand what she was typing. He was irritated that she could not follow his thought any more than she could keep up with him on their outings. She seemed always to be behind and, he suspected, 'somewhere else'.

Therese missed the ready excuse for not going out on fieldwork that she used to have at college, of her own work. The only excuse she had now was unfitness of one kind or another rather than something positive of her own. It was a great shock to both of them when one of these times, when she had decided to stay in bed, Horace suddenly found himself kissing Therese vehemently. Both of them were taken unawares. He had felt no warning of the power that had suddenly rushed up in him to make him do this. Though acting without consent by his normal, conscious self was disturbing, there was also relief because there had long been the sense of a pressing demand, an urgent unease that he was used to pushing back fearfully. It had taken over and taken him where he dared not go. He was little aware of Therese and the impact on her of the force by which he felt himself pushed forward as if by a great wave. He could barely catch his breath as he was carried on.

Therese felt shaken and shocked. Of course it was to be expected and yet she hadn't expected it. She had gone along with the vaguely reassuring idea that Horace was almost ludicrously work-absorbed. As he had given her no indication of sexual interest in her – awkwardly holding her hand when they were out together or planting a kiss on her cheek when they parted hardly suggested it – this assault came out of the blue. Below and beyond the physical and mental soreness with which it left her, there was some barely acknowledged reassurance that they were now in a mainstream of life from which she generally felt painfully separated. Far from being brought closer to Horace though, she felt more wary of him. In this respect too they were similar.

They did not speak about what had happened. They were both alerted to a new force to be reckoned with in their fragile set-up, both unsure of what it might do to that. Their corresponding needs had made them erect a joint shelter from the fullness of life for which neither was ready. It had reinforced their individual defences and let through a minimum of natural life. Now there had been a disturbing influx of such life that carried them off to a main road. They moved along that road by fits and starts. In Horace's 'ill-sprung vehicle' it was a bumpy road and the journey an uncomfortable one, but they did move on. Fear of the consequences that were too serious not to be realistically foreseen drove Horace to take every possible precaution against making Therese pregnant. Nothing was more intolerable for him to contemplate. Living on the same premises as Therese, he had been led where as a rational being he could not have chosen to go; but he would make sure not to be carried further into a whirlpool!

In those days Therese wished she still had girls around her as at college. She would not have discussed her relationship with Horace but it would have been a comfort to be able to speak about it indirectly and get their reactions. They could be relied on to take every hint. Where they had found their little flat she had no friends. They would have stayed near the university, where Horace would have the benefit of the library and other facilities, had accommodation not been scarcer and more expensive there. So they moved to a small village that was too far out for regular students. They had not considered that they knew no one there. Therese only realised the importance of even the diffuse friendship that she had had with a group of her contemporaries at college, when she had got over the novelty of having 'a set-up' of their own. They chose to call it that because even 'their flat' sounded more established than they felt at ease with. 'Home' was out of the question; it would arouse the same embarrassment as much of normal life caused them; like the rash that readily afflicts people susceptible to a wide range of allergies.

Rather than seeing their set-up as a shelter, Therese now felt exposed in it and needing to withdraw into a comforting background of female companionship. Lacking that kind of support behind her, she needed somehow to protect herself against Horace. She needed to increase the distance between them. She became less communicative. Horace did most of the talking anyway; he could be relied on to initiate conversation because there was always something on his mind that interested him and he assumed that it must be interesting to her. Although he did not expect her to say much, he depended more than he realised on her interest; her readiness to come along on his conversational as on outer, geographical expeditions. He was put out when he found her 'not there'. He could see no reason why she should not be there; could not think of anywhere else she might be. 'Why wasn't she there?' was more a complaint than a question in his mind. As far as he could see there was nowhere else for her to be.

She became restless and ill at ease. She slept unusually badly and wondered if it were because she was afraid of Horace wanting to sleep with her. Having listened with interest to the girls in her little group at college exchanging notes on their nights out, she thought they would treat her fears lightly. She could hear them say, 'Just nerves, like before exams! It takes time to get used to, let alone enjoy it. Like everything, it takes practice', but such imaginary reassurance did not touch her unease. She realised it concerned not only sex but seemed to be everywhere. She resented the imbalance between her and Horace. Everything was on his side, nothing on hers.

She had not liked him having more possessions than

she in the place they shared. Especially with all his books, maps and files, he had much more. She bought some things but they were not the same, being newly bought. She knew that she could not shop for things that she would care about as truly her own. She became a less responsive or obliging companion both on their outings and in their daily life. She wished she could somehow make Horace aware of her. Her moroseness did not attract his attention to her because, like a child, he missed what he was accustomed to having and regarded as his right, without questioning why it might be absent.

Therese registered the uselessness of her withdrawal. She gained nothing from it because she could not find or be anything of her own. She reluctantly returned to her previous part of compliant companion. At least it was familiar; she acted it well and it went down well with Horace. When he got a research grant his workload increased and her help became more valuable. More and more of her time was absorbed by it. She was led to organise his files by her need to find things. They had become a headache because Horace had no idea of order, except with regard to maps, which he naturally saw as part of a fixed geographical order. Therese could not understand his blindness to the obvious order in which she saw things asking to be arranged. At least she fulfilled a necessary function but Horace, blind to order, did not appreciate it. At best he would admit that she saved time by finding things more quickly than he did. When he started lecturing, she not only had more word processing to do but did more of the preparatory work for excursions.

Chapter 6

They got married largely on the basis of this working partnership. When Horace suggested it as a good idea Therese was doubtful. He said that it was the sensible thing to do in the circumstances. To hesitate and be wondering about it was a waste of time and would only distract from the work they needed to get on with. He thought that their rather rough physical relationship might be a cause of her hesitation. Of course he was not wonderful in bed but neither was she. They were both inexperienced. At the beginning it had all been rather unpredictable and he had been baffled by surges of sexual drive overtaking him, but they had taken him where obviously he could never have gone in cold blood. Now matters were not quite as much out of his control. He still could not understand how men could plan campaigns to win women and strategems to please them. Since he and Therese lived in the same place he had come to see the necessity of their physical relationship but he could see no reason for dwelling on the matter. It would be pointless and boring, in his view.

Horace persuaded Therese that it was only practical to get married. The set-up they shared might just as well be upgraded to a home-of-sorts until it became too small for his growing library of maps and slides as well as books, and until he had earned enough to buy somewhere bigger. Her hesitation was unwelcome. Once he had decided, he saw no advantage in their present state and saw nothing beyond these alternatives. What else was there? Therese was not interested in anywhere or anyone else, so he could see no reason for delay.

Therese had nothing substantial with which to counter his reasonable proposition. She mustn't be romantic, she told herself, when she felt a great sadness at Horace's sensible view. It made her feel cold. She pulled her cardigan tightly round herself but knew the cold came from inside, not outside. She saw a great void around herself and Horace, not only in the outer world because they had no close friends and exceptionally few close relatives, but also internally. Horace's unawareness of what she felt about their situation seemed to contribute to the void. It was surprising how dreadful nothingness could be; as much as any particular horror. He was wanting her to join him permanently in this void. She could hear him say, were she to speak her thoughts, 'What do you expect? I don't see anything wrong with where we are', and speak in terms of their outer circumstances. She could hear his tone, making her feel an ungrateful wretch with extravagant fantasies. What was the good of wanting what was not, and they evidently could not have, she told herself. Perhaps she still had adolescent, idealistic views.

She had precious little experience but had always had a sense of warmth around a couple who had decided to be married; of a warmth given out by those who had a marriage in which things grew. What grew depended on the people who owned the garden. Unexpected things would come up. There would be all sorts, including weeds, but the place would be happily alive. It would be the opposite of the dead place where she had lived with her aunts, where even the few little plants that grew along one edge of the concrete slabs looked artificial. She had never doubted that this was an aberration from a real garden and from life. She might never have lived on anything but a starvation diet, but knew that there was proper food and that something had gone wrong when one had to do without it.

When Horace could not see why she did not welcome his proposal to get married, she was at a loss to know how to explain why she felt so despondent at the thought of this sensible marriage. Her heart ached with sadness when she let herself think about it. Once in the middle of the night she was furious at his blindness and outraged by his expectation. She could feel something like a deep well inside her which she could imagine being filled with a wonderful glowing warmth by the man who would marry her. They would meet in its light and it would fill them both. This transformed the world that was without love.

She could only just perceive this without ever getting near putting it into words, even to herself. All she knew clearly and painfully was the world of things with hard edges and sharp corners where nothing merged and people like herself and Horace existed inside a bare, box-like space. Since this appeared to be hard reality and her perception of the opposite fantasy, she agreed that it would be as well for them to be married.

One evening, during supper, Horace made a statement about the social and economic *raison d'être* of marriage. Every marriage, he claimed, was basically a marriage of convenience. He stated it as a matter of fact rather than an opinion. She saw his point but she felt hurt by his inability to pay any tribute to feeling associated with marriage. His seemed a bitterly cold and hard world in which to marry.

Nevertheless she felt some satisfaction at the prospect of being a married woman, which meant becoming 'somebody'. She would be the wife of this man who was somebody in the world, recognised for his knowledge, even an authority in his own field, however minute that was. His work made him someone solid and knowable, as she was not. She felt that there was no texture or colour to her. No one could say what or who she was. Even her name was floating on its own because she knew no close relatives with the same name. As the aunts had been childless there were no cousins on her father's side. Her mother's sister had emigrated to New Zealand and married a New Zealander. She died young and her husband did not encourage his two daughters to contact their English relatives. Therese felt her name was like the name-tag people have pinned on them at conferences or even at their workplace; something attached to them for usefulness rather than an essential part of them.

As Mrs Carruthers she would be someone recognisable and bear a name given weight by others. 'Carruthers' sounded much more substantial than her maiden name 'Lyle'. It would be a good change to be seen as Mrs Therese Carruthers, but in the background there was the unadmitted, painful knowledge that the name was only a facade for lack of the love between Horace and herself which would have given it body.

Therese later remembered with surprise how cheerful and bright she had been on their wedding day, after an acrimonious time leading up to it. 'No fuss' was Horace's overriding command. Therese could hardly disagree, for how could she have made a fuss? Who or what would provide a fussy wedding? She had no family to play their vital part and when it came to it she didn't want to ask college friends. She felt downhearted at the lack of surprise an invitation to her wedding would have for them, and at the thought of their opinion of Horace. It would have been different if she could have startled them with a name unknown to them, exciting their curiosity. She imagined their depressed reaction to this wedding and decided not to ask them. The implication that she had done nothing new since she left college reinforced her feeling of being a failure; being nothing in her own right.

She said to Horace that if she asked one or two of the

group, she would have to ask them all and this was too many, considering the small total number they wanted. He made no objection. 'The fewer the better,' he said. But this annoyed Therese and made her insist that she must meet all available relatives of his, especially as she lacked family. She would throw herself into being as much a Mrs Carruthers as possible, rather than protecting herself against the imbalance of the much greater weight on Horace's side. His parents had lived most of their married life in Colombia and his father, both on health and business grounds, was unable or unwilling to come, but his mother had every intention of meeting the wife of a son with whom she had had minimal contact all his life. There was a brother with wife and children, about whom Horace would never say anything good or bad. Although this brother had been at the same school for many years, he could say nothing more personal about him than about anybody else.

She urged him to tell her more. He hadn't the excuse for saying so little, which he made in the case of his parents, of not having seen much of them. When he was small they had a nanny, which was both customary and necessary because his mother was determined to carry on with her public work, which she regarded as more important than child rearing. She had no doubt about her value in the welfare field, in which there was no one to do what she could do, while anyone could have and bring up children. When the children were old enough to be sent to school in England, she was relieved to be able to carry on with her work single-mindedly. Holidays might have been a problem, if for reasons of economy they had not been rationed to one annually back in Colombia, with arrangements made for the rest in England.

Therese understood from Horace that brothers at the same school were as likely to have nothing to do with each other as to stick together. Either one was ashamed of the other or they were both determined to disown any family feeling that could be cause for mockery. Therese had no experience of siblings, but what Horace said sounded sadly true. For all the lack of a joint family life in Horace's immediate family, it was a fairly large family and Therese was curious to meet them. She was slightly nervous of being criticised by Mrs Carruthers senior. She surely filled the formidable name in a way Therese could never hope to match. Odd, she thought, how two quite different women could bear the same name. Her feminist friends would object to their being more or less compelled to do this, but though she had joined their chorus sometimes, she couldn't get worked up about it. Most of it seemed to her like jealousy, though she conceded that the jealousy might be justified.

Therese's apprehension of Horace's family melted like snow in a burst of sunshine when she first met his brother Daimeon. She had been intrigued by the name, which seemed out of place in that family, and felt happily surprised when she found herself looking up at a warmer, maybe weaker, version of Horace's face. She naturally warmed to him because here was a much more approachable Horace. He lacked Horace's intensity. He was not driven by any daemon as Horace was in his work and she could imagine him rather being criticised for being a dreamer. She was delighted with his courteous friendliness.

Her feeling that Daimeon might be considered rather ineffectual was reinforced when she met Hildegard, his wife, who she realised with a shock, was of course a third Mrs Carruthers. Rather, she told herself, Hildegard was the second Mrs Carruthers, and was certainly much better qualified for the name than she. She almost felt that she should withdraw, since Hildegard was so eminently suited to the name she could never fill anything like as well. The formidable new sister-in-law was evidently as strong-minded as she was big-boned and tall;

the opposite of herself who was always described as petite. Daimeon's wife confirmed her view of his gentle character and for a moment this seemed to throw light on her own relationship to Horace. In their case was she the weak and Horace the dominating one? She quickly dismissed any such insight.

Therese found herself inwardly swerving away from Hildegard, whom she felt driving at her, but readily turned towards the unintimidating, almost inviting Daimeon. As if there were an instinctively known affinity, each happily welcomed the other. The tone of Daimeon's remarks about his workaholic brother, suggesting a mixture of respect and disrespect for his excessive work, were a happy surprise for Therese. She had become so accustomed to living under the weight of Horace's workload, never questioning its virtue, that she had not realised how oppressed she was by it until she heard Daimeon's critical remarks. 'The motor is never allowed to stop, is it? I suppose he wouldn't know himself without it. He couldn't stop revving even at school. He must depend on it. It gets monotonous to others.' He laughed as he said, 'Or worse!' Wanting to soften this, he added, 'He certainly makes himself an expert in his field, even if it is a small patch that others don't find all that interesting. He always was an authority on something, even at school.'

Though she would not admit it, to find someone else's experience coinciding with her own and making it more explicit was perhaps the happiest moment of Therese's wedding day. Her face beamed as she looked at Daimeon. She could have flung her arms round him. She was on the point of asking, 'How do you know?' when she realised that of course Daimeon had lived with his brother, even if it was mostly at school, for many years.

She didn't say anything but Daimeon noticed her marvelling smile and thought it rather nice. He thought Horace was doing well in marrying her. 'Better than he deserved' was a stifled comment. It belonged to an underlying anger at his brother which was in contrast to his general mildness. A glimpse of his anger startled him. It was quickly put away in a mental drawer which he kept firmly shut.

Therese drank more than she could remember ever drinking. As she became increasingly light-headed she felt that it was to celebrate having met a kindred spirit in her brother-in-law, rather than her own wedding. She saw and felt her marriage as a heavy undertaking. The position of permanent assistant to Horace was one role in life for which she had found herself eligible. This dark image of her undertaking seemed reason enough for her unprecedented light-headedness. It felt right to float high in the light before going down into the dark trench where in her inebriated state she saw her married future.

Horace had expressed to his mother his surprise at Therese's state. He remarked in a puzzled tone that she was generally a very sober, quiet person. He was relieved when the familiar person had returned the next day, although she was evidently rather unwell and not surprisingly cheerless. He was glad that there was not likely to be another occasion for her to change as disconcertingly as she had done yesterday.

Chapter 7

They had a quarrel a week after the wedding. Therese registered with surprise a different quality of this quarrel within marriage to any before. She was shocked by her own angry resentment, whose unfamiliar strength troubled her. Why did it suddenly appear after being married? Their joint life was the same after, as the days and months before, the wedding. She had a vague realisation that even a wedding like theirs that only paid lip service to a convention had a more powerful meaning than she had recognised.

They had decided to postpone going away till the spring, when Horace looked forward to combining a professionally interesting exploration with the delayed honeymoon. They were now in the same room in which they had lived for months. But Therese felt shut in as never before. She felt that a door had been firmly shut on them which had never been shut before. Someone seemed to have said, 'OK, this is it. You get on with it. That's what you asked for.' The shock of this made her turn against Horace, like a child fearing and hating the person with whom she was shut in.

Therese could not openly express fear and anger, as a child might, but found herself instead rejecting things Horace said and did in a despising, even mocking tone that was as new to her as to him. She was hearing someone she had not met before in herself. It was alarming but at the same time she felt a certain satisfaction as if this were something she had not been able to afford to do before. Perhaps the closed door worked both ways. It was safer to do this after the door had been closed when Horace couldn't get away easily. They were on their own as they had not been before. Each was at the other's mercy.

In Horace's view nothing had changed, but in this atmosphere he felt a particular chill and tightening in himself that went with an unspecific memory of his parents' home. It had never been a family home. The chill, even in a hot climate, and that same tightness, had made it a relief to go away to boarding school. He now turned to his work, trying to ignore the chill, past and present. When odd people phoned to say it had been a nice wedding party or because they had left something behind, and asked how they were faring, Horace's reply was that they had soon got back to work. That was the reassuring fact.

Yet sometimes in the evening that winter, sitting under the lamp over the small square dining table, Therese had a comforting sense of their being a married couple. She felt enclosed in a good way, in contrast to the unmarried, alone in an indefinite space. Marriage then seemed a good idea because, even when they were living in the same place before they were married, there had not been this kind of enclosure that she valued. She did not ask Horace, as she would have liked, whether he felt the same, because he would most likely get up saying he had just remembered something concerning his work that he must make a note of. Then she would feel disappointed and even angry, which would spoil what she enjoyed. She told herself that it was better to keep these silly things to herself. But belittling them saddened her.

Therese felt that Horace's expectation of her had increased with their marriage. He seemed to assume that she was now more at his disposal than before. He regarded this as one perfectly legitimate reason for getting married. Sometimes she liked his treating her help and her accompanying him on his expeditions as his natural right because it gave her a place where she was expected and evidently wanted. With more experience she became more useful. Horace regarded this as only to be expected and therefore calling for no comment. Then she felt painfully that he never really noticed her. She was part of his life because she had become part of his work. She thought she was his work processor; processing rather than contributing to what he did. He assumed it interested her. He would have said that she had chosen to do it.

Horace could no more imagine that she could get tired of his work than that he might do so. He was puzzled when she once said that she did not want to come on an expedition; surely she would not want to miss it? He reluctantly accepted that she would not come. One day Therese was shocked to hear herself saying internally, 'I shouldn't mind if I never went on another expedition again'; knowing that, except very rarely, it was impossible for her not to go. It was not just a matter of Horace's need and expectation, but of her own. Her occupation with his work covered a frightening void that would face her if she gave up her role as his work processor. She remembered saying to a girl at college that she knew she had never yet got her act together. Now she was assisting in Horace's because she still hadn't got one of her own. Sometimes that made her angry with Horace but at others she told herself that she mustn't let him down and he needed her help. She believed it, and that gave her strength to carry on.

When they had been married three years, the regular work trips started arousing a peculiar anxiety in Therese. Intense anxiety came with no indication of its source or meaning. She often felt as if a messenger were standing at her door whose very presence was deeply troubling. She seemed to see him standing there in silence and she could not even read any message in his face. The anxiety made her feel ill, so she dragged behind Horace. To speak to him about a groundless, peculiar fear or foreboding was impossible. As she felt it gripping her vital organs, she could not eat; she felt weak and cold.

She often felt the anxiety affect especially the lower part of her body, which made her wonder whether it was to do with not having children. She had been inclined to agree with Horace when he said that there could be no thought of having a family until he got more established and they might afford a house. It would be intolerable to have a child about the place where they were. He could not afford any interference with his work. Only if he could complete the research on which he was engaged would he get the established academic post that he wanted and that would also make a family financially plausible. Therese agreed that a house would certainly be better for a child or children than this flat.

If the intense anxiety that now settled in her abdomen were a complaint about the want of children, there was nothing she could do about it. Horace must be right, for when she thought of a baby it just did not fit into this set-up of theirs. Their marriage had after all not stopped it being a set-up. She could certainly see no place in it for a child. As usual there was only Horace's way to follow.

Whenever the painful anxiety left her she hoped she was free of it but it always returned. Its coming and going was unpredictable. She felt it like a blackmailer in her life. Most of her energy went into coping with it. She came to be convinced that she must somehow assuage an inner demand that was now added to the outer ones which she could never meet. Although painful, this inner state was something private and of value as such. One night she had a dream in which she faced a tall, masculine figure standing before her, whose face she knew to have been deliberately obliterated so she would not recognise him. The tall, dignified figure was shrouded under folds as of a Roman toga. The figure was connected in her mind with her dreadful anxiety, but it was imposing and she knew this was someone to be respected. The august presence seemed to reassure her that the anxiety was not just a devilish device aimed at her destruction. She woke with a faint idea that if she would only pay some attention to this figure, even do something he wanted, the terrible grip of anxiety might be relaxed.

So there was an element of hope in the night's experience, but she was glad to get on with the business of the day and escape into the ordinary world. Although she readily settled at the word processor to edit the latest addition to Horace's dissertation, she found her mind wandering from the minutiae of a geographical landscape to an indistinct inner one which nevertheless had a reality and power which the outer one lacked. She was like a child drawn into a mysterious wood, and had to be brought back to the flat, factual landscape on her work table.

Since her marriage she had persuaded herself that this was a quite proper life, which would get better as they got established. Now she could not help feeling it had become worse. Sometimes she felt that everything in her world was like scenery in the theatre; when she touched things she assumed to be real, she had the shock of finding only a flat painted surface. There was no structure behind all the convincingly painted things. The frightening lack of 'body' of her world made her sometimes feel as if her own being were like a balloon from which the air was escaping. The prospect of it shrivelling up at the end – not at the end of old age but in her present life – was so frightening that she did her best to dismiss the idea.

Sometimes the anxiety brought her near to breaking point. She carried it like an invisible cross that it took all her strength to bear. It also made her insistently aware of herself as a separate individual. While she was constantly straining to keep up with Horace, whom she saw always ahead of her – not just on actual expeditions but in the demands of his work and even in their domestic life – she felt herself drawn backward by anxiety. When she fought it, it became in her mind like a crab-like creature that would hold her in its grip.

One day a helpful idea came into her mind, that whoever she felt was pursuing her was not wanting to seize or harm her but wanting her to look, or move in another direction. It seemed that someone had been trying to convey this to her for a long time. She had refused to pay attention but would now try to do so. It even seemed that the one within, claiming her attention, knew mysteriously more about her situation than she did.

Chapter 8

Horace was coming out of the library, where he had been trying to find a small area in the Fens in as many generations of maps as were available. For weeks he had been on this search. It was always a delight when he identified the area, sometimes so differently presented at different periods that it was hardly recognisable. When his find was confirmed by some unmistakable distinguishing mark, he felt triumphant. Now he had found it in a sufficient number of maps to have won his case against a regular imaginary opponent who maintained, 'You can't find it. It's not there.' It was as if he were searching for one person in different guises, against another's assertion that he was wasting his time.

He had been intent today on finding continuity below evident change. He had recognised a particular area of Fenland in five generations of maps. He went into the nature of the historical as well as geographical changes. He knew of no one else who had taken such an interest in this area. He felt possessive and proud of his findings. He felt that such an exceptionally successful conclusion of a morning's work deserved celebration, while knowing of no way to have this.

Of course he would be telling Therese of his achievement but the prospect gave him no joy; rather the opposite. He foresaw that spoiling rather than enhancing his pride and pleasure. Her words would be praising but she would fail to express the appreciation of his work that he wanted. That would make him angry, and then the suppressed anger would put him into a bad mood when he had cause for satisfaction. He always tried to put aside his disappointments with Therese. He was not going to be troubled with personal difficulties, especially not the marriage problems that other people had. He hadn't the time to spare. He believed he could avoid such wasteful preoccupations by expecting nothing in particular and carrying on their life within strict limits. That way he would avoid the pitfalls that were the downfall of people who lived more freely.

This was his most satisfying achievement for a long time; all the more so because his chosen area was so unremarkable. He had put the little area on the map in a way it had never been because now it was recognised for itself rather than being an insignificant part of a bigger landscape. He had chosen and established it as a proper subject of geographical study. Horace was smiling to himself as he walked down the steps of the library. He was smiling at the image of his Fenland area. A bright, quite joyful 'Hi!' startled him from his preoccupations but happened to fit his mood.

He was still smiling when he looked at the bonny, glowing face of the young woman who faced him on the steps and was saying 'Hi! It's good to see you!' It was good to see this man smiling as she had never seen him during the three university years she had known him. Amanda Cleveland had a plump face with a plait of hair around her head like a crown, emphasising the full rounded look, not only of her face but her whole appearance. Her eyes and mouth seemed more generous and rounder than other people's, though her nose was rather delicate. Her body perfectly matched her face. As far as it was apparent under a full, long skirt and loose top, it was as plump as the face, in a comforting rather than gross way. She exuded a sense of fitting comfortably into life which was very strange to Horace.

'How are you? she asked joyfully, as if he could only be well. When Horace had answered more convincingly than usual that he was well, she replied with pleasure, 'You look it! Wonderful.' She was ready to make the most of everything and added a laugh as if all good things were an opportunity for laughter. Horace could not think of Amanda without this laugh that he now remembered. In the past he had thought it pointless, and because he couldn't see what it was about, it made him uneasy. Today he didn't mind; it even seemed rather nice. He went on smiling as, standing on the sunny steps, he nodded approvingly when she told him she too was fine. He was not aware that he went on smiling while looking at her appreciatively, but she was. Although they had met many times, she felt this was the first time he had ever looked at her, certainly the first he had done so with a smile. Wonderful, she repeated to herself, wonders never cease; another cause for her natural joy.

He seemed to her almost like someone in a trance when she suggested that they go and celebrate the lovely day with a drink and maybe a snack, as it was lunch time and so not really worth her while going to the library. His more than willing compliance confirmed her impression of intriguing change in Horace. For a moment she looked at him questioningly but decided to make hay while the sun shone rather than waste good time with questions of why and wherefore.

'The Nag's Head?' she proposed. Horace readily agreed. 'And there are benches outside although it's so early in the year. The first warm day,' she said, as they started going down the broad library steps. He thought of Therese standing on the hard, frosty ground of a field only a short time ago, miserably cold, waiting while he took notes. He too had been cold but he was interested in what he was doing. He wished her interest were greater so she wouldn't be so troubled by the cold. He regretted that when he said this to her it did not help. Her inadequate interest was unfortunate. It was not for want of effort on his part to engage her in his work. By contrast, the present warmth was very pleasant.

Amanda asked after Therese just when he had left her in his mind, standing in the cold. He felt like saying spontaneously, 'She is cold', but of course that was nonsense and he said that she was well and working hard.

'Doing what?' Amanda asked interestedly.

The question took Horace by surprise. 'My work,' he replied, only just cutting out the 'of course' because he could not think what else Therese would be doing.

It sounded depressing to Amanda but she had no time for being depressed and she laughed at her own hilarious remark about a feminist version of the ploughman's lunch they had asked for. It led on to 'the ploughman's wench' and then it all got mixed up, with the wench becoming the food, in a surrealist picture she painted in words with such gusto that Horace doubted that this was her first drink. But he was fairly amused, when normally jokes that other people found great left him stone cold; as cold perhaps as Therese in the field. He felt amused most of all by this woman whose high spirits could not help rubbing off on him.

Horace found himself offering her another drink when they had already had several with a longer meal than he had expected. He was aware of behaving more how he was used to seeing other people behave. Another drink postponed ending this pleasant change. She was enjoying seeing him apparently melted in the spring sunshine and by her own warmth. Knowing Horace, she felt this a special feather in her cap. With the justification of a first-day-of-spring, she thought, Why stop here? What a pity not to strike while the iron is hot. Her reply to a moment's doubt, that surely this was going too far with a man like him, was, You never know! Challenging that doubt within, as much as Horace, she said, 'Come and see where I've found to live; a really "bijou little place". I'm sure you'll hate it!', with another peal of laughter.

Horace felt her enjoyment in making mild fun of him surprisingly acceptable. It was an affectionate teasing that was a sensation like having warm water lapping round him at the edge of the Mediterranean when he was only familiar with the cold Atlantic. Why not enjoy a rare indulgence?

They had sunk into her small, deep, floral-covered settee – proportionate to the cosy little attic room – where she naturally started to fondle him. The deep, soft sofa and the whole room with its profusion of things – bunches of sweet-scented dried flowers hanging from the rafters, silk drapes over the backs of chairs, and odd colourful clothes lying around – was so different from his customary comparatively bare and tidy surroundings that he was like someone in a foreign country. Going along with its strange ways was the only thing to do, unless he turned round and went back home, which would seem extremely rude.

He was amazed by being made love to. Before he had time to think, he felt a pleasant shock, like being overwhelmed by an explosion of delicious, almost intoxicating scents released on him; or having shaken over him a cornucopia of exotic fragrant petals. He realised later that the scent must have come from Amanda's face and body. He was the recipient of the cornucopia of her gifts.

It was something he had never even imagined. No one, nothing, had ever given him any idea of it. He could not blame Therese for never having given any indication of this extraordinary thing that a woman could be or do. How could she have done? It was inconceivable. He was inclined to believe that other people also did not know this but realised that some, probably few, other women had this capacity; his intelligence would not allow him to believe that it was Amanda's unique gift. Nor could he believe that Therese alone was devoid of it. It certainly did not just come with the feminine body.

On his way home especially, and on occasions ever

after, he wondered with great curiosity about the women who had and those who had not this amazing gift; also how many men had experience of it, like him. The two questions were obviously linked. His research-attuned mind was eager to investigate. He could not even start by questioning another man because he had no men friends. So he had not only to keep his extraordinary experience to himself but also to frustrate his enquiring mind by keeping his questions under lock and key.

Sex had always meant a very different sort of explosion for him: he visualised power accumulating in something like a balloon within his own body which at a certain point must escape. Since the first explosion that had been a shock to him and Therese, he had become accustomed to it being a regular occurrence. He reassured himself that it was proper for the woman to be overwhelmed by it, that she was made for this and would more or less expect it. He had managed to ask 'Are you all right?', not the first time, when he was too baffled himself, but other times, and she had nodded her head. He could not discuss these things as he knew others did readily. He told himself that he had more important things to think about and simply had to accept this, like other physical facts. He would not waste time talking about it any more than he would discuss food and drink as others did with enthusiasm.

In his experience and picture of sex there was no place for any active role for the woman. He thought of Therese as the 'target' of his explosion rather than recipient which she would have been were she to bear children. She had only to accept the eruption of energy of which he was then relieved for a while, and for this he was grateful. In this fantastic experience in Amanda's attic everything was different in an unimaginable way. Her release of the indescribable effusion of whatever it was that overcame all his senses, activated that great force that had always burst out by its own momentum and never been called for by another person. He was amazed by that communication; a possibility of which he had had no idea.

When he had eventually left Amanda, he was still dazed. He left, looking at her in wonder; like a child who had had showered on him presents that he could never have asked for. He was more or less speechless leaving this fairy tale donor, while she looked at him with amused satisfaction. After blowing Horace a kiss from her landing when he looked up from the bottom of the stairs, Amanda went back in her flat and spread her arms wide. It was a happy stretch to express her oneness with all around her; well beyond the flat which was an extension of herself. Life was good and she felt good. It had gone through her and she had embraced it which, more than embracing Horace, gave her satisfaction and gratitude.

She went to the little round table on which were the glasses and drinks they had had, and poured herself another. She drank it to what she called the goddess of love. She saw her as a light-hearted, flighty and delicious goddess who did not go near the god who was concerned with serious business of life. Amanda wanted to enjoy the floral fabrics and sweet incense in her room, not sackcloth and ashes. She would say she believed in celebrating life and if only there were enough people of the same mind, and body, there would not be all the dreadful killing in the world. All right, it was simplistic, she would admit when having to meet others' objection to her immature views. At least they provided excellent sport when she expounded them in a group, who tossed them about like a ball from one to the other with some mockery.

When she thought of Horace a faintly mischievous smile came on her face. Horace was like a child to Amanda. She enjoyed his innocence or naivety; whether it was one or the other depended on whether she felt romantic or down-to-earth. She thought she had never seen anyone to whom she had made love look so staggered. In another mood, she realised, it could have been irritating but on that lovely spring day it was fine. Fleetingly she wondered what he and Therese were up to and thought it wouldn't be very exciting; she would rather not think about it and leave people to their own devices, especially as she did not want to be depressed.

She plumped up a few cushions, picked the dead heads off some flowers and picked up a few of the things lying on the floor. But then, like a child who is deliberately and provocatively disorderly, she scattered the petals of the dead flowers and a few things she had picked up elsewhere, as if to show that she did just as she liked. Was this what she liked? Yes, everything spread all over the place. No order, OK? Somewhere, barely distinguishable in the back of her mind was a female figure in dark, plain clothing that was the opposite of her light, flowing layers. Although this person was permitted no entry to her world and was almost unseen, she aroused a strong feeling in Amanda.

Standing before her full-length mirror, Amanda leant forward, so her long blonde hair fell right round her head, which she then shook energetically so the hair went in all directions. She drew her head up and back, and with another shake made the hair fall backwards beautifully. Though there was no one there to admire it, she knew and enjoyed its beauty. She then stood, giving it long, leisurely strokes with her brush. The rhythmic movement confirmed her satisfaction and apparent peace. She was like a cat who had had a good meal, cleaning and cherishing itself. 'Love thy neighbour as thyself.' Loving yourself was the starting point.

Chapter 9

For Horace this day remained a fantastic secret that made his heart beat louder and faster than normal every time he thought of it. He didn't like to go back too often in thought to Amanda's 'bijou' place and particularly into her arms, in case the magic lessened with excessive returns. Too much use of it would become misuse of the experience. He feared being punished as one might for using God's name in vain. God might no longer be God to you if you reduced the word by casual usage.

Far from feeling any sense of guilt towards Therese, he felt satisfaction in his possession of what Therese could not have. It never occurred to him that Therese might be in the equivalent position. In his mind she was permanently locked in their joint set-up where she was a safe possession. Feminists would enjoin battle in vain. He would not be found on their battleground. He had no theory about woman being man's inferior or her place being in the home. He knew his deficiency in his ideas about marriage or sex. He had never managed to get interested in student discussions, and any woman challenged by his negativism to 'take him on', either to try and convert or fight him, gave up in exasperation.

Therese found Horace somehow lighter in those days and though their work schedule was the same, there was an easing of the grip in which they were usually tightly held. It released some little part of her from the entirely Horace-orientated life. It occurred to her that it might be possible to go for a walk; a wonderful new idea! Apart from necessary shopping, outings were exclusively on

Horace's projects. One did not think of going out for pleasure. She could not mention the idea to Horace; it would disintegrate under his scrutiny. It seemed to have come to her on the first breeze of spring.

That spring and summer odd little ideas kept coming to her with a tempting light or freshness about them. The first innocuous idea of a spring walk for its own sake, which it seemed strange never to have had before, had opened a way for other thoughts that had never entered her head but seemed to have been waiting for an opening. As they multiplied she resisted their pressure, however inviting they might be. She felt as if someone were having a game with her; enjoyed making her look up from her work to see a picture of a lovely place of whose existence she had been unaware. She was annoyed with herself for being caught out again and again, forgetting that she had told herself not to be distracted by irrelevant ideas that would stop her working.

There grew an idea of something or someone living inside her with power over her, and over which, or whom, she had no effective power. 'For goodness sake!' she would exclaim to herself when her concentration on a piece of Horace's work was yet again broken. This became more serious when Horace expressed surprise and increasing irritation at her falling behind in her work rather as she did on expeditions.

Their nights were rough. One or the other was always tossing and turning and occasionally both. It became commonplace for one to give up trying to sleep and get up, mostly in the early hours. Therese would go and make herself a drink and sit on the stool in the kitchen, feeling mangled inside, especially when she was aware of having had dreams that now eluded her. She seemed to be given them only to be deprived of them. She suffered the effect of her dreams and from being cut off from them.

*

Horace was sitting at his desk, looking at papers on which Therese had been working. There were two sets of diagrams of the essential features of the same area as shown in two maps, 70 years apart, with text discussing the differences. 'Quite straightforward,' he said emphatically. 'If only you read the text and looked at the diagrams, there would be no problem!' He was exasperated. It was intolerable. He was up against more and more absurd obstacles, apparently specially invented to prevent the completion of his work just when that was within view. He felt his goal being regularly moved away, or that he was being pulled back from it until he felt frantic. He could not understand how Therese could be so stupid! He did not like calling her stupid even to himself. He would say that of course she was not brilliant. There was no question of her being 'research material' but at the ordinary level she could be very useful.

Now Therese's part was to transfer the conclusions of his research, which he cared most about, to the word processor. When he had made sure that there could be no possibility of misunderstanding, the confusion she nevertheless produced in the script was unbelievable. How could she, how could anyone, have produced such confusion when he thought he had left no room for it?

Therese standing to the side of his desk was seeing Horace's head in profile. She saw and felt his exasperation, not just in his frown and tight lips but in every muscle of his body held taut. Perhaps such tension holds the tiger of fierce aggression that would otherwise spring out. Therese looked down on Horace's thick wavy hair, which she had always admired and which had made her call him handsome. When he wanted to make love and she had to overcome inner resistance, feeling his thick hair encouraged her. Now it might have been a hedgehog's off-putting spines. She felt him bristling and herself in an indefensible position. She had neither excuse nor defence.

She felt worn down by the last many months of having to drag herself to work against invisible resistance. Something like an enormous weight inside her would stop her going anywhere near Horace's work. It needed an enormous effort for her to sit down at the word processor and get to grips with the papers. She seemed to have been struggling to get on with her task against a small army inside her fighting her every conscious intention. When she stood by Horace's desk and he was glaring at her work, she felt the enormous struggle she had had to produce it, and the impossibility of conveying this to him. It left her so hopeless that she felt such strength as she had draining away. Her arms were limp and her legs so weak that she felt about to fall to the ground and to pieces.

Then the weakness suddenly turned to strength. The limbs were weak because overpowered by an immeasurable force that rose in the centre of her body from a deep underground source. It filled her to overflowing so it seemed to come out of her fingertips and every pore of her whole being. She was swallowed up in it. It swept her round from where she was standing and led her to seize the knife she hadn't known was left out of the kitchen drawer. The great wave carried her back towards Horace, where without any effort she lifted the knife with a wonderful lightness. It was something different from the sensation of lifting an object lighter than you expected; was rather as if all the usual taken-for-granted weight of the world was taken away and one was deliciously free of it. The question flashed through her mind whether being weightless in outer space felt like this. The lifted knife with that lovely lightness came down into Horace with no sense of resistance whatever, guided by the great force that had her in its charge. For once she had made exactly the right move.

She stood facing Horace – he had slumped forward and his face now rested on the desk – calmly looking down on him with the sense of having performed exactly what had been wanted of her. There was no mistake this time, and this rightness made irrelevant all the indefensible mistakes in the manuscript before Horace that had seemed to demolish her. It was as if she had been transformed into a bird that could fly above them.

The super- or sub-human force that made this murderous act more easily and perfectly performed than anything she had ever done was the expression of an overriding natural strength, unadulterated by anything like a thought. That force had risen from the depths to slay the dragon by whom she had been possessed. She had suffered the utmost humiliation of being appropriated by another. An absolute power had arisen like an avenging angel from the depth – rather than descended from heaven – to deliver her.

Then the hidden, mysterious presences within her had made her return to the scene to acknowledge the incredible fact of Horace having been murdered, by her. There she was able eventually to nod her assent. She stood before this body. She was now someone with her own boundaries and not part of someone else. But she was in confusion. The dragon from which she had been delivered was not the same as Horace slumped on the desk, though the two were connected. Nor was she who had slain him the same as she standing there, but the two belonged together. There was no doubt about that. She would swear to it both in the inner court, where she was questioned by a judge inside her trying to establish the facts, and eventually in the outer court, where she would on no account plead diminished responsibility. No! She resolutely rejected all persuasive arguments by her lawyer that this was the obvious and only sensible course for her to take. She shook her head vehemently. No!

Chapter 10

It was a relief to be on her own, when she was able to feel the pain inside her more than when she was with other people. It was like a sound which she must keep hearing but which was drowned in the company of others. Sometimes it became so strong when she was alone that she welcomed the temporary relief of having it dampened by others. Tonight she did not want to see the shiny bright paint or the brash pattern of the thin curtains of her small room that were supposed to promote a cheerful rather than depressed state of mind. She wished the light were not so bright. She had learnt that she was to be bright rather than penitent. The officers were trained to look out for signs of morbid guilt that must be counteracted in case it led to serious depression, needing treatment. This was why it was so important to keep prisoners busy and engaged in communal activities for a good part of the day.

They discouraged Therese from making her room dark and then just sitting, often with her face hidden in her hands. One warder tried to cheer her up in a friendly way; she called in to offer her some more books (that Therese had soon learnt were magazines) for which it would be worth putting the light back on, but Therese said, 'No thanks.' Another felt so put out by her sitting in the dark, different from all the others, that she told her to snap out of it and finally said it wasn't allowed to have lights out before the fixed time. 'What does she think she is doing?' the officer said to herself angrily; her sitting there like that got her goat. 'It shouldn't be allowed!' But

Therese stood on her rights. They could not stop her sitting in the dark in the evenings, when she was at last safely shut in from 6.30 p.m. till 6.30 a.m.

She was alone, free to feel, hear, be attentive to whatever there was inside her. She had still to persuade herself that the strange beings inside her need not be threatening and that it was necessary to give them her attention. They had driven her to free herself from Horace and had helped her to go back and actually see what she had done. Here, they had not left her. Her communication with them was a curious business; not a wordy conversation. Sometimes she thought it might be like being in contact with relatives from a distant country, neither knowing the other's language.

She felt safer sitting on her own in silence than with other prisoners, with whom she felt the very odd one out. Trying to keep up with the other women was hopeless. To speak a foreign language or even to be dumb would have been easier than being with these women when she and they supposedly spoke the same language yet didn't. Nor could she afford to get on too well with any warder who liked 'a quiet one' because of the jokes, at best, which that provoked from the others. She knew that some warders despised her 'class'.

Some of the other women marvelled at Therese, in her presence. 'You wouldn't believe it, would you? A "wouldn't hurt a fly" kind of creep, probably teacher's pet who never used no bad language, in here for murder! I was telling Ron, "You would never believe it!" Maybe they'd give her a career in the circus, like a midget that can act like a giant. Great!' Babs, the biggest woman, holding forth, gave one of her big belly laughs at her own wit that made her huge, loose body shake.

'What's so great about her?' a disgruntled woman next to Babs said. She could see nothing funny about this dull bitch to cheer anyone up.

'Why, it's marvellous, don't you see?' Babs answered.

'If that tasteless bit of cheese that hasn't got no sharpness in her anywhere so that no mouse even would want it, if that can slaughter a man . . . God! What can't you or I do?' Another roar of laughter rocked the enormous bulk. Therese looked away to avoid the sight, if she could not avoid the words. The laugh followed her down the corridor. Others weren't as explicit. Either they looked at her contemptuously or ignored her emphatically.

It was not so different with the warders. They were at least suspicious of anyone out of the ordinary. The one who objected to lights out before time could have kicked Therese when she had to leave her sitting there in the dark because she had had the cheek to say there was no rule that forbade her putting her light out early. 'There damn well ought to be', she had muttered, and she had a good mind to bring it up at the next meeting. She shouldn't be left powerless and a prisoner allowed to get away with it. A prissy, pale, little piece too, so smooth and bland you couldn't get hold of her no more than a jelly! She felt happier any day with the rough ones. You knew how to handle them, except the occasional one that could be a tough proposition needing two of you. But that was fairly rare.

One big, broad woman officer, with whom Therese felt better, was solid enough not to be bothered by her. She saw no need to get excited about Therese any more than about any of the others. It took a lot to make her even raise her voice to a warning note. She couldn't see how this dull one could upset her colleague, even to the extent of acting like a red rag to a bull. She could only see a wet rag. When, on her round in the early evening, she saw Therese already sitting in the dark, when no one in their senses would choose to turn off their light, she just muttered to herself, 'It takes all sorts, evidently.' She took another look at Therese in the dim light that came in from the corridor. The face struck her as 'not bad'.

She could even imagine liking her, but she would never say that to anyone.

The last few months since Horace's death, and since she was released from the invisible prison in which she had felt locked when he was alive, had given Therese experience of herself that she had not had before. She had the surprising reassurance of unknown resources within her coming to her aid. She could still hardly think of them as parts of herself. At first they seemed like some sort of superhuman intervention at a critical moment; it took her a long time to believe that these sources of help could actually be within her always.

She still found it difficult to see her extraordinary experience in court as anything other than a case of divine intervention. Getting up in court, feeling terrified and weak, she had heard a voice speak out of that weakness; speaking clearly, without hesitation, mainly of her life with Horace but also of before that. She heard the truth spoken as she had never fully recognised it. She heard herself with astonishment tell what she had not known she knew. She suffered for it afterwards. She had never seen more than a fragment of the truth that she had heard herself tell here, and, once spoken, it did not go away again. After it had been declared, it hurt. It had produced mitigating circumstances convincingly and even movingly. After that she had to bear it, presumably for life. But her sentence was for years not life.

Chapter 11

Freddie, Amanda's current 'regular', was returning to her from work one evening. He let himself in, and stepping skilfully over the various little heaps of things that littered the living room, he made his way to the tiny kitchen where Amanda was. He was talking to her, while avoiding things in his way as if they were permanent landmarks rather than unexpected obstacles. 'Do you remember Horace? The gangly fellow in our year who behaved more like a Fellow with a capital F than an ordinary mortal even before he got his degree? He insisted on doing research alongside all the degree stuff, he was that sold on his subject, geography. What a subject to be so passionate about! But passion was hardly his line; possessed by it he was, which is rather different.' Freddie sat down on the chair nearest to the kitchen door that was permanently open. 'Never thought of him since we last saw him – when? Is it really more than three years ago?'

'What about him?' Amanda asked from her kitchen that seemed so tiny because she had it filled chock-a-block, so that Freddie could only talk to her from the doorway. Much of the time she had her back turned to him while she was chopping vegetables, so she didn't see the newspaper cutting he was looking at while talking about 'this fellow in our year'.

He continued, 'I'm not surprised if you don't remember him; you wouldn't have been interested. He wouldn't have seen you because you weren't a geographical feature.' He laughed because he knew that Amanda tended to have no time for anyone who showed no interest in her, unless they were worth a lot of trouble, in which case she'd set about making them see her. 'I was going to say he was oblivious to women, but there was that rather mousy girl who seemed somehow tied up with him.' He was looking into the distant past rather than at what was before him when he said, 'I remember her looking at this bloke in quite a strange way, even then.'

'Of course I remember him,' came loud and clear from Amanda. 'What about him?' She sounded impatient, to Freddie's surprise.

'Oh good, then you know who I am talking about. Quite a story in those few lines,' he said, savouring the fact that he held something dramatic in his hand to present to her.

'What few lines?' The question made her turn around to look. She held a carrot in one hand and a knife in the other. Her hair was all over the place and the generous floral apron that hung over her full-skirted, long dress added to the 'overflowing' impression she gave. The tendency had to be checked sometimes, by forcibly holding in her hair against its inclination and putting some severe belt on, as at least a mark of containment.

The emphasis in her appearance now on freedom rather than restraint provoked Freddie into wanting to contain her himself, in his arms; or to plunge into the overflowing waves. He already had his right arm round her back and the other hand was about to seize hers holding the knife, when she protested, 'I am full of food!'

'You always are, you greedy little girl, and I want mine now,' he said as he pulled her face towards his to kiss her.

'No! You know I mean I've got my hands full of food and I'm messy with it,' she complained. 'You know very well I've not eaten for hours!' She waved the carrot in his face as she held back her head. 'Look how messy my hands are.' She laughingly held out her hand with the knife. He stared at it with surprising seriousness and stood still, so she was free to turn and go back to cutting her vegetables. Then she remembered what had made her come out in the first place. 'Those "few lines" you were talking about. Let me see.' She leant her head towards the piece of paper he was holding in his hand, which she would have taken from him, had her hands not been wet.

'Was that the way the knife came . . .?' Freddie was muttering.

'What are you talking about?' she interrupted him impatiently. She wanted the gist of what he had to say quickly, so she could give her full attention to getting their meal. She couldn't be sure whether Freddie was talking to himself or her when he asked, 'Do you think she was busy cutting up vegetables? It would have had to be meat with a large knife.' She was getting fed up with his rambling on in riddles. 'Do you think that she just turned round, like you did, knife in hand, and . . .' He stopped short of 'cut him up instead', which he was about to say when it felt too sick a joke. Also it would have let the cat out of the bag. He rather enjoyed keeping Amanda in the dark and playing on her curiosity. When he came to think of it, it gave him something of the pleasure of foreplay in sex; a very particular enjoyment of power to arouse the other. He usually missed that with Amanda, with whom there was no place for it because she was always ready, if not leading the way. Perhaps he was making up for it here.

'What the hell are you talking about? When are you going to stop talking in riddles? I'll spoil your supper if you don't spill the beans. I'll put too many into your stew and make them jolly indigestible.' She went and added something to the vegetable stew, put the lid on firmly and, rubbing her hands on her apron down her hips, said, 'Let's have a drink.'

Freddie felt he had to re-start his stimulating game. He no longer had her in his power; the thread of interest had slackened. It was like playing with a kitten; when the thread you were wriggling on the ground before it was no longer 'alive', you had to wriggle it some more, with the right accompanying noise.

'These mousy women . . .' but he interrupted himself, asking, 'Why do they talk of a mousy woman when they mean an unexciting one, when a mouse is the most exciting thing you can imagine for a cat!' Amanda looked at him, drink in her hand, trying to fathom what all this was about, without asking. Her insistent gaze was meant to show that she expected an explanation. He decided to ignore the silent demand but offered her a lead by observing that the so-called mousiest, most insignificant women can evidently be the most shockingly violent. 'You wouldn't remember her, the girlfriend this bloke Horace had; if he did. I shouldn't be surprised if it had been a platonic relationship, they were both so uptight. One doesn't know of course what happened after that . . . until now.' He savoured his power over the mystery.

Amanda still held him fixed in her silent gaze. Maybe she had him in her power, like the kitten making him react to the line, rather than the other way round. He turned towards her full face so their mutually challenging gazes met. As they did, they burst out laughing. 'You rat!' She pushed him further back into the couch. 'You great tease!' As he moved closer to put his arm round her she picked up the newspaper cutting that had dropped on the floor without his realising, and read it. 'Good God!' she exclaimed in a tone that amazed Freddie. She sounded as if she had experienced a personal shock, rather than read a news item about people they had known, even if it was horrific. She looked so shocked, he thought she had lost some of her natural high colour.

Her subsequent silence flawed him. He was the one kept out of something now; as if she knew something more than he. He wanted to say, 'Why should you be so affected?' when she repeated 'Good God!' and sat back in the sofa as if too weak to do anything else. Aware of his bewilderment, she said, 'I met him not so long ago.' She did look pale, Freddie decided, there was no doubt about it. She picked up again the little paper cutting she held in her lap, trying to make more sense of what it said. This man she had briefly known intimately; she could still see vividly the look of wonder on his face, as of a man who had never been made love to before, which she found rather touching. It was about him. Of course she had remembered the girl with him at college, before Horace talked about her. Men had no idea of women's memory for people, quite different from theirs. He had told her that they had got married. Whatever had gone on there? She felt a painful sensation in her solar plexus and then a nasty contraction from her stomach downwards. Her instinctive body was better able to comprehend than her intellect. The news seemed to settle in her lower body, which felt dark and heavy with it. Anxiety then spread upward.

'You look quite upset, darling. You shouldn't take this so personally. You aren't usually so sensitive about these things. After all, these horrific things happen all the time; there are enough nutcases around. But you don't mind the odd crime. I've seen you poring over the gory details.' He tried to bring his arm over the back of the settee and reassuringly round her shoulder. But she was unresponsive. 'Come on, what about that supper? Those beans you've been spilling. Aren't they over-cooking now? I am ravenous and you look as if you could do with something inside you. Shall I pour you another drink?' He was getting slightly impatient with this exaggerated reaction to his innocently produced bit of news. He had just been amazed at their knowing the people in such high drama. The last thing he wanted was to upset her for the evening. Women! Unpredictable.

She looked so preoccupied even when they sat down to eat and he said the food looked excellent, and then talked brightly about things that would normally amuse her, that eventually he said, 'I really believe you are still with this absurd news item!' She put her paper napkin to her mouth – he thought as if she feared she was going to be sick – while she stared at him. He thought he had not fully realised how very round her eyes were. She might have just had a hiccup and put the napkin over her mouth for that, as it soon went back into her lap.

'"Absurd news item!"' she repeated. 'Perhaps "theatre of the absurd"? Wish it were. Sorry, I shouldn't let it spoil our evening. I'll put it aside.' She went to put the scrap of newspaper onto a high shelf and came back to sit down, as if she had put the whole subject away. She smiled at him, 'a good girl' smile. He got up to change their plates and stopped on the way to kiss her thick, wavy hair.

After Freddie had gone to sleep contentedly, Amanda lay on her back, glad to be alone with her thoughts. The shocking puzzle of Horace and wife was now allowed into the forefront of her mind. But rather than taking up the offered place, it made itself felt, as before, in her belly. It was uncomfortable there and she wished she could have some sensible or illuminating thought about it instead. She could not relax and became restless. Instead of anything that shed light on the mystery that bothered her, there suddenly came the compelling idea: 'You better go and see Therese. "Therese". Of course that was her name.' She had not been able to think of it, however well she remembered her and although Horace had mentioned it when they spoke of her.

Could anyone visit someone in prison? Didn't you have to be a relative? She supposed she could apply. She imagined visiting times might not be too mean nowadays. You never knew; Therese might be quite glad of a visit. As long as she kept it light. She could trust herself to do that. Perhaps that was what Horace liked about her. That's why Freddie was upset by her state early this evening; it wasn't like her to take things very seriously. She went to sleep.

She dreamt she was on a turbulent sea. She was being thrown upwards by huge waves and fell again as they did. When they thrust her up she saw that she had left a little boat below her. She seemed to land back on the floor of the shell-like little dinghy. Though the surging sea had soaked her, she was never submerged nor was she afraid of drowning. All she could do was to try and catch her breath as she was thrust up again above the water, then down again on the crashing waves. The force of them made a thunderous noise which seemed to envelop her.

The turmoil was going through her as well as going on about her; there was no distinct inside and outside. She was no longer herself, apart, but like a tiny fleck tossed on the waves; one minute visible and the next lost in the waves. The roaring sound inside her ears went through her head and filled her whole being. She had a sense that, even as she was thrown about in this uproar, there was some way in which she could and needed to remain still. It was the way to stay alive. To lose that stillness would mean being destroyed by the vast forces. She was holding on to that point of stillness when, cast on the shore of consciousness, she found herself on her back, not daring to move, in her bed.

Freddie, still lying in bed, was stretching his arms up and wide apart, and said with evident surprise, 'I dreamt of Horace.' He seemed to be looking to Amanda for an explanation of this peculiar fact. Why should he be dreaming of Horace? His memory jogged him. 'I suppose we talked about him yesterday evening. You talked about him, didn't you?' He looked at Amanda for confirmation and then felt uneasy. 'You said you had seen him recently and had liked him better than before. That was it.' He didn't much like remembering that.

'It wasn't me talking about him but you bringing that newspaper cutting that brought Horace up,' Amanda reminded him.

'Brought him up from the dead?' Freddie asked with a flicker of humour. A shudder went through her that chilled her though she was lying in the warm bed. Freddie felt that he had dreamt about Horace because of what Amanda had said about him, rather than because of the sordid newspaper story of his death. That did not matter to him personally, as did Amanda's remark. 'Oh yes,' he said absent-mindedly as he got out of bed leaving his half of the bed open and bare. She pulled the duvet over and tightly round herself. He felt himself excluded from the bed. 'Aren't you getting up too?'

His tone struck her as slightly critical. 'I don't have to yet.' She wasn't going to tell him that she had had a rough night. Rough! It hardly described the sea she had been in. She couldn't find words to describe it. She felt frightened remembering the experience. She needed to stay in bed to get over it or to take leave of it before she got up and into the day. 'I won't be long.'

Leaving Amanda in the morning, Freddie usually felt fitter to start the day than when he had been on his own. He was usually so pleased with himself and her that, of course, he was pleased with life. He was usually feeling desirable, and master of his life, whatever the world might be up to. He didn't believe that a murder, even of someone he had known a little, could stop him feeling fine after a good night with Amanda. Something spoilt this morning. It was not that newspaper cutting that she had made much of. It was she, he felt reproachfully, who was the cause of the trouble. He wanted to find fault with her. She was all right in bed last night; he couldn't complain about that. She never really let him down there, not like so many women who made one excuse after another. Either they felt too tired, so you had to work to wake them up or it was the wrong time of the month so you couldn't expect them to be at their best. Amanda seemed made for love. You felt she was in her element. There was a danger that if you had a lot of her you expected all women to be like that and got a nasty shock. You had been spoilt. The reason for his niggling complaint against her now was outside bed.

'I didn't think I slept badly,' Freddie said in reply to Amanda's question. She had caught up with him and was standing, with a cup of coffee in her hand, at the table where he was sitting eating his toast. He didn't notice her faint smile at his 'upset' look. He was too sorry for himself at being denied his normal state of feeling on top of the world, to look at her properly. It was easier to feel aggrieved at the injustice of this lapse in his good fortune than to question seriously what made him feel as he did. He could only think that he had not done anything to deserve this loss of form he took for granted. Had he seen Amanda's smile, he would have been even more put out.

In the office he did his best to get on with his working day but then the name 'Horace' appeared, uncalled for, on his inner screen for the second time and he had to remind himself that the man was dead, because he seemed to be thinking of him as someone alive. All the more reason to object, 'What the hell are you doing here? Why should I be bothered with this man who isn't even alive?' He resented the intrusion, especially when he couldn't just tell the intruder to get out or ... It wasn't unlike finding a squatter in your flat whom the police say it isn't their business to get out. You are left more or less helpless and extremely indignant. He was exaggerating, he told himself. It wasn't like him to get into states like this; most unlike.

Perhaps he should ring Amanda and suggest meeting at their favourite pub. They might go on somewhere else from there. Only when he phoned and she sounded not as game for anything as she usually was, he thought that perhaps she too had not been her usual self this morning. Usually she was bubbling with playful life so that he accused her of stopping him getting on with the serious business of the day. She enjoyed seeing him having to resist her wiles in order to get to work. There had been none of that game this morning. Realising this, aggravated his troubled mood now. Without admitting it to himself, it made him doubt his appeal to Amanda. Her usual games made not only her so desirable that he had to escape – to her amusement – but made him the object of desire. He seemed to have had no effect on her last night. He remembered her rolled up in the duvet this morning. He felt almost insulted and angry with her. He put down the phone without any firm arrangement. Usually they said something in the morning about what they were doing that evening, together or apart. Everything seemed to have been abnormal today and he felt put out.

Chapter 12

Amanda had been grateful in the night when Freddie had gone to sleep, and felt a relief when he had gone in the morning. She did not give him a single thought after the door closed behind him. On her way from the door she was stopped short by a movement inside her, as of waves. 'Did I dream of the sea? Yes of course; it was terrific.' As she picked up absent-mindedly the dirty breakfast plates from the table, she recalled, 'I was on a turbulent sea. On or in it? No, not properly in it, certainly not swimming nor on any tangible boat. God, yes – what a sea! I've never been in anything like it. Though it was boiling – don't they say "like a cauldron"? – I was not terrified, just battered as I was thrust about.' And just in this tumult, she now recalled, she had found a precious point of quiet, a kind of full stop. Those words were oddly apt for an essential point in herself. Curious! It was great to have found this 'full stop'. She laughed at the odd meaning which no one else would understand. Not that she understood what the dream was telling her, and she did not want to hear what some clever psychotherapist might say it meant. She was satisfied with how it was. It was hers and no one else's; she would have no one poking their finger into it.

Later in the morning, however, she wished she could share her dream with someone who had no pretensions of any claim to it; just someone to marvel at it with her. She imagined that someone as a woman; it could not be a man. She was astonished when she realised that she was imagining herself sharing her dream with that woman,

Therese, who must be in prison. That was as odd as the dream. Why, she pondered, should she have been seeing herself telling her dream to this woman of all people, whom she had not seen or thought of since their time at college several years ago? She might never have thought of her again were it not for Freddie's newspaper cutting. What had happened to that? She had last seen it when she was sitting on the sofa last night, and believed she had left it there. A quick search round the sofa now recovered the scrap of paper.

After reading it again, she thought of all that she could remember of Therese, which wasn't much. She thought of her as a light-coloured moth flitting about when she was with other people but an inconspicuous, dull-coloured one with folded wings the rest of the time. Had she been the fluttering or the dull one with Horace? His few remarks suggested the latter. Could someone like that wield a knife, as she was said to have done according to that paper? Incredible. It made her shudder and drove her to wash up. At the sink she decided she wouldn't be put off by sensational newspaper reporting from making contact with this woman. She no longer questioned that that was now her purpose.

She didn't really want to be bothered with Freddie for the next few days. She did not worry about his thinking her unfaithful or whatever. He could look after himself. He would not hesitate to follow another attraction should one lure him and would make some lame excuse whenever he returned. She would make her own lame excuse; she was preoccupied with tracing Therese and this was a private enterprise. She did not want Freddie's nose in that.

'Do you remember me?' Amanda asked cheerfully when she came face to face with Therese, as if they had just met in the street. Amanda had been shown into one of the prison visiting rooms to which Therese had been brought and where ten prisoners could have their visitors at the same time. She found Therese not altogether tallying with her memory of her, which may have been faulty, but then Therese might also have changed. The question whether she herself had also changed flitted through her mind. She naturally set out to put Therese at ease, though she felt that it wasn't clear who was hostess under these circumstances. She had invited herself. Weird business, visiting someone in prison, and different from hospital visiting. That seemed always to have a show of brightness with all the flowers and cheery nurses flitting about. Seemed incongruous when someone was very ill and the visitor worried. No flowers or brightness here, she thought. She had been disappointed that the bright flowers she would naturally have brought were not allowed. What mattered was that she herself was allowed. She put aside the slightly worrying question of whether Therese wanted to see her. The brief exchange with her now seemed reassuring.

They shook hands – or at least Amanda shook Therese's warmly. She had to restrain herself from giving Therese a kiss, which was her natural way of greeting. The bare surroundings seemed to make that all the more necessary but she didn't want to overwhelm Therese, who looked at her with reserved interest. Therese had repeatedly gone through all the college faces of her year that she could remember; like looking through a series of photographs. The features of her mental images by which she identified people were exaggerated and others were blurred or missing. Sometimes the identities got mixed up when the wrong name was attached to a set of features. She now looked at Amanda with interest to see how the image of her related to the real person. She was amused by the picture she had produced from memory. She had got the florid impression but had made her a lot bigger than she was. Poor old Amanda! she thought.

What a good thing she couldn't see the picture she had had of her!

She looked at the face before her questioningly and a little anxiously. What Therese called her 'old self' made her instinctively want to offer something to her visitor. She looked about her in vain, as if hoping to find something to offer. 'I am afraid they don't even offer cups of tea here,' she said, lifting her hands in a helpless gesture, showing their sad emptiness. She shrugged her shoulders; obviously there was nothing she could do about it.

Amanda said, 'They provide cups of tea or coffee for visitors to buy while they wait, but of course that's not the same thing. What about you? I suppose you get yours at fixed times. If it's anything like hospitals, you've probably had your tea ever so early.' Neither wanted to dwell on these practicalities and shrugged them off.

The outside world from which this woman had mysteriously appeared felt nearly as strange to Therese as that of the women amongst whom she now spent much of her time. She felt, and was regarded by them, as a foreigner. This person come to see her from another world did not seem to see the gulf that she felt separating them. As far as Amanda was concerned, she might have come to talk to Therese at the hairdresser's, where she also had to sit in a peculiar, fixed position but was not therefore 'out of the world'. Therese could find no trace of the unease she expected in anyone come to see a person convicted of murder. The unease was rather of neither woman being sure of her place. There was no established relationship to provide a prepared pattern into which to fit.

Amanda was not sure who she was in relation to Therese. Throughout the long process of getting a visitor's permit she had been describing herself as a friend. In fact she hardly knew Therese but decided she was a new friend. She had briefly been her husband's lover but, she decided, that would hardly have cut much ice with anyone. They both felt like fish suddenly put together in a tank. There weren't any plants behind which they could shelter and be concealed, nor were there other fish to distract them from each other. There were three or four other prisoner-and-visitor pairs in the bare room but each was in their own tank. To look at the others, let alone comment on them, was impossible and the place seemed deliberately stripped of any pleasant landing place for anyone's attention, so each person was fixed on the one opposite.

There was no escape. The visitor was temporarily imprisoned too. For Therese it was a shock to be locked into this situation that demanded spontaneous communication rather than the exchanges on fixed lines she was learning to have with other prisoners and staff. She looked at Amanda uncertainly; Amanda thought suspiciously. It was no good going back to college days. They shared no subject and Therese felt no inclination to go back there in thought or talk. On the contrary, in killing Horace she had killed her life as an adjunct to him. On no account could she reminisce with this woman. Fortunately their minimal acquaintance, several years ago, was too little for a talking point and could not be the cause of her visit, which was a mystery. Yet asking Amanda what brought her here was the last thing Therese would do.

Amanda, always trusting the moment and taking little thought of before or after, had not troubled to think in advance what she would say to Therese about why she had come. Now the situation demanded it, she told Therese, 'It came to me one night, the middle of the night, that I wished to come and see you; a wish quite difficult to realise, as it turned out. It took more than a month,' she said with a laugh, as if the wish itself were nothing strange. It seemed rather like deciding she wanted to fish in a particular river for which permission was needed. Had she come fishing? The matter-of-fact, rather impersonal way in which she told Therese this made 'Why?' out of place. Therese accepted it as this woman's private business. 'I am glad they checked with you that it was OK for me to come,' Amanda continued. 'Thanks for accepting me.'

There flashed into Therese's mind a question whether this woman could be doing some project on prisons, perhaps 'Women in Prison'. Perhaps she was a social scientist. That hadn't occurred to her when she was asked whether she agreed to have this visitor. It now made her look sharply at Amanda, but what she saw and heard disposed of that disturbing question. Amanda laughed. 'Do you know what they asked me at one point? I think they are a bit paranoid; I mean the prison authorities. They asked whether I was working for a newspaper or on some sort of research; just because I wasn't a relative, it seems. I said, "Sorry, nothing interesting like that. It's just for myself." Luckily they accepted that.' She laughed as usual and Therese smiled sympathetically. 'Do you find at least some of the people "on the ground", rather than higher up in officialdom, quite pleasant?' Amanda asked hopefully.

'I find the men rather better than the women,' Therese replied. It was as new an experience for her to hear herself talk, as to hear Amanda. It was the first time she heard herself, after three months in prison, talk to an outsider. 'There are just a few of them, and maybe for them we're a pleasant change from their usual male prisoners. They are more relaxed than the women, perhaps because we are "little fry" for them; and I am afraid women take authority badly.'

Therese realised that her eyes, wandering over Amanda while she was talking, had become fixed on her dress, like bees or butterflies feasting on a field of flowers they had come upon unexpectedly. Her eyes were feasting on what they had not seen for ages and clearly had been missing. She only realised now how deprived she had been of anything to delight the senses. It struck her poignantly that for months she had been looking only at harsh surfaces, crude colours, shoddy and garish fabrics; nothing soft, subtle or rich. Amanda's clothes, with the many different patterns of the different layers of fabrics she wore, all in muted, rich colours, were a feast. Therese's talk tailed off as she let her attention go with her eyes to enjoy what they had found. The pleasure was mixed with pain as it made her long for something she had always missed without realising it. Although she had made their flat quite nice it was not as she would want the place she lived in to be. She felt it would be more like this woman's clothes and yet different. She was longing for her own colours, patterns and particular feel of a place.

Prison seemed to have formed in her a more distinct taste than she had ever been aware of having. Where most people feel stripped of their individual personality, she had escaped from where she had never found her own. Though there was no stimulation here, she had ideas that she had never been able to formulate before. The books people talked about were mostly shoddy magazines and the few real ones she had found on offer were old copies of novels by unknown authors. There was officially a library service from which it was possible to order books but it was made difficult to do so. She suspected that you made yourself unpopular by using it and had lacked impetus to test this. She was enjoying a new experience of hearing herself think, of finding in quiet, solitary times that she had ideas appearing as from nowhere. She felt blessed when this happened. She had not known that there was good enough soil inside her for ideas to grow.

'I wasn't allowed to bring food in but when I asked they said a book would be all right,' Amanda said. 'Not knowing your taste, I wondered what on earth to bring: old or new, fact or fiction. Impossible to tell. In the end I picked up Lear's *Nonsense Songs*, the only thing I felt enthusiastic about bringing. So sorry if you were wanting something serious; I'll have to make amends another time.'

'Oh no! I couldn't have chosen better myself.' Therese meant it. Someone else knowing the right thing, choosing better than you could have done, was a rare and special pleasure. It made one feel known, which was an amazing experience for her. Perhaps she could not have been known by others while she had hardly any knowledge of herself. 'I shall enjoy looking at these,' she said, looking through the book with its illustrations. 'I don't think I'd want to read a novel just now and certainly no learned tome.'

The mention of learned books made Amanda wonder what subjects would be in Therese's mind; what had been her subject at college? 'Your main subject wasn't geography as well, was it?' It was the first time they had come anywhere near Horace.

'No, it was a subsidiary.'

Therese's brief, subdued reply was the first time she had looked and sounded on the defensive. Amanda saw her looking grey and sitting in a huddled position, as she had feared to find her. 'No,' Therese wanted to say fiercely, 'geography was not my subject! It was not! It was not!' She wanted to throw off and throw right away any garment she had been made to wear against her will and which she refused to wear any longer. She suddenly looked totally dejected.

Amanda thought the subject was sore because of its reference to Horace and the crime. 'Of course, it was social science, wasn't it?' she remembered.

For a minute Therese hated her visitor. She felt herself being put back into the prison of the world in which she had to be and do according to others. She longed for the evening when she would be left alone in her little room for all the hours till the next day with its demands. She had to resist the intense wish to get up and leave this woman. She felt hate rising up against Amanda, a big woman who would dwarf her to nothing and who seemed to be putting her back into a pattern of straight, dark lines by which she felt society obliterating one's individual, irregular lines. She felt it was like having one's unique fingerprints replaced by straight lines.

Amanda was shifting about in her seat. Goodness, this woman looks black, she thought. She looks as miserable as sin now, when she was cheerful before. It must have been too good to be true. She gave Therese a short, questioning look before daring to go straight into the dark cloud by saying, 'It's not surprising that geography is a sore subject for you. I suppose it was damn foolish on my part to ask whether it was your subject.' She paused before going on. 'I tend to blunder about, so friends feel they're rising up to the ceiling with embarrassment when they witness my rushing in where angels fear to tread. They want to hide under the table! Apart from it being one of your subjects, I believe you helped Horace a lot. He said so.' The last words came out of her spontaneously but she was not sorry that they had escaped censorship. Perhaps that was partly why she had come. She even welcomed the words that had slipped out. They might have been designed for the effect they had.

Therese came out of the grey huddle. Her face, from being blurred with suppressed emotion, showed interest. From being lost in herself, her attention was focused entirely on Amanda. Her eyes were intently questioning, searching for the meaning of those last three words 'he said so'. Her eyes demanded an explanation from Amanda, insisting on it with the force of her earlier anger. She would not have known where to begin in words because there were so many questions that could be asked but which were essentially all one. Only Amanda could know the precise question that would go to the heart of the matter. Amanda nearly lost her light touch faced with the intensity of Therese's gaze.

'I had a chance meeting with him in the spring. The first time we really met, because you know how for those three years all we saw of each other was in the crowd round the bar, or at some meeting; just as little as you and I saw of each other. It was quite surprising that on the strength of that we stopped to chat on those library steps; he coming down and I going up.' Amanda had the sense of Therese following her every word as if she would not allow her to pause, always immediately behind her to make her move on. 'Yet I suppose we weren't just meeting each other individually but also greeted each other as representatives of that period, you know?' Unusually for her, she felt herself trying to reflect rather than simply giving her overriding impression of Horace's face as he looked at her, seeming to take her in, as if he were tasting something delicious with wonder. It made her smile in retrospect but she turned the satisfaction into a more impersonal one for Therese. She said, 'It was an amazing day, a foretaste rather than beginning of spring.'

She tried to get away from possibly treacherous to firmer ground. 'I suppose that, because it was such a fine day, one felt rather more expansive than one would have done on a cold or wet one when we might have hurried off after a "Hi!" and "How are you?" On the spur of the moment I asked him to come and have a drink.'

To her relief Therese's face relaxed. 'Of course! I remember him telling me that he had met you. He had said "Do you remember . . .?" She did not repeat his attempt at a description, 'A big girl . . . big woman', assuming that the name Amanda would not mean anything to Therese, and anyway he felt it sounded too personal when he needed to be as impersonal as possible. 'He had to remind me who you were; after all, it was quite a long time ago. Horace never found it easy to describe anyone. He couldn't say whether someone looked well or ill and least of all who they might be like.'

Therese was pleasantly surprised to hear herself talking of Horace calmly and, she thought, objectively.

Encouraged by this response, Amanda went on freely, 'It was odd because it was a new meeting, as we had never really talked before and yet seemed "old" because it was based on the past.' After this thoughtful comment she allowed herself the light relief of a giggly laugh. 'I can understand what you say about him not having been good at describing people.' She had to stop herself saying 'being good' rather than 'having been' and so avoiding the dominating fact. 'It took quite a lot to bring him down to earth, I imagine, though you'd think that's just where a geographer would be! But I suppose he could be under the sea and in the heavens too with climatic studies! But of course I don't know what I am talking about.'

On a more serious note she said, 'I guess that geography was a scientific and almost abstract subject for him.' She had not got this idea from their meeting, she thought. There was no concern with abstract things then. His work was only mentioned, she recalled, when she asked about Therese. She had forgotten her name and asked about the girl he used to be with. He told her they had got married. His only answer to the questions she had asked about her was that she assisted him with his work for his Ph.D. 'Mainly word processing,' he said, 'but also on expeditions,' where she evidently accompanied him.

'Now I remember! We only came to his work . . .' She interrupted herself with, 'By the way, I know nothing about geography whatsoever so I couldn't talk about it. I just learnt to draw an outline map of the British Isles at school but show me a globe and I am stumped! Frequently people talk about countries, even say they come from them, and I have no idea where they are. But what I started to say was that we only came to talk about his work,' she felt afraid to say 'Horace's' as if that brought him too close, 'when I asked some question about you. I had just remembered you with him at college but of course didn't know you were married.'

'Why did his work come up when you asked about me?' Therese asked.

'He told me you helped him with it.' Amanda looked at Therese compassionately, feeling sorry for a woman, especially a wife, who was thought of by a man first and foremost for her help with his work. She could not help sharing the other woman's pain in such a sad situation. Would it be the first thing to come to a man's mind when asked about a woman, if he were in love with her or loved her for herself? Impossible. Horace's remark had given her a glimpse into a bare, hard place where those two lived, which made her just want to keep away. She did not go on thinking about it except for regarding it as a clue to her particular encounter with Horace: his amazed, innocent as well as ignorant delight at what was, unbelievably, new to him. She had not liked to think what an arid life that couple led.

Amanda did not want to be involved in feminist politics. She wasn't going to go to the defence of a woman whose husband thought of her as an aid to his Ph.D. She felt better employed in giving him a taste of the real thing, showing him then and there what a woman was like; her gifts and his place in the show. Far more valuable, she felt, than all the clever and basically stupid talk about women's rights and role. In her view those feminist women, young as much as old, had gone to seed, so everything was sprouting out of their heads instead of lower down where things ought to be growing!

That night, after Freddie had brought that shocking newspaper cutting, when she had lain awake next to him, fast asleep, that glimpse of Horace's married life had returned to her. The brutal facts in the newspaper report had brought back the grim view she had had, as though they belonged together. Only when she had accepted the simple message that had come into her mind: 'You must go and see Therese', had she found a way out of the restless misery in which she had lain there, and had been able to go to sleep.

'Oh I see!' Therese said slowly while taking in that this surprising visitor had known Horace more than she had realised, and more recently. It made her feel that Amanda had perhaps come on account of this recent contact. She almost felt as if Horace might have given this woman a message to give her after his death, which was of course fantastic. How could he have known that he was about to die, in the prime of life? How could he have left a message for her, with this stranger? Had he had any foreboding, such a message would have had to be terrible. But this whole train of thought was on a crazy track.

The idea that Amanda was here on account of her recent meeting with Horace carried no menace. This woman was no avenging angel or messenger of horror. She seemed oddly unconcerned with Horace's death or the manner of it. Amanda behaved as if she did not know the circumstances. For a moment Therese felt this a strong possibility but reason interposed: she is visiting you in prison! For goodness' sake, how could she come here without knowing! Whatever the facts and however absurd it might be, Therese could not help being pleased to hear of Amanda's fairly recent contact with Horace. In a world of strangers, Amanda was like a compatriot whom a homesick person in a foreign country is very pleased to meet.

To Amanda's relief, Therese looked pleased. 'So you've known him recently,' Therese said slowly, as if marvelling at it. 'I mean, you have not just known him as a student but when we were married.' She was on the point of asking, 'What did you think of him?' when she thought better of it. Yet she had a wish to share impressions of Horace and found herself saying, 'How did he strike you?' The question surprised Amanda and the interest she saw in Therese's face made her a little uneasy. She felt the first link between Therese here with that newspaper cutting, and the first suggestion of a strange state of mind.

Although Amanda had anticipated a sort of triumph in going back to Freddie and saying, 'She was perfectly OK, no different from any other woman I might visit in any other place,' happy to disprove Freddie's view of some sort of monster, there was some relief in finding something curious about the woman who could do such a deed. Would it not have been worrying if there had been no hint of a difference? She wanted it both ways: to disprove those who, like Freddie, put a woman who could do this into a category of the mad or monstrous while she maintained that any woman could be driven to it; but also she wanted the reassurance that the capacity to murder belonged to a distinct personality.

What might Therese be looking for, she wondered. She looked and sounded so expectant, as if there were something particular she hoped to have confirmed. Amanda would have liked to please but the other's expectation put her off her stride. 'I thought he was well,' she answered feebly. Her overriding memory was of Horace's rather dazed look; not only as if he were seeing her for the first time but seeing a *woman* for the first time. This odd impression displaced any other that might have been more suitable for Therese. 'Although, as you say, I now knew him as a more mature adult, he had remained quite young, hadn't he? Perhaps I mean inexperienced.' She did not want to fail Therese by just saying that she found him well, and for her own satisfaction she wanted a real conversation.

The response in Therese's face was appreciative. A hungry mouth seemed to have received something that it eagerly consumed. 'Young? Do you think so?' Therese said disbelievingly. How odd when she had often felt like a young woman married to an old man. She had tried to dismiss that feeling and told herself that this remote marriage had many advantages. 'I used to think of him as rather old, even when he was a student,' she said. 'I suppose it was his seriousness, being really only interested in his work,' she added sadly.

'He was a workaholic, wasn't he?' Amanda said, 'and I suppose that meant he was inexperienced in life.' To Amanda, life was other than work.

Therese felt rather like she had done in court when all those feelings about Horace inside her, so much in the dark that she could not see them properly, became explosive. They were making her feel that the truth about Horace had never been properly known or heard and insisted on coming out. They were so pressing now that for safety's sake she must speak about Horace, even if she had no idea how. She was in the position of a child who is driven to make up vivid, lurid pictures of people and situations to express its feelings about them; and in so far as they do that, the pictures are true.

'He wasn't just a workaholic.' Amanda heard the change of tone, like the resonance of a big drum compared with that of a flute. Therese was again seeing herself trying to keep up with Horace, always ahead of her, never looking back, and expecting her to keep up. She relived the agonising feeling of the impossibility of communication in that situation, of her increasing physical and mental exhaustion and inability to call his attention to her plight. She now saw that she might have killed herself; that this might also have made him stop, but then decided that he might have just gone on regardless. To kill him had been her only sure way.

'He was as much a murderer as I,' came from her as a shock to both of them. Amanda stared at Therese. She felt afraid and hoped it didn't show. Was there going to be some revelation of as yet unknown murders? Would she have to tell the police? She dismissed her childish alarm and waited. 'His killing was pure cruelty; mine was not. He would neither look nor listen, anywhere, any time. Out on expeditions I used to tell myself that he was concentrating so much on what he was looking for in the field that he didn't see what was happening to me: whether I slipped or stumbled or just couldn't possibly keep up with his pace. He was too far ahead when I cried out with pain because I had hurt myself. But it was the same at home. He was impervious to me.

'You called him a workaholic, but don't you believe it!' came in a voice that again was a shock. There was the same resonance of the drum, of Therese's whole body and an unknown depth, while the previous thin tone seemed to have been only of the head. 'He was a devil, not the obvious sort with horns for all to see; perhaps the devil's disciple. That fits his scholarly nature. Horace continually, silently, cruelly cut me. Perhaps that's why in the end I used a knife, in one deep, sharp, plain cut, that showed the blood honestly while he never let it be seen.

'I'd rather go to prison for what I did, than live as he did with undetected murder. He cut me so that I was bleeding to death internally. That was the devil's device, ever so clever. You keep it all inside so nothing shows. That's why the devil is so impossible to defeat. People won't believe what they can't see. That's the devil's joy. When you talk of the devil they only think you are mad; that you are something escaped from the Middle Ages because they still look for the devil of that time and haven't caught up with the contemporary versions.'

Brilliant fantasy, Amanda thought, but fantasy with a ring of truth. Her fear had given way to satisfaction that the person now talking in this extraordinary way made their meeting a true one. It hadn't been believable before that she was sitting here with a woman who had murdered her husband; and with whom she, Amanda, had made love not long ago. The ordinariness of their conversation seemed to make nonsense of the facts. The facts made nonsense of that ordinariness.

'I was a ready victim,' Therese seemed to rush on breathlessly. 'He knew I couldn't escape and that there was no one I could call for help.' She gave a little laugh. 'It's brilliant!' she exclaimed with an excessive brightness that hurt. 'You don't have to be marooned on a desert island or in the desert; we lived in total isolation on one of those monotonous housing estates. Though there are a lot of people close together, it's possible to know no one and for people to keep their ears and eyes shut so they hear and see nothing. They are the opposite of the village neighbours that know everything. Nobody knew us or cared.'

Amanda thought longingly of stepping outside the prison and feeling the closeness of other human beings and breathing fresh air. She did not want to be seen looking at her watch and was grateful to see for the first time a clock on the opposite wall. A quarter of an hour before her time was up. She ought not to leave Therese all worked up. She was afraid of the feelings that had been stirred up. She could not see how she had brought her to this depth but, however it happened, she did not want to leave Therese there.

'It was hell, yes hell! Prison is better.' Therese broke down. Her head dropped towards her lap, where her hands received and hid her face. One's own body can have within it the pattern of a family; the hands were acting like a mother receiving the distressed child. Amanda wondered whether she was allowed to get up and go to the other side of the little table that separated her from Therese. The table might be supposed to act as a barrier not to be crossed. She instinctively got up to put a comforting hand on Therese while looking anxiously towards the prison officer standing near the door on their left. He either caught her glance or, prompted by the change in the back view he had of Therese, came over to them.

The 'all right' from the officer was not altogether reassuring. It might have been a threat to Therese: 'You'd better be all right. This sort of thing is not allowed here. You can't have visitors if you don't behave according to the rules.' But he only said, 'Time's nearly up; it'll be as well to go back now. Won't be long before supper.' Amanda looked at the clock in amazement. She was going home to tea; but of course prisons had an absurd timetable for meals, evidently even worse than hospitals. She felt that the officer's idea of supper was like a dummy put into Therese's mouth to keep in the distress that had been coming out, threatening to upset the ordered calm. If supper didn't do the trick, there were drugs that kept trouble under control.

Amanda was glad to see that he put a hand on Therese's shoulder to guide her out in a kindly way, waiting for her to say goodbye to her visitor. Amanda said, 'I'll come again. It shouldn't be so difficult to get permission now I know the ropes.'

At the officer's appearance Therese had regained control and made his hand on her, whether comforting or restraining, unnecessary. 'I am sorry,' she managed to say, 'that I let all this out on you. It came as a surprise to me too. Sorry!' She gave a barely perceptible smile.

Amanda repeated encouragingly, 'I look forward to our talking again.' On balance she believed it was probably better for Therese to have a chance to be upset in this way than to have everything locked up in herself.

Chapter 13

Standing in their bedroom, Hildegard Carruthers exploded at Daimeon, 'I really think this has gone on too long. You really can't go on harping on your brother's demise as if it were the world-shaking event that obliterates everything: your work, family, social life, everything! It's absolutely ridiculous. After all this time! No one expects anything but disruption for a week or so. Not for a month, let alone months! Every Tom, Dick and Harry knows that "life has to go on". But not you!' Here her tone became enraged. She felt at the end of her tether. For a split second there was a shocking recognition that she felt murderous. It linked her with this murder in the family that she regarded as outside her world. She also thought of such murder as 'lower class'. The contempt she felt for her husband as he lay in bed before her fed her fury.

Lying in bed like this, late in the morning, with no reason such as a high temperature or a shattering migraine, was a personal offence against her. She felt him the weakling wallowing in some feeling – she couldn't say what – but certainly not grief at his brother's death! In any case it was unhealthy. One would have thought Daimeon's public school education would have provided a safeguard against such infections. She felt that having to look at her husband lying there was an indignity inflicted on her and grossly unfair.

Daimeon heard and saw her as from an enormous distance. She expected him to participate in what was to him an unreal world. He could only stay apart, saying and doing nothing. When she said something to do with the children, he felt differently, He knew this situation wasn't good for them. He managed to say that he was about to get up. She must still drive him on. 'You know perfectly well that the partners will not, simply cannot, take this much longer. You must know that their patience must be wearing thin.' She stopped the accusing words that were about to follow: 'But you don't care!' because they would have driven home to herself her own miserable helplessness. She would not admit defeat but admitted that his inexcusable behaviour put her in a dreadful position.

He had never before let her down like this. Of course she had always known that he was weak. It was passed over when she first knew him and when they got married because everyone agreed that he was charming. When people said to her, 'What a delightful person,' she knew what they meant and felt flattered. The light of his big blue eyes, his blond hair and his benign face were as pleasent as a balmy, sunny day. One could do without strength while this charm shone so reliably. But after a year or so, she got a bit tired of it, as she would of living in a permanently sunny climate; she would miss a blustering English wind. In spite of her Christian name that acknowledged her German ancestry, she felt English and would miss the Yorkshire moors had she to live in a Mediterranean country.

However, she had managed living in the mild climate of their marriage. She was 'the manager' in every sense. She had seen herself as the backbone of the family, while Daimeon had given it a desirable appearance rather than anything more substantial. Yet now that, what she had preferred to call a break in his work, had alarmingly turned into a breakdown of his whole life, she found that he was after all more essential to the family than she had recognised. She was enraged by his letting down the structure he was supposed to maintain. How dare he lie there instead of being in his place helping to uphold it! She did not see him having a personal breakdown. He was not real enough to her for that to be conceivable. She only felt his incredible weakness in not getting up and getting on with their life, which he owed the family. After all, she had made the best of him all these years. Was he repaying her like this? She dared not think that she might have underestimated him and that this situation might be beyond her management.

She felt she might be looking at a corpse. Why did such morbid ideas come into her mind? This absurd way Daimeon was reacting to his brother's death was affecting her. All right, it wasn't an ordinary death. She hated having pointed out to her by friends, only trying to be helpful, that it was the manner of his brother's death that had the extraordinary effect on Daimeon; that had his brother died normally, he would have taken it normally. She now felt that it was part of Daimeon's weakness that his brother could not have managed a normal death; that there was a shameful abnormality in the family. There had been nothing like that on her side.

Daimeon had got up while she stood there trying to contain her contemptuous anger. It was some relief for her to see him pick up some clothes and go into the bathroom. He had had to get out of her glare. He felt her directing a glaring light on him that threatened to paralyse him. He must get away from it but he had no idea where he could go. Had he been able to feel Hildegard's indignation, it might have been a relief to feel such life. He had no access to such energy. It seemed not to exist in his present state.

He was glad to have had the strength to crawl out of that glare in which he had been fixed, and avoid being blinded by it. But now he felt lost. He didn't see why he was here, nor where else to go. Downstairs or outside the house had for long felt impossible. He not only had no place there but would be actively rejected by these places.

He had only been able to take shelter in his bed. That had felt like the end of somewhere like a very long corridor, where at least he could go no further. There was some safety in that.

Now, driven out of that little shelter into the bathroom, he automatically wetted his flannel to wipe his face and then picked up his shaver. He was being wound up like a mechanical toy engine by the actions performed habitually, which normally led to his going downstairs and into the working day. When he realised that this end was in sight on the track, he stopped short. He had been reminded with a jolt that he must not go that way; there was an obstacle on the track. A horrifying, insurmountable obstacle. He could not go downstairs into the living room. To go there would be like walking into a trap that would fatally mutilate him.

Down there he had heard of Therese. Her name had become hugely enlarged in his mind. It was for him both beautiful and terrible. He felt its terrible power. He could not help admiring it but knew that this very admiration was a danger to him. It had hovered about as if showing off its magnificent wingspan to impress him. It seemed to claim his recognition and praise. She – the great eagle that merged with Therese in his mind – was circling round him. He was her target because she had some secret knowledge of his spirit being at one with hers, so he might even be an accomplice. She needed that to come into the open and was wanting him to confirm it.

Wherever he went from his bedroom shelter, she would make herself felt, even if she would not seize him as the eagle would its prey. She wanted him to acknowledge his link with what she had done. He had been terrified by that demand. Yet he could not keep it out of the house since the inspiring and terrifying bird had first come in the living room, as out of a blue sky.

On that apparently ordinary day, he had been in the living room when there was a phone call. He always left

Hildegard to take calls. They both wanted it that way. He had been busy fixing the video for the children when he was alerted by a strange sound at the phone. He looked up at Hildegard because the voice he heard was not her usual one. His impression was confirmed as she put down the phone and stared at him. It was such an intensely uncomfortable, even eerie moment that he had wanted to laugh, but the laugh came out as a strangled sort of noise that only emphasised the eeriness. Hildegard had then sat down by the phone and said dully, 'Shocking news: Horace has been killed by his wife.'

He had not been in the living room since. After two days he was so unwell that Hildegard had reluctantly called the doctor, who she thought might prescribe a sedative; feeble though it seemed to her to need this. After all, she had rallied soon enough after a stiff whisky. Daimeon had been too absent-minded to drink his. She would grant that as a brother he was obviously closer to the victim than she and that it was a shocking way for a close relative to go. It was extremely unpleasant for the whole family, whether you were a blood relation or not. When she had said this to a friend, the words 'blood relation' seemed an unfortunate choice. It had brought into her mind a horrid idea of the actual blood of this death, which she did not wish to think about. After this she became very careful in what she said to anyone about Horace's death. It was not safe to go near it. She would never discuss it with Daimeon.

Contrary to her determined expectation, Daimeon was nowhere near normal after a week. He lay in bed stiller than she had ever seen anyone, which she found particularly unnerving. Had he groaned or been sick, she could have told him to pull himself together or taken appropriate steps. There seemed to be no fitting technique for dealing with someone lying there, still as a corpse. Then she decided that he probably knew this and did it on purpose, which made her recover her aggressive capacity to cope. She dared challenge the white-faced figure. 'Don't lie there like a corpse!' made even her hold her breath for a moment at her own temerity in choosing these words. She imagined a shudder go through the figure. She bustled about tidying things around him and declared that it was time he had some light food. He made so weak a negative response that the strength of her feelings about him was painfully incongruous.

She had to put up with several days of this deathly stillness in which she stuck to her 'firm treatment' with increasing unease. She struggled to maintain it against the fear of some ungraspable mental phenomenon. It was like working against a ghost. She did not believe in ghosts and must behave accordingly. She was too afraid and ashamed to call the doctor after the first time, when he had prescribed the sedatives. She was afraid of what more he might say about this remote state that he had described as an extreme response to shock. She was ashamed both of her husband's weak nature that could not take a shock, and her own unusual position of not being in full command.

Until now Daimeon had felt being upright, let alone walking to the bathroom, was dangerous. He had lain still in bed for a purpose. It had been the only safe thing to do, to keep out of the way of the threatening bird. He felt that if he moved around he exposed himself to the accusation of murder. If he lay quite still in his darkened bedroom, giving no sign of life, he was as good as 'not there' and was therefore relatively safe. He almost did not exist for himself. While not presuming to have a place in life, not claiming anything from it, he would not provoke any judgement. If he claimed no life, he could not be shown that he had no right to it on account of his guilt.

Daimeon was living by the Old Testament law of 'an eye for an eye'; therefore 'a life for a life'. He saw his life demanded for his brother's, as if he had killed him. He was both horrified and terrified by the murder of his brother. As he lay still, he was rigid with fear. He was both fascinated by his so little-known sister-in-law, Therese, and could hardly bear to think of her. Drawing near her in thought, he marvelled at her actually coming to do such a deed but then got to such a pitch of terror at the idea of her wielding a large knife at Horace that he wanted to shout out 'No! No!' and black out the vision, as one does waking from an intolerable nightmare. The thought 'She actually did this!' incapacitated him.

He was alone because everyone else was going about their daily business. After the shock and exclamation 'What a terrible thing!' they turned away from what was not fit to enter their lives. It was not real to them; it had nothing to do with them. It had everything to do with him. He felt closer to his brother than he had done for years. Some of the time he regarded him with awe; as if by virtue of his death or the vileness of it, Horace had become a heroic figure. Regarding him like this, he returned to his earliest position relative to his big brother who, by the advantage of two and a half years, was always ahead, always able to do everything better than he. Horace was praised by his parents for working hard at school and by teachers for his studious concentration. His parents did not know that other boys despised and mocked the swot. He was tempted to take their side but mostly he was not allowed to do that, by being branded the swot's brother and suffering from their ridicule.

That had turned envy into hatred of Horace and fed the feelings which now gave him this terrible link with Therese. It had only now become terrible. When he had first met her at Horace's and her wedding party, he had enjoyed her apparent pleasure at meeting him. She had made him feel that he was the member of the family she was delighted to meet. It seemed particularly odd that she seemed to compare him favourably with Horace. Therese had even suggested jokingly that meeting him was a wedding present for her. It was funny, Daimeon had thought, how easy it was to please this new wife of Horace's when it was impossible with his own. He had been pleasing to her at first; rather like a pet who is a darling at first but then no longer what is wanted.

At that first meeting with Therese an alliance seemed to have been formed between them. He and Therese unconsciously recognised their corresponding positions with a dominant, demanding partner, though the nature of the domination and demands was different. They enjoyed the appreciation each had of the other's situation. A link had been forged there and then. In the following years they met rarely and only fleetingly but the rapport always seemed to be confirmed by their mutual pleasure at seeing each other.

The present terrible aspect of this link had also been apparent at that first wedding meeting. He remembered his conversation with Therese about Horace revving his work engine unceasingly; about his work having its own momentum, like a motor that was running him, rather than he running it. They agreed that the motor was never allowed to stop because Horace had become identified with it. It had only finally been stopped by killing Horace. Daimeon not only shockingly understood Horace's murder but saw himself as having underwritten it by what he had said. What had happened appeared as the terrible conclusion of their conversation. Such things pass secretly between people, unknown to the rest of the world and almost to themselves.

Moreover, he remembered after all these years the anger he had felt when he had thought that Horace had done better than he deserved in marrying this girl, Therese. He had banished it but it had been real enough for him to remember it now. After what had happened such feelings now seemed to put him into the position of accomplice in Therese's crime. He felt as if he had helped a killer to his weapon.

At this point in his lone deliberations, Daimeon had felt that he was about to be blown up; that his chest would explode with feelings that were beyond anything he had known. A power that was beyond human capacity to contain was rising from a region where everything was infinitely more than life size and therefore unbearable to a human being. He could only be shattered by such forces. The danger of this horror was so great and close that he had to do everything possible to keep himself from it. After suppressing what was boiling up inside him, he lay there in a cold sweat.

When the immediate danger receded he was left helpless by the experience and the knowledge it gave of the immensity of a power, beyond any that one is aware of in normal human life. Even the memory of that glimpse was hard to bear.

He then wished he could lay down his life for his brother, an innocent victim by whom he felt condemned to hell. He felt within him 'Ye have heard it said . . . Thou shalt not kill. But I say unto you that whosoever is angry with his brother without a cause shall be in danger of Judgement . . .'.

Chapter 14

Hildegard was shaking out of the window everything from Daimeon's bedroom that could be shaken; giving vent to her accumulated rage at what she saw as his stratagems to thwart and incapacitate her. She beat these things as if they were a substitute for the body she felt like beating. She was needing to pay him back because he had won; he had cunningly undermined her superior power that had reigned unchallenged all the years of their marriage. By lying there, as if ill or disabled, for no visible reason, he made her rule inoperative. It was as if he had got the power switched off in her house so that a great variety of sophisticated mechanisms by which she ran her household were all rendered useless. Apparently by a brilliant piece of sabotage, he had overcome the power against which he had been helpless for years and seemed likely to be for ever. Hildegard could only see this as the contemptible treachery of a weakling.

She had suffered the indignity and bitter frustration for weeks. Now, as she beat rather than shook his duvet out of the window against the wall, she seemed also to have shaken Daimeon out of his intolerable inertness. Instead of getting out of bed only to go to the bathroom and back, he had taken his clothes with him to get dressed. She had never been able to strip the room as today or express her feelings as now. This slight relief brought the full force of her pent-up feelings into view so it took all her energy to control them.

She overhauled the room more and more thoroughly and gave no thought to what Daimeon was doing. She was so absorbed in herself that the sound of the front door shutting only struck her after many seconds. For a moment she was frightened. Had Daimeon left the house? She had been longing for him to do so, reminding him regularly that his place was in his office, where he was lucky to have it kept all this time. Had she become so accustomed to his presence here that his departure was a shock? Had she driven him out of the house? Where might he go? What was she afraid of? She made short shrift of such unusual concern. Indignation remained supreme amongst her many feelings.

It was a fresh, sunny morning; still too cold to open all the windows to the spring air but she eagerly opened those of Daimeon's room for a good airing. She relished the fresh air coming in, as if the house had been shut up for weeks or they had been in quarantine. She breathed in deeply. He was out of the house. She could carry on with her business without that dead presence weighing on the household.

At lunch-time it was a relief not to have to go through the ritual of presenting him with food, which he only nibbled at, and removing it again. She would have given him none if she had not had to go on being the dutiful wife. But she did wonder where he was. Had he taken any money with him? Did he know what he was doing out there after such a long time? Was he 'all there' after keeping himself shut in his room for so long, and mostly in bed? She would hardly admit her concern, and the uncertainty fuelled her anger against him. Why should she be put into this position? This was a continuation of the insult against her.

Daimeon too felt some relief when he had shut the door of the house behind him, wondering how he could have contained the magnitude of what he carried in a place that seemed like a doll's house. He had no delusions of grandeur but had now had a view of life and death on a different scale from that on which normal active life operates. From where he had been recently, he saw Hildegard at a great distance, preoccupied with minutiae that he could not see. What she said was meaningless to him. She had come nowhere near him since she gave him the news of Horace's death. He had realised from the start that she was too far away to understand or even hear anything he might say. So it had not been possible to talk.

Whereas he had had to lie motionless to give no sign of life to which he felt he had no right, he now felt bidden to leave the house where there was no place for what preoccupied him. In quiet streets he wandered, observing ordinary things and people. Sitting in a café with the outer world around him was an adventure after his long absence. Sitting on a park bench he was lost in stray thoughts and daydreams. He spent the night in the station, pretending that he had missed his last train and felt it not worthwhile getting a room somewhere for the few hours till the first morning train. In pretending that he was only waiting to go somewhere, it occurred to him that perhaps this was more true than he realised. He seemed to wake up to the question 'Where am I meant to go?' The answer 'Therese' came like a bolt from the blue. It was a shock but appeared to be no real answer. He wanted to dismiss it as absurd but his heartbeat would not let him. How could that be the answer? It was a practical impossibility. Though he could see no practical way, he was held by the idea and knew he could not get rid of it. He must find this way because there was no other.

Hildegard never knew what had happened during that night. She always thought of it as Daimeon's secret that never failed to rouse her curiosity. She imagined some dramatic encounter or brainstorm that kept him out all night. She sternly resisted the temptation to call the police because she could not bear the sensation that this might cause. 'Distraught wife reports missing husband: mentally disorientated after the murder of his brother by his sister-in-law!' No! Never would she play any part in that sort of game. She was not going to be turned into a weak victim by her weak husband. The mere idea roused such strength in her that she felt she could win whatever battle lay ahead.

In spite of her long, largely sleepless and fearful night Hildegard was not caught out by the anger that tends to overcome relief when suddenly the agony of waiting and worrying is ended by the safe arrival of the missing person. Being determined that whatever might befall Daimeon, she was not going to be the victim of his situation, she had already set off on her own route. Her nonchalant reception of him on his return in the morning seemed to be a triumph, until she found herself thrown off her perfect poise in a way she could not have foreseen.

She had not been prepared for the change in him that startled her as soon as he spoke to her. Where had he been, what had he done to come back so different? He was no longer in that maddeningly inaccessible state she had had to endure for weeks. Nor was he the charming Daimeon everyone knew, whose charm she saw as a disguise for his weakness. Far from being the pitiful figure for which she had been prepared, he struck her as rather preoccupied and in some odd way commanding respect. What shook her most was a strange independence which made all her own attitudes disconcertingly inappropriate. She felt out of place and unable to make her usual way through the day. It was like getting into her car to find nothing in its familiar place so it was impossible to drive off as usual.

Although she was used to looking down on Daimeon

inwardly, he had been a fixed point to which everything else in her life related. She had been waiting these exasperating weeks for his return to his usual place. He now appeared astonishingly returned to life from his inaccessibility and yet she could not tell where he was. He seemed to be in some place of his own, unknown to her. To her consternation he no longer fitted into the place she had for him.

Hildegard had relied on Daimeon's prompt return to his office when he returned to outer life with his faculties apparently restored to normal. To her intense irritation he maintained that there were other matters to which he must attend before he could return to work. She was about to explode with indignation at this presumption towards his long-suffering employers, but there was something about his preoccupied air that made him immune to her pressure, which in the past he could not have resisted. He was not in his usual place to be targeted, so she was as good as disarmed. She felt her world had been shaken as in a kaleidoscope; there was no familiar pattern. Everything felt in disarray.

Daimeon was back in the world for a purpose. While he lay in bed inaccessible, he had been in the depths like Jonah until he was spewed out by the whale to fulfil his mission. For him this was centred on his brother's murder. To say 'murder' even to himself, rather than 'death', was difficult. He had to say it to make sure he took the right way to his sister-in-law in prison. He needed all the strength and assurance that comes from following a direction received from an inner authority. Only the power emanating from there is able to move one in strange directions and do what would be inconceivable otherwise.

To make his own way in the world Daimeon had to be more fully in it than before. To Hildegard's amazement he spoke to his boss on the phone about his situation without his usual prevarication. She could hardly believe that he was doing so without having talked about it for a long time beforehand or having had to be persuaded by her. She could not stop herself standing outside the door to catch as much as she could of the conversation. He spoke briefly but genuinely of the profoundly shocking experience that had, regrettably, made him unfit for work during the last month; that he was now back in action but must attend to matters concerning the death of his brother before anything else, so he would greatly appreciate their patience for another short while till the time when he returned to work.

Though Hildegard could not help admiring the maturity of his words, the final request aroused her regular indignation at such a preposterous demand when he had already taxed their patience inordinately. But she found herself once more out of place when it was evident from the affable conclusion of the conversation that Daimeon's request had met with sympathy. She later accepted without comment the information that he was putting off his return to the office because he needed to look into things connected with Horace's death. She wondered what he meant but only said 'Oh?' He was glad that he could ignore this.

Daimeon's new self-containment discouraged questions or discussion of his affairs. Since they had always been part of Hildegard's sphere of influence this was a striking change. She seemed too perplexed to fight it. But Daimeon was not secretive so Hildegard soon learnt from letters going out and coming from prison authorities that he was concerning himself with his sister-in-law. She realised that he intended to see her. The determination he showed in this was new and prevented her questioning the wisdom of what he was doing. It impressed and alarmed her. She realised that as a brother-in-law he would be an eligible visitor. Or might the authorities be wary of trouble from the victim's brother? Might they scent danger or suspect trouble with the prisoner?

Daimeon's sense of complicity with, and compassion for, the murderer was the most unlikely reason for his behaviour to occur to anyone. Hildegard had no idea of it. She could not imagine what Daimeon might want to say to the woman who had given herself up for killing Horace, but feared some perverse approach. Was he going to say 'Well done' for going to confess? She could hardly have done otherwise, Hildegard thought, for how could she cover up a bloody murder with a kitchen knife! Hildegard could not bear to think of it; anything as crude as that was beyond her and should surely be kept out of her family. She never dreamt of marrying into a family that could bring her near that sort of thing. That her children should be even remotely associated with it was a new, enormous accusation against Daimeon. The least he could do was remove himself as far as possible from the whole deplorable business; yet here he was intending to visit the woman who was the murderer. It was unbelievable but she remained silent on the subject.

Chapter 15

After her visit to the prison Amanda wished she had found out whether Therese had other regular visitors. She had every intention of going again but would hate to be the only visitor. She had no wish to be a life-saver for one inside by becoming their one link with the outside world. She liked Therese, and would enjoy carrying on their first conversation another time. There was also her curiosity to know Horace's and his wife's story from inside.

When first committed to custody, it had been a relief for Therese to be shut away from the normal world. She could not have continued out there, which was why it was natural for her to go to the police to ask them to take her in. She still could not tell how long she had spent alone before returning to Horace to own what she had done, which naturally led her to the police. That time did not fit into the measure of days or weeks and certainly not hours.

There was no one to visit her inside. She was in a different position from most prisoners who, if they hadn't a husband or boyfriend with or without children, had a mum or girlfriend or somebody. Only when one woman asked her, 'Haven't you got nobody?' did she feel a pang but told herself that that was a reflection of the questioner's attitude making her feel sorry for herself, rather than what she felt. As there was no one out there she really knew or who was a real friend, it was safer and simpler to be kept locked in here by herself, however hard.

She could hardly believe that the formal request for a visit on a printed form which was handed to her one day was not a mistake and was for her and not someone else. She had said that she had no relatives because the nominal, distant ones did not count and those by marriage were strangers. They would be the last people to come near her here and now. When she saw Daimeon's name on the form, she did not know whether to be pleased or put out. At the sight of his name she felt lit up by pleasure but quickly she put out that light, as if to say, 'I don't want it.' Why should he want to come and see her? She had thought she was well and truly shut away, and here was the prospect of a breach in her security. Staring at the printed form, she realised that it asked for her consent. She could refuse it. The form was left with her to sign or not.

She said to herself that coping with the people around her was enough for her without this extra, but the pleasure of her past contact with Daimeon flickered across her dark view. She would not give it any importance, treating it as irrelevant in her present situation. What could the pleasure she had felt years ago, when she had been surprised to find Horace had such a likeable brother, mean in her present situation? It was ludicrously beside the point. But the pleasure became like a temptation that would not leave her alone when she was going to withhold her consent to the visit.

She sat for ages with the form in front of her, resenting this intrusion into her privacy. But when she saw the absurdity of that when every day was a struggle, it made her more miserable. Was she that much of a nutcase, as others here evidently believed, that to be shut up in a cell on her own was all she wanted? She now felt more of a misfit than ever; as despairing as she had ever done here. She must see Daimeon, at least to refute such a picture of herself.

But then came the worrying questions. Why should he

come and see her when she had killed his brother? She was frightened. Could he come to do anything to her? There was always a prison officer nearby who would presumably protect her. Thinking of Daimeon she found it hard to imagine him coming as the mouthpiece for a vengeful family. On the other hand she was thinking of him as he was at their wedding party. If he was happy then, presumably wishing Horace happiness, this was all the more reason for his being upset and angry now.

Circumstances change people and no one could be expected to see her point of view. Her view seemed to her so simple and clear that she had regularly to try and drum into herself that other people could not see how you could kill your husband 'in cold blood'. They could understand if you had a history of being violated which had driven you frantic or you had turned on him in physical self-defence, but with someone as harmless as Horace? It would be inconceivable and she must be a monster. They were unaware of how many forms violation can take. Some people, baffled by her gentle behaviour and ordinary appearance in court, concluded that she had suffered an extraordinary fit of madness and insisted on a psychiatrist's report, in spite of her insistence that she did not wish to plead reduced responsibility through temporary imbalance of mind.

She said that she had known what she was doing and saw it as necessary though she had certainly never imagined doing it, let alone planned it. Yes, she had acted on the spur of the moment, and yes, it was a complete surprise to herself. But no, she could not say it was as if someone else were doing it because it made complete sense to her. She could still hear the gasp there was at this. She apologised to the court and especially the presiding judge, who she felt was trying to help her, for sounding so contradictory but she was only speaking the truth. Trying to find out if she lacked normal human feeling, suggesting she was a psychopath, they asked her if she judged other murders, which she must have read or heard about, as also making sense. She had said that she could not remember such a case but now she came to think of it, hers could not be the only one in which it made sense. She could remember an audible sigh that puzzled her. She could not tell what it meant. There was no way of knowing and it worried her.

She must not fall into the same trap now of believing that others could understand why she had had to kill her husband. People didn't see these invisible things that happen to you, perhaps not even those that happen to themselves. They could not see things like the shackles of Horace's everlasting expectations and demands which held and cut into her, and from which she could not free herself; that she had struggled against these in vain, until she was driven to cut him off forcibly. If these things were truly invisible to other people, life must be even more surprising to them than it was to her. Her living in a different world from other people was troubling and sometimes filled her with alarm.

She told herself that Daimeon could not have the slightest idea of how she came to kill his brother. It might be terrible for him to find out. Now for his sake she was inclined to stop him coming. But, after all, it was his request; no one was making him come. Perhaps someone was. She could not know. Perhaps he was being sent as a family representative. What would they want him to say to her? She arrived at the same place of total, worrying ignorance.

She had a restless night before the day of Daimeon's visit. She could eat even less than usual. When she was supposed to be getting ready to be taken to the visiting room, she felt this one of the hardest things she had had to do in prison. One of the women who had got wind of the impending visit said to her enthusiastically, 'You better get out your beauty box.' Perhaps because she looked blank she added, 'Haven't you got none? You can borrow some things.'

Therese wasn't sure whether this was meant seriously or whether the other was making fun of her and muttered, 'No thanks.'

'Stuck up thing! You don't half need it,' her disappointed fellow prisoner muttered as she walked off. It made Therese give a glance at the mirror but she did not register what she saw.

The last thing she could do was to put on a bright face. She wanted to hide. Even in prison you were not allowed to hide. She felt herself being marched along by the officer on duty, having to walk before him as if she were going to court again. Was she just going to be looked at? If expected to speak, what was she meant to say? She felt as if all the life in her had frozen. She didn't know where in the room she was to go and looked into it fearfully. With all its small tables and chairs it reminded her of a classroom. She felt relief at the sight of a blond head that was familiar. She was surprised by her own spontaneous smile that met Daimeon's.

He held out a hand to her that she took hesitantly. It was a wonderfully warming human contact. There was an echo of the happy surprise of their first meeting, and of learning that he was her brother-in-law. Both were reminded of that meeting and struck by the comparison with the present one, which made Therese lower her head. But Daimeon needed to look at her. He had been waiting for this impatiently. He had not been able to give a satisfactory answer to the questions: why did he need to see Therese? What did he hope to get from seeing her? He had dismissed the questions as not answerable in advance. The answers could only come from seeing her, which made him say, 'It is good to see you,' with a sincerity that made Therese look up in surprise. She was released from her frozen state; a thaw could begin. She felt what she called 'a good pain'; one that meant life.

She was glad of his presence but not able to look at him for more than a moment. For the first time she felt great sadness at the reality before and between them, even remorse at what she felt she had had to do. She lifted up her eyes at him with a plea for belief, if not understanding; they said what was in her heart and mind but was beyond her to say in words. Her truth was so real and strong to her that in an inarticulate way it was conveyed to him. They seemed to share it, which was a painful relief to both of them. They knew themselves in some way more surely together than any map could tell them. 'It is good to see you,' Daimeon repeated.

'It is good of you to come,' she said, surprised at how important she found his visit.

She was on the point of asking 'Why have you come?' but dismissed it as irrelevant. She was confused by the impact of his visit. 'It's such a long time since we met . . . I am sorry to bring you to this place.' Her expression as she looked around the impersonal room was not just an apology to his aesthetic sensibility. It was like the simple mark a primitive, illiterate person might make for something immensely complex. A simple mark like this had to serve where there was neither time nor words to express what she meant. He understood that.

'Are they treating you all right? Is it not too rough?' He did not like asking because he was afraid it must be gruesome. He felt lily-livered, afraid of hearing how she had to live day and night, for what must seem for ever. He had been in so strange and distant a place while he lay in bed, since he heard the news of Horace's death, that factual details of her conviction and likely sentence had escaped him. He was never sure what he had forgotten and what he never knew. He could not ask Hildegard.

He looked at her anxiously. 'I think it could be a lot worse,' she replied. 'I don't altogether mind being shut up, so far, you know. It's a shelter I wouldn't have outside. A prison sentence is not just imposed on you but a natural sequel when you could not just live outside as if nothing had happened. It's a bit like being taken into care, into a very bleak institution. It would be easier if I were left alone more; just the opposite from the others, for whom that's the worst part. Being left alone is the one thing some of them can't stand. Pity we can't swap. I'd love to give one of them my social times, specially "recreation".

'But it's stupid to talk about these things. They are bad enough without my wasting time talking about them . . .' She was about to say 'rather than . . .' but withdrew, afraid of what might follow. What would she talk about? She gave him a dejected look as if she had been rebuffed. After all, he was Horace's brother! How could any of that family talk to her or she to them? She asked herself again whatever had made him come and see her, and almost blamed him for doing so. The depressed look became an angry one.

'I don't know what makes you want to come and see me!' she burst out. Then, aware of her roughness, she added uneasily, 'I mean, I don't see what there is to say.' Her deed was unspeakable and she obviously too dreadful a person for the family to speak to. So why this tease? She felt a remnant of honour that she wanted to defend and felt like saying, 'Leave me alone then.'

Daimeon said dejectedly, 'I am sorry.' He was made to feel an intruder who had no business to be here. He remembered the night he spent in the deserted station where, having no idea what to do next or where to go, he had found out his destination. 'Therese, in prison' had been like a place written up on one of the station indicators. It must help him answer Therese's hostile-sounding question.

'I had to see you. I was certain I must see you.' He mumbled, 'I'm sorry if it has upset you.' Then suddenly thinking that she might have been offended that he had not come earlier, he said, 'I'd have come before if I'd been well.' He was too intent on trying to state his own position to see her incomprehending eyes and frown. 'I was in a strange state ever since I heard the news; I mean, since Hildegard was told of what had happened. It seems extraordinary that for so long we knew nothing. Our family are not good at keeping in touch, as you must know. Apparently one side of the family assumed that the other had told us. It is shameful that one literally did not know whether one's brother was alive or dead!' Daimeon was reminded of the guilt by which he had been crushed.

'I don't know quite what happened after we heard. It was so overpowering, all I could do was just lie still to try and survive – like you might in an enormous storm or some cataclysmic event beyond comprehension. What I heard the doctors say up above me had no connection with what I was experiencing.'

He was relieved when he sensed a flicker of interest instead of the earlier hostility. It helped him to dare go on as he knew he must. 'I could only lie still, in terror of an indescribable power, and depend on mercy. It had something to do with penance. All this sounds ridiculous because we don't see things like that nowadays but it's actually the nearest to the truth as I experienced it. I haven't talked to anyone about it till now. Old words that have been made redundant come to mind as suitable for what I am trying to describe. I know that one's state is filed in the computer by the doctor as one or other mental disorder, which bears no relation to the experience. That experience, however shattering, is more real and true than anything else. The doctor is only concerned with removing the pain, not with the truth.

'When you get to somewhere as deep as the bottom of the sea, you know you are at God's mercy. You know your need for mercy. It makes me think of what we used to read about in scripture, of people going into sackcloth and ashes and fasting for forty days. I shouldn't be surprised if I had been out of the world for forty days. I just was not there to talk or be with anyone. I knew no time or anything in the everyday world above, below which I lay at a great depth. The rest of the house did not exist. I can see now that it must have been worrying for the family. In the end I had to come back to the room, where I lay also.

'I was made aware of Hildegard being upset. Where I had been is more real and true than what we think of as "the real world". It is terrifying partly because we behave as if it were not there. I have no doubt about it being God's reality, and to be separated from it is terrible. One must dare somehow to be in or with that other world while one is in the everyday world. One can be there in a deep, painful trust that the reality is as wonderful as it is terrifying; trust that love and mercy are to be found there.'

Daimeon put his face in his cupped hands, needing the darkness. Therese sat in silence. She felt amazed and peculiarly privileged to be given this account of his experience; a strange, precious thing brought here, of all places. But then she looked at Daimeon apprehensively when he lowered his arms and looked like someone come ashore from a tumultuous sea. She did not know what to say but knew that she must say something. 'Thank you for telling me,' she managed, hoping it might do. They sat in silence for a while.

The duty officer came up from behind Therese, as if he were just taking a stroll, with a casual 'All right?' He came just far enough for a quick look at Therese. Having seen her visitor's odd behaviour, hiding his face and then sitting in silence, he wondered what was going on. There was of course his colleague on the opposite side of the room who had a full view of Therese and would have signalled if there were anything amiss but he thought he'd just check for himself. 'Not long to go,' he said, which usually was a warning but now went with his idea that the two of them might be having an awkward time.

'Thanks,' Daimeon said. He was reminded of being warned as a child 'just five more minutes . . .'

'I don't know why I had to come and say all this to you. I don't understand but I know it is not an accident, nor a case of needing to unburden myself. It seemed as if I were sent to do it for another purpose. I realise that it must seem very strange; I hope not upsetting.' He looked at her both fearfully and hopefully. 'Perhaps I can come another time and we can talk about other things. Would you like some books or anything else that you are allowed? We'd like to know.' He was used to saying 'we' as practical things were done by Hildegard because she did them better, but realised that it was inappropriate here. Hildegard would not have anything to do with his visits here.

'Thanks. I can't think of any book just now . . . but . . .' she hesitated because she wondered if she could really expect him to come again.

'Go on. What were you going to say?' Daimeon encouraged her.

'Some paper, I mean writing paper, I would appreciate. But please, of course, any time . . . whenever . . .'

Chapter 16

Therese was puzzled. Daimeon had talked of terrible guilt that had taken him somewhere like the bottom of the sea; and of the need for mercy. It was to do with the death of his brother; of Horace murdered by herself. Her guilt then, not his. But he had not talked about her, only himself. He seemed to have taken her place. She was troubled. Could this be some roundabout way of talking about her guilt? Of letting her know that he wanted her to be forgiven? It was a preposterous idea. It would be devious and the mere idea made her angry. But then she reprimanded herself for putting such a peculiar interpretation on his trusting account of a strange experience. Was she being offensive bringing herself into the picture? But there remained the question of some connection between what Daimeon had told her and herself.

When Daimeon had left that day, she had been full of gratitude for his visit. It had seemed like a gift. Then it had become more and more disturbing. It was as if she had drunk some potion that was working in her with strange effects. She could not purge herself of it. She could not appreciate her solitary times as a longed-for relief from the social times, as usual. When she came back to her room that had been a refuge, she seemed to come back to where she was open to attack by an unseen inquisition.

She felt harassed as she had not done since she forcibly freed herself from Horace. She had supposed that her confinement here, the fact that she was unable to escape, satisfied those inner strange beings who had for so long been clamouring for her attention. They had even allowed her to forget them. Had they turned against her now? Had they been roused by Daimeon's words? She could believe that they belonged to the world Daimeon was talking about. She had felt it a deep, awesome, true world when she saw it through his eyes, but now she felt frightened.

What had she to do with Daimeon's inner world? Why had he come here anyway? 'Been sent' were the words he used. How? Why? He did not say that he had been sent to give a message but perhaps implied it. In that case it was a perplexing, mystifying and disturbing one. If he were a messenger, why couldn't he have made his meaning clearer? She told herself that if she could not understand, she must wait till he came again. He had said he would. Then she could question him. But that didn't help now. If you have a nagging tooth, it doesn't help to say that next time you saw the dentist you could mention it. She could not ask to see Daimeon, and would not if she could.

After several miserable days and restless nights, with the equivalent of not one but several teeth nagging her, she sat wretchedly in her little room. Its space became threateningly small when she wished she could get away from where she now felt herself being undermined. She was afraid of becoming claustrophobic in prison. She told herself that if she were able to walk out she would be assaulted by the same things that were getting at her here. They did not belong to this cell which her room had now become. It had been altogether different when it had meant a place of her own to be in.

Therese paced up and down the little room more and more frantically, as she had heard described 'like a caged animal'. She had never done this before. Her body might sometimes have wished she could climb a great hill that would match its energy but she realised that her spirit had also demanded the confinement. It needed her to be inside. She needed to be her own prisoner, to bear being with herself, even talk to herself.

She now had the idea of someone waiting for her inside herself, who was quiet and not one of the clamorous presences that had previously demanded her attention. When she turned her attention to this unknown one within, it appeared to be a woman who would never ask for attention but would wait to be approached. Her very presence seemed to be 'a waiting' without pressure. Therese felt guilty of having ignored her until now. She could defend herself by saying that this person had not made herself apparent so she could not be blamed for not seeing her, but she knew that somehow she had known of this unobtrusive, yet not self-effacing, person in the dark recesses within.

She stopped her frantic pacing. By not running away, she could reach the other, who was quietness personified; a lively quietness. Most remarkably this mysterious, modest person seemed to provide limitless space. The walls of the cell-like room became insubstantial. The infinite space was that of limitless acceptance; space for the truth. By its very nature that space could have no barriers or limits. Unlike empty space, it felt actively receptive, as if made to receive all truth lovingly. The modest woman led her to this space, not only ready to embrace all that Therese had been keeping locked up in her small dark interior, but prepared for all truth to be given its rightful place and due recognition. This boundless receptivity with the right measure for everything, though beyond the limits of any one person was at the same time essentially personal in that its very nature was unconditional love. There could be no criticism or judgement here. It was plain to Therese that these did not exist here. As if she had come to a very light, spacious place she had never been in, Therese was overcome by the marvel and had to find her bearings.

There was no confusion about her cell and this great

space she was experiencing. She realised that a spiritual presence gave this limitless space within. It might be within everyone, mostly ignored, as it had been by her. She approached the female presence hesitantly but not guiltily because guilt seemed unable to exist in the atmosphere of this all-embracing love. Nor could self-justification exist here. Her murderous deed, far from disappearing, was more real in this setting than it had ever been. It was here in its own right rather than to be condemned or defended. Weighing up, even in the scales of justice, was seen as a trivial pursuit where there was a closer, more far-reaching encounter with the truth.

This was an admission of the truth, more awe-inspiring and humbling than she had known anywhere. It was a silent admission because words would break up the wholeness of the truth. They would distort what needs to be known in its entirety. The mind gives up its customary selecting, discriminating and assessing when it finds itself in a realm where these become pointless. Therese was awed by the immensity of where she had arrived. She felt cold and shaking. There was a great surge, as of the sea, within and without her but with no threat of drowning her. It was a painful wave of belonging to all, giving up all the reservations of having to belong to one thing or person and exclude another, be on one side rather than another, which destroys one's true whole humanity.

Therese was now content to be led by this person whom she could trust as no one else. She felt as if she were taking the other's hand when she came near the fact of murder, as she could not bear to go near it alone. It would utterly crush and overwhelm her; not just kill but grind her to dust through ages of unimaginable torment. Murder, she now knew, was infinitely more than her cutting herself free from Horace by making him incapable of taking her with him wherever he went, expecting her to serve him or his work, which was dead matter to her and made her dead.

She felt herself before something no human being could stand, when she became aware of something emanating from the unknown yet very close woman which was both gentle and powerful. She felt it like an invisible stream surrounding her which not only assured her of safety; it assured everything and everyone of a place in my life by forgiveness and acceptance. Without forgiveness she could not live. If this stream had not reached her, or she not been brought within its reach at that moment, she would have perished in an unimaginably terrible way. She would have gone down 'into the pit', into a hell that was worse than being consumed by fire. Now the strength of the surrounding stream enabled her to breathe freely, apparently for the first time. She was alive in her own right, like everything and everyone else. The proportions of everything seemed to have changed. People were not dwarfed by their deeds, however formidable for good or ill. The all-encircling stream confirmed a fundamental state of Being.

Being there of right did not mean that she had 'a right' to be. It could not have been more different. Having a right was obsolete. There was nothing to claim when, like everyone and everything, one was there because one was one of God's creatures, of life and of love. This was the simplest and most astounding conclusion of all. It was a plain fact that love and life were one. Therese saw that this was the foundation which gave everything its place; and that without knowledge of this we flounder disastrously.

'You look as if you'd had a night out, and not on your own!' Sharon turned from Therese to the other women. 'Just look at her! She looks like she's had all she wanted, all calm and relaxed as she is. Looks like someone had really done her good, given her just what's wanted. What this place is crying out for, I'd say! What your right man can give. One who knows, not one of those to whom it's a quick come and go like having another fag.' Her whole body heaved with a sigh.

Therese's calm had been spotted at once. Last night she had eventually gone to sleep wonderfully comforted. The taunting, envious remarks were both true and off the mark. She felt the acuteness of the women's longing for men that was a constant outcry in their existence here, and made her aware of the deficiency of her own experience. She felt unnatural compared with them, inferior for her lack of experience but also frightened by the evident intensity of their need and what she saw as the great size of their bodies.

'Just a good night's sleep,' she mumbled in answer to Sharon's remark and the others' supporting laughter and echoes.

'I guess so!' one of the women continued on the same track with emphatic innuendo.

'Wouldn't have thought we had one up to it here, would you? Maybe they hide their lights under a bushel,' was someone's surprising contribution. The others, giving the words their own interpretation, roared with laughter. They went on, not for the first time, to an assessment of various officers, which, with variations on the common obscenities, always produced laughter and relief of some sort. As usual, Therese felt out of it, though this time she was in the unusual position of having stimulated the fantasies in the first place.

Chapter 17

Hildegard breathed a sigh of relief. 'It does seem,' she said on the phone to her friend Ursula, 'that he has turned a corner. Mind you, one can never be sure. I've learnt that the hard way with Daimeon. But it's a fact that after being out most of Tuesday afternoon, he came back looking more all-there than I can remember. It was quite amazing to see him actually right here, as if a sort of veil had been taken off his face.' She stressed the word 'veil' self-consciously, aware of talking rather peculiarly and not in her usual sensible way. 'To see him without that absent-minded look is quite amazing. So . . .' and she gave an audible sigh, 'wish me luck, dear, that we might be back to some sort of normality.'

Walking away from the phone, she realised that she had been on the point of saying, 'Wish me luck that I might have my husband back' but would not because she had always felt that she had no real husband. She had regarded him rather as a kind of puppet who played a part for family and social purposes. She had treated him with a certain respect but her real feelings were expressed in private; like in childhood, where in private you kicked another child to whom you were made to be nice in public. She could not help despising Daimeon's apparent inability to hit back. The child who kicked you back might even become your friend, but never the one who didn't. That sort of person remained a thorn in your flesh for ever. In a way he or she won by leaving you with your bad feeling indefinitely.

Now there was no doubt that Daimeon had emerged

from that anaesthetised state, as she called it, yet he seemed not to feel her sharp jabs. If they did touch him, he would move with an unsuspecting 'sorry' as if he had just been in her way. At first she was surprised but then irritated, suspecting this blandness was meant to deny her the satisfaction of showing he had been struck. She told herself that that was too sophisticated for him. Nor did she believe that this apparent insensitivity was a remnant of his illness, whatever that had been, which was a friend's suggestion. He seemed remarkably clearheaded these days; surprisingly more so than before. It was disconcerting that he was not back where or how she expected him to be.

She was reluctant to admit some change that floored her. To be floored went right against the grain. She liked to have things taped. It would have been easier to slip back into the familiar old pattern. She had had trouble enough from Daimeon without now having to reorientate herself. She was amazed how quickly he caught up with practical family affairs and how he dealt with them. Once in a rare reference to his illness that was neither treating it as a disgrace, nor an inexcusable trial for his family, she said, 'Your time off seems to have cleared your mind.' Taken aback by her own generosity, she added, 'Just as well, considering what there is to make up for!'

She gradually realised that Daimeon's apparent imperviousness to her jabs, which meant a loss of power for her, was due not to a decrease in his sensitivity but rather an increase in his strength. All right, she responded internally, so you are more your own man, are you? She felt in the position of a mother faced with the adolescent's new self-assertiveness. She might have to learn more about Daimeon, and their partnership would have to adjust. She could no longer rely on having him taped, which was a bother and dampened her over-confident manner. After so many years she found it hard to grant that there might be something in Daimeon that was not in her possession, well-known and labelled. Her assumption was that she must know it all.

Of course she had not known what was going on when he lay there, out of this world, but that was so extreme that he was just labelled 'ill'. After all those weeks the recovery seemed to have come suddenly. It was most striking after the night when she was worried stiff because he had gone out for the first time and not returned till the next day. She had told herself in the course of that night that this was something scores of wives experienced, but she had never expected to happen to her. She had then been prepared for him to return as a wreck, if not brought home by police or ambulance. She had not been prepared for the inexplicable fact that he returned in a better state than when he had left; better than she had known him for months. It was not her imagination but a fact for which she could not, for the life of her, think of an explanation. Obvious suggestions like 'a night out on the tiles' simply did not fit, let alone convince.

She became aware of his preoccupation with some business of his own after that first outing. Later she realised it had been a visit to his sister-in-law in prison. She was not surprised that he had not told her about it till well after the event. She would have been dead against it. She could barely face the apparent fact that Daimeon's startling improvement coincided with contact with the person whom she was determined to cut out of their lives; whose name she had decreed to be unmentionable.

Daimeon's brother could not be cut out but the manner of his death could be. You could speak of a relative who was dead but not of one in prison, let alone for murder. How could she do other than ban mention of this woman to her children? It was bad enough that they might find out when they were grown up. By then the woman might be out and about, considering how lax the law was nowadays. Of course there ought to be no question of her ever leaving prison but apparently the prison service couldn't cope with the numbers if all killers were truly in for life. Hildegard believed that they were forced into this appalling leniency by the abolition of capital punishment.

Yet contact with this woman coincided with Daimeon's recovery! Everything in her wanted to deny it. She must be mistaken. In any case, she told herself, it was a waste of time to be worrying about what caused Daimeon to be more *compos mentis,* as long as she did not have to see her sister-in-law. God forbid! Yet the peculiar link between Daimeon's improvement and that skeleton in the cupboard was disturbing. It put a fearful shadow over her relief at Daimeon's return to normal life.

Hildegard was not one to pay attention to dark shadows. She believed in disregarding them. 'That is none of my business' must apply to everything to do with her sister-in-law. Anyway, Daimeon's prison visit must be a one-off, so if there were any worry it was of the past. She was not going to look for his reason for making it. She had better things to do! The vague idea of his needing to speak to his brother's widow on business was acceptable. The great thing was that he looked and behaved more normally; the last thing to do was to start looking for anything abnormal.

Daimeon had internally never left Therese since his visit to the prison. He felt himself naturally linked to her as to a blood relation. In some sense he felt Therese and himself sharing a single bloodstream by which they were united for better or worse. He did not think about Therese as someone good or bad, whom he liked or disliked. Choice or judgement seemed irrelevant. They simply were together, sharing 'one blood'. They might have been united by Horace's blood, since Daimeon was convinced of his shared guilt in Horace's death; but he felt that they shared not the accusing, spilt blood, but lifeblood.

When he had talked to Therese about his experience after Horace's death, it was like talking to a compatriot of a country others did not know. He did not think of her as having greater understanding than others but there was no possibility of his being able to speak to anyone else of the same things, and he believed that his words had had meaning to her.

It seemed to Daimeon that until now he had always struggled to be in 'the world' where everyone else was naturally. He felt inferior because he never quite made it, being always somewhere below the level on which he was expected to be. They were unaware of anywhere below. The shock of his brother's death had made his hands let go of the ground above so he had plummeted to a depth where he was separated from all above.

Eventually he had begun to hear and see others again and had risen to where he could move alongside and amongst them. He could only do this after his experiences below had penetrated and filled him. They remained in him wherever he was. Therese's life had also taken her to this deep level, which made it possible for him to speak to her of his experience. Afterwards he was surprised by his faith in Therese's understanding.

It came as a surprise to him that he coped better than before with the demands of outer daily life. They were more real to him than before. Small things that had been so enlarged in his vision by anxiety that he was not up to managing them, were now reduced to a size he could handle effectively. Considering his long absence, his colleagues were still remarkably patient. Assuring him that he must take his time to get back into the business, they expressed not only concern for him but their uncertainty of whether he could cope.

'Remarkable,' Mr Timson muttered, to his partner Saunderson at the end of Daimeon's first day back. 'Very much better than was to be expected, from all reports of the extent to which he had gone overboard. Astonishing, I would say. Let us hope he can keep it up.'

Saunderson, the senior partner, said, 'Perhaps our waiting so as not to be accused of dismissing him on account of his illness will turn out to our advantage.'

When two years later Timson packed up suddenly after a heart attack, Saunderson blessed his acumen in keeping Carruthers after his breakdown. Daimeon Carruthers, who had become more capable after his illness than he ever was before, was invaluable. Saunderson and he found themselves complementing each other in a most satisfactory way. Timson had been closer to him in outlook and character, but that, he realised later, was not nearly as productive.

Though Hildegard would have agreed with Saunderson that Daimeon coped more effectively with the mechanics of life than before, she did not have the happy experience of finding Daimeon and herself complementing each other in their partnership. Rather, she felt put out by his greater competence. She was put out of her position as the indispensable person who keeps the family running on track.

Hildegard realised that the difficulty of adjusting to Daimeon's recovery increased rather than decreased with time. During 'his absence' she had become used to organising everything in her own way. Although she had felt deserving of sympathy for having to shoulder the whole burden herself, secretly she had been relieved not to have Daimeon muddling things that she dealt with so much more efficiently. Her way was so much more rational than his. She had enjoyed being in command and began to think of a business career when the children were settled at their final school.

Daimeon not only went back to dealing with the things

he had struggled with before, such as their finances and house maintenance, but took a greater interest in school problems. He thought he was only doing his bit belatedly and did it without any ado. To object to what he was doing made Hildegard sound unreasonable even to herself, which added to her feeling put out. It made her angry with herself as well as Daimeon, which led to more quarrels over trivial matters. She knew that these only served as an opportunity for an explosion waiting inside her to happen. But instead of clearing the air these disagreements intensified her sense of being in the wrong position. She seemed to feel jealous of Daimeon, which, she told herself, made no sense.

Chapter 18

Daimeon realised that the two months he waited before applying for a second visitor's permit was too long. The wait till he got it was a terrible strain. He seemed to be saying to a person inside himself, 'I am sorry. I had no idea of the vital importance of seeing Therese again sooner.' After that, he knew that his visits must be at regular, shorter intervals. He was so grateful that, as brother-in-law, he could claim a relative's right to visit, especially as she lacked others wanting to do so. When he saw the woman officer dealing with visitors' permits, she showed signs of approval that there was a relative taking up the prisoner's right to regular visits. They didn't like prisoners having neither family nor anyone else taking an interest. Visitors could cause trouble but 'no visitors' could mean more trouble for the prison authorities, and reduced the prisoner's chances of keeping out after release.

At first Therese had felt embarrassed when Daimeon told her that he was claiming a regular visitor's permit. She could only think that he was doing it for her sake, perhaps from pity because he had realised that she had hardly any visitors. She had mentioned Amanda to him once; telling him of the book she had brought her, but in the course of a conversation that explored their family background, Daimeon had learnt that Therese had no living relative with whom she had had real contact since she was adopted as a very young child by the two aunts. He understood this was the result of the tragic loss of her parents as a small child and the unsuitable adoption to which it had led. It was like a grim tale calculated to make children feel sorry for the orphan and themselves lucky, however awful their own parents might be. He could understand much less easily how she came to be friendless. Therese felt ashamed of that.

Daimeon had no idea, and she could not tell him, that even before and without Horace, she had not existed sufficiently as a person for another to be able to make a relationship with her. Horace could only do so, and she relate to him, because he was equally limited. Their different extreme limitations were the foundation of their relationship. It was finely made to exact personal measurements, as, on close scrutiny, probably all relationships are found to be.

Daimeon was also puzzled by Therese's attitude to her imprisonment. He had dreaded finding her so depressed that he would not know how to cheer her up because he could only share her depression at the terrible prospect of years in jail. She had in fact behaved as if it were a natural place for her to be. He had asked her about prison hesitantly, but she had not complained, except about meals, nor given the impression of intolerable confinement. After his first visit he was worried that he had been incredibly selfish, talking at length about himself as if this were of any importance when her experience and need for attention must be paramount.

It was her incomprehensible acceptance of prison that allowed his visits to be so good. Far from being depressed by them, he even came away elated and was sustained by them. He would never have believed that prison visiting could be like this and sometimes wondered guiltily whether he was feeding on her hardship. But these doubts were dispelled by the extraordinary conviction that 'their visits', as he thought of them, were a joint, good experience for both of them. This seemed to be unquestionable in all his puzzlement. Although the hour was sometimes shockingly short, they both had a sense of continuity that gave a reassuring permanence to their relationship which would have been difficult to establish 'outside'. This sense of indefinite continuity gave a sense of time and even space to their meetings in externally cramped and strictly regulated conditions.

Therese had never had anyone come to see her regularly, to talk to her and apparently want to listen to her. She wondered whether one had to be in prison to have this, and could not imagine it elsewhere, though, she told herself, people evidently had friends whom they met regularly. She wondered, could she ever elsewhere have the regularity that she valued so much? Of course it could fail here too. Sometimes she looked forward to Daimeon's visit so much that she felt it dangerous and warned herself that things could happen to prevent him coming.

She was more than interested in anything Daimeon told her about his life. It was like being told about a country, even her own native one, in which she had never managed to live. He told her about his family, a bit about his work, and they both talked about their past. Their different maps joined at only one point: Horace. Minimal though their first meeting in the outside world had been, she saw it as essential to their present relationship.

Therese was protected by the prison sentence from any questions of where these visits and the relationship might lead. It was an extraordinarily secure situation that suited her. Though they could never meet alone, their relationship was well guarded against intrusion from the outside world. But it was exposed to unflagging interest and questioning by Therese's fellow prisoners. If she did not question her relationship with Daimeon, there were no questions that these life-starved women would not ask her. When they found Therese more extrordinary than ever in not wanting to talk about her man, they compensated by discussing the pair amongst themselves. 'Burning with desire' they saw them. Their interest kept burning, however little fuel Therese gave them for it.

They did not give up trying. 'Tell us about him. We didn't have no visitor that day so we had no chance to see, except for Doreen, the lucky devil, and she says she was on the opposite side of the room where she could see you but not him, except for the back of his hair. We want to know more than the length of that!'

Doreen entered the fray. 'Go on! Don't be such a rotten can with no pull-up to open it! All that good foam inside, and us dying for a drink! God you're tight and mean!'

Therese felt like a stupid child who couldn't give the teacher the right answer, much as she would like to. She thought of Daimeon; he gave her substance inside but not the foamy pleasure that came out of the drink can they thirsted for. She didn't know how she could give them a taste of what she had. She doubted they would want it.

Therese's expression struck Doreen as incredibly feeble. She must surely know the desperate dearth inside that drove you to drink, but she wouldn't share what she had; the blunt need when you were denied a man that you were made for, which these prison bastards know and use to punish you with. She had had a rotten night tossing and turning, and fantasy wouldn't fill the bill. When she woke up she felt as frustrated as ever; intolerably so when she imagined that her starvation was satisfaction to the bastards who put her here.

Now that they were all supposed to be working together at the table, and the others were having a go at Therese, Doreen felt that damned woman just keeping to herself something she was dying for. She wasn't just keeping a drink can to herself; she was that can, in her eyes, that kept its contents and would not be opened. If anything was wicked that was! She was outraged. She felt the breach of 'Love thy neighbour as thyself' raw, in her body and soul. As far as she was concerned, she was fighting for the rules that God made, when she hit out to knock sideways that sealed can that wouldn't give a drop away. It wouldn't break open but at least she could dent it to show what she thought of it.

Doreen had leapt up and her fist had darted out in such a flash that some of the others jumped up with the shock, and the table tipped up and knocked Therese, who had instinctively ducked sideways to avoid Doreen's blow. The table, unbalancing, took her with it to the floor. She found herself there with a smarting temple that drew her hand to it. She held it there as if to protect what was hardly painful yet, when the duty officer was already on the spot.

A bell went that brought other officers in. One took charge of Doreen, who had failed to hit Therese but had been identified as the cause of the trouble, and marched her off to her room. Another put the table back into place and roughly told the others to sit down and carry on quietly. Pockface, as they called the woman officer on their corridor, after giving Therese a quick once-over, took her by the arm and marched her off. They had never found out what made her round face so pockmarked. Some said she had worked her way up from gang warfare on Moss Side, because they had found out that she came from Manchester. They said she had been promoted to prison officer on the strength of her useful experience in the gang. She now led Therese to the first aid post and then for examination to the prison hospital.

'So you've been in another fight, have you?' the woman doctor said while cleaning up Therese's left temple before deciding how bad the damage was. Therese wondered why 'another fight' but said nothing and no reply was expected. It was evidently not a bad case since the patient had not lost consciousness with the knock and fall and had walked to and from the van that had brought her. 'Can't you leave that to the men? They may accuse me of sexism but I'd say we'd be better without that bit of equality.' She gave a sigh as she got ready to give the local anaesthetic to sew up the cut, and caught sight of Therese's profile.

She had not looked at the patient's face till now. She was struck by the fine, almost delicate features and something childlike, even lost-looking, in the face, that made her halt telling Therese about the anaesthetic she was about to give. She wanted a quick look at her full-face. It wasn't that of a fighter, but you never knew. She asked, 'Did you get as good as you gave? Or more than you bargained for?' She felt uneasy with such apparent gentleness and tried to find it wasn't true. For a second she could understand someone wanting to knock this woman whose very softness was provoking. 'All right, I'm going to give you a local anaesthetic. I expect you've had one before and know what it's like.' Four stitches sewed up the cut and she put on Therese's notes that she needed to be watched in case of delayed symptons of concussion. She told Therese that, from the description of her fall, was unlikely. She had not been knocked over with force. The usual sort of fracas, rather than straight, more serious violence.

Chapter 19

Therese was as bewildered as she had looked to the doctor. Back in her little room, she was miserable and angry. She did not know whether she was angrier with others or herself. She hated being the victim. She hated being the feeble, injured one, which would make them turn on her all the more. She had learned that anyone unable or unwilling to defend herself provoked them. She had been slow to realise it, preferring to be in her private world most of the time. She was not interested in standing up to them or 'playing the game'. She only wanted to hold her own enough to avoid trouble. In her solitude she came to see that it was more than some could take, that in no way would she share with them her time with a man, which, with fags, was the most desirable thing here. She could even agree with them and hated seeing herself as the odd one out. She had had enough of that. She wept with a mixture of self-pity and anger.

She felt like telling Daimeon about all this but there was no chance of that as she had just had his visit; that had indirectly been the cause of the trouble, and she therefore had the longest wait till the next visit. She decided it was just as well because when it came to the point she would not have wanted to talk about it. She would feel ashamed before Daimeon, were he to know that she could not get on with the other women. She would show what she felt as her sexlessness if she could not get on with them, who were sex personified for her. The thought of Daimeon seeing her in this light was so painful – touching a deep humiliation – that she would bear any trouble in secret rather than risk being seen like this by him.

Until now Therese had marvelled at the other women's passionate longing – mostly not for a husband or boyfriend, but simply for a man. Their whole life and vision seemed to be dominated monotonously by a man to have sex with. The most remote thing around them, or conversation on any topic could lead in their minds straight to the sexual organs or act, which they found hilarious. This evidently provided them with some release and food for their obsession. The more they practised finding sex in everything, the more it was to be found everywhere and the more it dominated their life. As Pockmark said the other day, 'Can't you girls think of nothing else? You don't have no time nor thought even for your kids, do you? Never hear you talk about them like you do about any old man. Do your kids tag along or fend for themselves, I wonder, while you're hot on the trail?'

'It's "them" that'll be hot on the trail, won't it, girls, not us!' came a rallying cry from Kelly in defence of the girls' honour. She was reminding them of one of their favourite scenarios for their return to 'Civvy Street', of the guys queuing up for them. It served the purpose of boosting their self-respect, the spirit to keep on looking after themselves rather than slipping down the slope into despondent sluttery.

Therese felt herself in a familiar position, recalling her experience as a schoolgirl when she knew nothing of sex except some unpalatable facts, apparently made as off-putting as possible. She was then a laughing stock to a group of girls around her. Now she was at best a curiosity, having supposedly had a husband, but appearing to these full-blooded women unbelievably untouched by sex.

'Killed her husband!' ranked high on their scale of what got you here. Not many aspired to that. They had been ready to be sympathetic, whether it was rape or whatever that had driven her to murder. When they got nowhere along that line of enquiry they worked on the assumption of provocation by prolonged abuse and tried to find out the form this had taken. That too was a dead end. They could not find the right button to press that would produce the goodies. That was frustrating enough, but when she did deign to say something it made no sense. They would have said she was daft if she hadn't also the air of one who knew things. They had understood that she had had a good education so she couldn't really be simple, and she never claimed that she had been off her head when she put the knife into that man. Most of them, most of the time, had given her up as a bad job. But when she had got this bloke visiting her – a new man? – they couldn't help getting involved again, and that had led Doreen into trouble.

Therese wanted to cry like an angry child at being what she could hardly admit to herself, it felt so unbearable: a sexless curiosity. Even when, according to their lights, she had a man, she could not talk of him like that. Yet far from being superior to them, she now felt utterly, bitterly inferior. She felt they were alive, however vulgar or boringly one-track-minded, as she was not. She hated herself, seen as a grey, one-dimensional creature, like a shadow that painfully felt its flatness compared to the three-dimensional, living bodies of these women. She hungered and thirsted for their substance and life so fiercely, her whole body ached for it like parched earth for rain. Maybe this was equivalent to their dreadful want of a man. She so envied them their substance and colour that if these had been their clothes, she could see herself going to steal them by night. They seemed a treasure she would do anything to get her hands on.

She was frightened by such ruthless want. She saw with horror the force of absolute want, its power to sweep over everything in its way, like a fast-flowing river; a power that could lead people to do almost anything – even murder. *Even murder.* That's what she was here for. She had the greatest difficulty in using the word in her own case and when she did, it was not real to her. She seemed to say it just to oblige or comply with the rules but it had no reality to her. Now she had a fearful understanding of murder through experiencing an absolute, total need that could overrule everything, could make one do anything regardless of cost or consequence. Was that at the heart of murder? Then, she saw for the first time that of course she murdered Horace! She had never thought of murder like that. It had appeared rather to be killing by people who did not care for life. Now she saw that people who were desperate for life could take another's to attain something that had come to mean 'life' in their deprived, depraved state.

The dreadful incongruity made her want to cross herself. She could not remember ever having done this before. The gesture seemed to say 'God forbid', but God had not forbidden her falling into this dreaful trap. She had actually done this. She had stopped living what had stopped her living; stopped it once and for all. She thought that this was the only time in her life she had ever done anything determinedly and single-mindedly. Her familiar doubting self had been left far behind and something much clearer and stronger had taken over. She could not help feeling strengthened now as she recalled that self which was real and true. It was a relief to be one instead of divided and diffuse; but only in stopping another – Horace – from being at all? In killing him! Why had she come to this now?

She was afraid she must be crazy because the terrible truth of what she had done made her feel more real, rather than devastated or repentant. How could she ever admit this to anyone? It seemed to make her something even worse than a murderer: someone who finds herself through murder. What kind of perversion was this? She would have to be kept in prison for ever. She was frightened.

Having till now sat in the middle of her little floor, holding her sore head in her hands, she now crouched down on the floor. She seemed to have reached rock-bottom. She felt that, like everyone, she had been made for life but was forever denied it. Whatever forays she had made to reach the life for which she yearned, it eluded her. To be put into this position seemed like a cruel joke.

In her imagination she saw a malevolent figure watching with amusement her 'progress' into painful frustration. Contempt at this despicable mentality stopped her from being engulfed in despair. That malevolent male figure, surprisingly dressed in white, was the undoubted ruler of the game. She looked with horror at this figure smiling with gleeful satisfaction. Was he really without pity? The possibility made her go cold. It could make one freeze to death. But before she could freeze she thought of the many others on the same road. The inconceivably cruel, self-satisfied depriver might be in command but she could spread her arms round others who were aching for all that they were specially made for, and found themselves denied. She wanted to embrace these people protectively while she could only silently face the cruel one whom their plight pleased. Who was he? One who wants nothingness for the person made for fulfilment. She could not challenge whoever this was. It was no good trying to go forward and nearer that pitiless figure. That way lay death.

She turned round to where she was filled with compassion, and wept bitterly; not, as before in imagination putting her arms round others but now enclosed in what might be countless arms making one immeasurable embrace. In silence and stillness she became aware of a hidden sound and movement of a stream that flowed ceaselessly, like a tremendous bloodstream through a body that was countless bodies. It was not her body but one great body shared by all in a single embrace. She could sense the movement and sound and saw in her mind's eye a deep colour that meant richness and wonderful strength. It was like the richness of the purest, full-bodied wine. She thought of the wine of Christ's blood. That blood, that wine, brought fulfilment. It was fulfilment where she had least expected it, when she had turned from the exact opposite.

Therese sat up and could look around her again. She felt pain on the left side of her head. She thought of the stitches below the sticking-plaster and wondered about the comments this would provoke at the next meal. She was glad it was the table edge that had hit her rather than Doreen. She didn't want Doreen to feel guilty, because she could feel herself in her shoes. Was that because, after all, they shared one body which she had been led to know? She saw that the deprivation the other women suffered must be akin to hers and knew that they too, however full-blooded, depended on a deeper bloodstream of compassion that gave life, and that was more than any personal gratification.

'Any more trouble now the two of them are together again, Doreen and that Tess?' Polly asked Eric, the officer from whom she was taking over.

'Oh no,' he said casually as if nothing could be more unlikely. 'You mean Therese,' he corrected her. He regarded it as part of his duty to give people their proper names. Polly insisted on using Tess for Therese, which she thought fancy because she could never be sure she got it right. 'Perfect peace,' Eric confirmed. 'I don't like to say it but they seem better for what happened. Quiet though she is that Theresa, you could understand how she got under some of the others' skin. If Doreen hadn't blown her fuse someone else would have done, sooner or later. You could see it coming. It irks them, that quiet, wouldn't-hurt-a-fly look she has when they know she killed a man.' He looked thoughtful when he added,

'You would think she would come back even more of a thorn in their flesh with that stitched head. But she's come back different. She hasn't got that – you know, meek and mild, yet superior look that she had. Don't know whether it got knocked out of her in the accident. God knows!

'I am not saying that she's not still different from the others that Theresa . . .'

'She's not Theresa like you say, either,' Polly corrected him contemptuously. The contempt was more for the name than him. 'She should call herself something more like the rest.'

Eric did not see how her name could change unless they gave her a nickname but did not say so. Picking up his bag, he said 'Good night' and went off duty.

When one of the women looked curiously at Therese's stitches and said, 'That was nasty, I bet,' with obvious enjoyment, Therese shrugged it off with a nonchalant, 'It's all right.' The others watched with interest and Lorraine cracked a joke about the sausages for lunch, which distracted attention. Therese was on duty with Doreen to do the clearing. She didn't have what Doreen called that feeble, bloodless look that made her own blood boil. You could almost say that blow that never made it had done some good, as if it had knocked some sense into her. She struck Doreen as less of a pain.

Chapter 20

How extraordinary! was Therese's reponse when the following day she was handed a visitor's application form with Amanda's name on it, when I thought of her yesterday for the first time for ages. Something about Doreen had brought her to mind yesterday. Amanda might be insulted, but she had seen something the two women had in common, which made her feel better about Doreen, of whom she had been afraid. That had made her realise that it was a long time since Amanda's visit. Therese accepted that she would probably not come again; in a way that would be a relief because of her embarrassing outburst to this strange woman about herself and Horace. Not surprising she didn't want to come back! It might have scared off anyone.

Now here was Amanda asking for another visit! Therese saw in her mind the beautiful, rich, floral material of her dress; it was like the memory of a beautiful meadow. Probably Amanda wouldn't wear the same dress but she would have liked to see it again. Anyway, there was something about her, which the dress seemed to go with, that she liked. She supposed there was little hope that her outburst last time had been forgotten. She must try and forget it herself or it would spoil things.

Her first impression of Amanda on her second visit was of an even bigger person than she remembered. There seemed even more of the billowing, colourful figure so that she seemed to fill the room. There was the same refreshing impression of light and colour. It made her think of the movement of light on rippling water on a fine summer's day; it seemed to spread all over the place. Therese must find boundaries; find the woman's shape and features. She looked at her anxiously as if unsure of being able to do so.

Amanda arrived laughing, extending her hand across the little table. 'You may well look puzzled!' she said with what seemed a regular accompaniment of laughter. 'There's indeed more of me but it's no longer "of me"; it's "us" now!' She gave the happiest laugh yet, after which her expansive presence settled in one place. Only then was Therese able to identify the baby-sling Amanda had on her front, at the top of which a tiny head was visible. Therese gave a surprised gasp. She had no words ready for this. That was another occasion for Amanda's laughter.

'They let me bring her, wasn't it lucky? She's so much part of me, just attached outside now instead of inside, that I never thought of mentioning her when I asked to visit you. When I arrived they looked as if they were going to ban her. But even the male officer saw that she couldn't be left with them while I came in here, and when I'd made all this journey – not that I find it at all bad,' she hastened to assure Therese. 'But to have come for nothing would be bad.'

'Surely they wouldn't do that!' Therese said while she gazed at her visitors and looked floored. She could not think of anything else to say.

Amanda was ready to answer all the questions which Therese was too baffled to ask. 'Isn't she great?' she exclaimed, which struck Therese as incongruous with the tiny part of a baby's head that she could see. 'She was born a month ago.' Looking down at the baby's face adoringly she said, 'Happy birthday, darling!' her laugh recurring like a tune in different settings throughout a symphony. Therese managed to ask her name. 'How awful of me, I haven't introduced you! Melissa – Therese; Therese – Melissa. They make a good pair, don't they?

Both very feminine and quite dignified, don't you think?' Therese wondered about the child's father. She assumed that Amanda hadn't got married since they last met. Amanda had not said anything about any man she lived with.

'You didn't notice I was pregnant when I came before. People who saw me more didn't either.' She laughed. 'I loved having a secret inside that no one else knew. It was all mine then, before the world could grab hold of it.' It seemed that she might put the child back inside her if she could. 'With my shape and size, I could carry it off for a long time.' She moved her arms about her sides to give a voluminous impression. 'Can you imagine how those skinny girls you read about can get to the end of their pregnancy without anyone knowing? Sometimes not even knowing themselves! Unbelievable! No wonder they have the shock of their lives when the penny drops, and that they then try and put it down the loo. You should have seen me by the end; I was a mountain! Sorry all this about me – I mean us! I haven't even asked how you are. I am dreadful!'

But Amanda felt that surely such happy, healthy life coming into the prison could only be good; that Therese would be fascinated by a baby. She wondered whether she regretted not having had a child before 'all this happened'. Perhaps she wouldn't have killed Horace if they'd had a child. That brought her back to Therese and why she was here. Horace. In her particularly irrational state – for which it was rather nice to have the excuse of the birth – she felt like asking, if not 'after Horace', at least about him, as if he were still somehow with Therese.

Her attempt to shift her attention from Melissa and herself to Therese did not come to much. It just wasn't natural, she reassured herself when afterwards she realised that she had talked almost the entire time about the baby and herself. She hoped it was like a draught of fresh, natural water for Therese that might have been good for her. No reason why she should not go again and hear more about how Therese spent her time. That thought worried her. No lovely life like hers; no lovely child. None of all the things she had around her. It must be so bare there!

That reminded her of the awful mess she had left in the flat when she came out; things strewn all over the place. Freddie said it was getting beyond a joke and had made a list of all the things that she had to clear up before he came home. She was to check them against his list before she dared let him in. To give power to the threat of leaving her unless she mended her ways and lived in some order, he said he was ready to assert his right as father to rescue his daughter from chaos, which was of course nonsense. But nevertheless. . . .

When Freddie made heavy claims to his child, Amanda's answer was that Melissa was a love child and that was all that mattered. She wondered why married mothers had not mounted a protest against those who monopolised the term. One evening, after dwelling solemnly on Melissa being a love child, she added in a throw-away manner 'After that, what does it matter who the father is?' Her self-contained satisfaction with the product of love and disregard of the father, sowed seeds of doubt in Freddie's mind. She had said this playfully while changing the baby's nappies. Glancing up at Freddie sitting at the table a few feet away, she was taken aback by seeing a stock-still figure with a fixed stare in her direction. It seemed to try and fix her in the stare. That made her uncomfortable. She could not bear anything that impeded free movement; which was one reason for her always wearing loose clothes. She could only just bear the lightest possible bra; would have preferred none if that hadn't been also uncomfortable with her full figure.

She tried to throw her own remark away with a laugh,

like a pebble one picks up on a beach only to throw it away again; rather than a ball thrown to another person in a game. She tried to imply it was one of those remarks made for the fun of it. Freddie said nothing and she dared not look to see if he had relaxed, for fear of finding him in the same stony state. She kept up a flow of chatter, mostly to the baby but also to him, assuring him that he would get his supper, even if she was going to feed the baby first. He would not have to wait till midnight like the other day because, being highly organised – stressing that unlikely fact with great emphasis – their meal was not unprepared. 'At least in my mind.' she added quietly, in case he expected to find it already half made.

Freddie was quieter than usual but she made up for that. 'Be a darling and hand me the sling.' She held out her arm to point to the far corner of the room where she had thrown the baby-sling when she was supposed to have finished with it for the day, and the baby, fed and changed, was to be put to bed. But as often, she would not settle in her cot. After cooing at it for a while – didn't it want to lie in its nice cot? Did it feel lonely there? Wasn't she a sleepy baby? – Amanda announced, 'Melissa prefers to stay with her mother. She knows what is best for her, I am sure. If only you listen to your child you can't go wrong. "Out of the mouths of babes and sucklings . . ."' she assured Freddie. 'She had better go back in her sling while I get supper. Why don't you come and help so we get there quicker?'

Settled in bed at last, after yet another 'last feed', Amanda felt she had worked hard throughout the evening, not just with the baby but counteracting Freddie's moroseness. She had worked to keep it out of sight and hearing. The constant preoccupation with the baby helped. He not only did not join her in this as he often did but she had the feeling that he was only waiting for a break from the baby's demands to make his own. She suspected that it was one for illumination of her casual remark, now hours ago. All evening she had worked hard at keeping this 'out of the question', making sure that there was no place for it. Now she lay back exhausted.

She would never say 'no' if Freddie wanted to make love, especially tonight when it might help, but before she had a chance to know what he wanted she had dropped off to sleep. He hadn't the heart to wake her. He tried to read but couldn't concentrate, so he lay there alone with his nagging doubts.

It wasn't a joke, he kept saying to himself. He imagined her laughing at him for taking her remark seriously, as if that were the funniest thing in the world. But he was not amused. Was he falling into the trap of the classic jealous lover, making a fool of himself by taking so seriously and darkly the wiles of a typical woman? Tempting as that idea might be, it did not alter the heavy, dark state in which he had spent the evening, while outwardly he had let himself be carried along by the stream of Amanda's chatter and activity.

The ground had been prepared for the seed she sowed. He could not see her remark 'What does it matter who the father is?' as a casual one. Like a married couple, he and Amanda shared their friends. If they didn't actually know all, they knew of all each other's friends. Freddie used to be pleased if Amanda had some friend in during the day when he was working, so he could have her all to himself in the evening. He then had the advantage of being entertained by her amusing sketches of the visitor without the disadvantage of meeting someone who, in the flesh, might have been rather a bore. He enjoyed her descriptions of women friends and occasionally he would say deliberately, 'Maybe you could ask her one evening when I am around and she might bring another man?' Neither was supposed to be bound to the other; they were supposed to be free.

Amanda's wish to be as free as a breeze, or follow wherever the breeze might take her, had a special attraction for Freddie. He loved her billowing appearance. Even though she was substantial, she was always in movement and had something butterfly-like about her. He would not care for her to be 'just there' but enjoyed going after her as long as she stayed always within reach. Now lying in bed, he could not think how he could have been fool enough to play this sort of game with her. He felt heavy as a stone and saw his usual light-hearted self empty in the head, lacking any sense. He felt hate as much for himself as anyone else. There wasn't anyone else distinct enough to hate. He felt that having a particular, identifiable rival might be preferable to the awful present state.

Apparently close to Amanda, he felt at an infinite distance by being kept in ignorance. He was in anguish because he had no way of claiming closeness. They had chosen to have no right to each other so that their relationship would always be spontaneous. Neither had a claim on the other so their togetherness was bound to be one of love. The whole idea seemed to have been foolproof and to their mutual interest, giving perfect equality. Now, as he lay miserably isolated next to Amanda fast asleep, he saw it as an absurdity.

The baby cried next door. Freddie had almost forgotten her though she was at the heart of his anguish. He usually felt it his duty to get up and see if he could settle her again by turning her over or, if necessary, to bring her to Amanda for a feed. It had been assumed that he should play his part, for his own as well as Amanda's and Melissa's benefit. 'Amanda and Melissa', that was what he felt up against. It sounded beautiful but was a formidable presence subtly overpowering him. Would another man in his position feel excluded by the supposedly weaker sex or was he a peculiarly feeble male, feeling redundant? This was obvious nonsense, he told himself, but was reminded of how he felt as a new boy at school when he had no links with anyone.

'Melissa and Amanda', and all their kin, might appear to make a beautiful, self-contained life of their own but it was a deception, he assured himself, since the father was the source and foundation of it all. After all, we don't pray to 'God the Father' for nothing. He felt fervently the absolute rightness of this and that all questioning of it, suggesting that the deity should be female, was preposterous. For all their taking the centre of the picture – the pretty mother and baby – the father was behind it all. For heaven's sake, he gave her the baby and the chance to devote herself to it! He was behind them and kept them going with moral as well as material support. That was how he had always seen the father: a handsome, strong presence, the power behind the home, if not the throne. He was assured of his respected place. His view might sound old-fashioned but he believed it was still valid. He was ready to get up for Melissa, who had quietened but intermittently cried a little. Amanda was a heavy sleeper who was not easily woken.

Then came a question that cut through all this talk with himself with one sharp thrust. Father OK. But was he the father? That question was the root of his trouble; of his black fury now. He wanted to shake Amanda and get the truth out of her. He turned to shake her by the shoulder. Of course he must know. It was his right. 'Amanda! We've got to clear up this absurd situation. I can't lie here like this!' He was talking at the body whose spirit was in another world.

Hearing herself called from the outer world, she asked, barely conscious, 'Is she awake?' and in defence of her sleep, added, 'She's had her feed,' and rolled over, away from him.

'She's cried on and off. She's quiet for the moment but I need to talk to you. You've got to talk to me, Amanda!' Freddie said urgently. 'We've got to get this straight; do you see?' She didn't see at all. She felt the wonderful comfort of her sleep-laden body in the warm, soft bed and the lure of sleep waiting to receive her back. 'No, Amanda, don't go back to sleep! You've got to talk to me first or I can't sleep. We absolutely must sort this out before we go to sleep. Please!' And with this he shook her shoulder again gently but urgently. 'Listen!' he more or less commanded. It was extraordinary for him to assert himself like this and not let her follow her own inclination.

Amanda turned round to face him, resting her upper body on her elbow, as she stared at him with astonishment. 'What?' It expressed puzzlement at his extraordinary behaviour, hesitating on the threshold of anger. 'What?' she repeated as if to say, 'Is it possible that you wake me to talk to you? Now! Whatever has got into you? I don't believe it!' He seemed to get the gist of her message without words.

'I have a right to know!' There were rights, after all, though this went against their code. She looked at him amazed, as if he had turned into some incredible creature. 'It's obvious, quite obvious that I have an absolute right to know' – which he could hardly bear to assert since it implied a question – 'that I am Melissa's father.' He could not bear to say 'whether'. That would admit more plainly a negative possibility that, he felt, could rouse him to murder. 'I must be the father!' was a desperate, true expression of what he felt.

Amanda gave a look of exasperation, let down her elbow that had lifted her up to face Freddie, as one would let down a shutter that had been briefly lifted, and turned her back to him. That was her answer to as inopportune a call as she could have had. She was off to sleep. 'No, Amanda, no! You can't do that! You've got to stay with me. Can't you see? God! Surely you must understand that we must get this clear.' On the verge of outrage, there was a flicker of hope at the back of his mind that her impatience meant there was no question; that she thought he was mad to see a question where there was none. He also felt hurt that she had no sympathy for him but, as in a battle in which one knows one has been wounded but is too actively involved to feel it till after the event, he was carried on by the urgency of the situation.

He touched her shoulder again, which made her turn to him angrily. 'Do you have no consideration at all for my need of sleep? When I am regularly woken by the baby, do you have to keep me awake as well?' She was not only feeling sorry for herself but doing her best to make him feel guilty. 'It really is a bit much!' She meant it but the protest served also to keep what she did not want to discuss out of the way. Surely her case for sleep was good enough. Her milk supply might suffer if she went into emotional discussions in the middle of an already short night. 'Please, Freddie!' she now pleaded, apparently totally reasonably. But he had no choice. To go back to lying there as before was impossible.

'No!' he said with such iron strength, she was impressed. It was new to her. 'No, this cannot wait. Now! Now! I need to know and it should have been before now. There can be no question about Melissa's father.' There was a pause. His whole attention was riveted on her face. He saw it go into neutral, out of her previous righteous indignation, but rather than getting into the position for answering him as he asked, she hesitated as if considering which gear to go into.

When she said, 'Whatever makes you ask?' she seemed to come close to the answer for which he wished – like 'how can you doubt it?' but her words carried none of the finality of the few words he was waiting for. Rather it evaded the question by asking another. It was meant to give her time. But Freddie was not his usual easy-going self, perhaps because it was the middle of the night and he had not yet slept; though, she thought, at other times he was cheerful enough at the same hour. She saw he was tricky. He was like a trusted dog who, on the scent of something important, turned into a different creature from the amiable domestic animal he usually was. He became a bit frightening. As he said, there was no way she could simply put him off.

'I don't see that there is any good reason for doubt, you know,' she then said thoughtfully, suggesting she had considered the question and come to a fair conclusion. That there was a question was in itself a shocking admission. It was like a bullet hitting Freddie when he had believed he was coming out of the battle with only the incidental slight wound. 'Doubt' imprinted itself on his mind. He had a confusing sense of Amanda presenting him with the question he had so urgently put to her.

He was right. She would have asked him, if she could afford being honest, whether the little doubt in her mind deserved any consideration or if she could ignore it, as she would much rather do. She saw that to question Freddie's paternity would cause a lot of unnecessary bother. She didn't like seeing Freddie fussed. She didn't like this new view of him, all macho, so he became a nuisance. It would be a real shame if he couldn't just go along happily with Melissa and herself. Why shouldn't he be the father when he probably was, and was ready to enjoy it, as a lot of men would not.

Freddie was extremely uneasy. 'You don't sound very certain,' he said tensely. Her uncertainty was the one clear meaning he could discern. 'What do you mean by "you don't see any good reason to doubt"?' He repeated the words with difficulty and doing so made the tension inside him snap. 'What the hell are you hiding? You are skirting round something! Unpack the lot! Just get it out! At once!' he added threateningly. He was standing over her, now certain that she had something to hide, and making clear that she was not going to get away with it. He was fiercer than any customs official; more like police with a caught suspect.

*

Amanda hated it and him. Not since she had been a small girl had she been made to feel like this, miserably cornered. She had made sure by her whole lifestyle that she would never be in this position. She had hated the woman in whose care she had been as a child and who did her best to make her an orderly person. Order had been that woman's mission in a life that was always threatened by chaos. Her priority was to make one's island of order as secure as possible and the sooner children were trained for this the better. She had been hired by Amanda's father when his wife had left with their other two children, the twins. She had left Amanda with him, apparently as a generous gesture, as he had fortunately taken a fancy to the little girl who had come at a most unsuitable moment for her mother.

She had become involved with another man early in her pregnancy, which she therefore resented throughout. She often regretted not having terminated it but had kept putting it off for fear that it might arouse her husband's suspicion because she had originally been pleased by the prospect of a third baby. She had to go through the whole business, pregnancy and birth of a child, when all the time she was longing to be with the other man, who put up with her going through it all, saying he would wait for her. She felt it was marvellous proof of his loyalty. During the first year of Amanda's life her mother kept trying to decide the best moment for her to leave. It took her longer to go than she intended and it was well into Amanda's second year when she finally made it.

After a series of short-stay nannies, Amanda's father at last found the woman he believed would bring some discipline into Amanda's life. In Pamela Hastings he had found a woman who was strong on order, which was urgently needed, even if he could see that she was also rather unimaginative. She seemed a sticker, having lasted a long time in previous jobs, also in difficult circumstances. She would provide the most desirable contrast to the more than two years of disruption and change the child had experienced.

Amanda had smarted under the new order. At first she was baffled and vacillated between being morose and obstreperous. An important change came – which she later saw as a landmark – when she gained a sense of herself wanting to be and do things, as distinct from what others wanted her to be or do. She became aware of herself wanting to be as different as she could be from what Pamela wanted. She would never call her 'Nanny', as other people called her. 'Governess', which some called her, was to her a horrible word that later expressed perfectly her feelings about the woman. The idea of her being there to govern her was dreadful. She later disliked governments and would have joined an anarchist movement if her intelligence had not baulked at their ideas, and common sense made her see her interest in a basically ordered society.

As right and might had usually been with the governess, Amanda was regularly defeated, frustrated and furious. Once she was free of others' rule, she was determined to follow her own sweet way. She continued to kick over the traces of Pamela Hastings' order every day. She kicked out of the way things that littered the floor, rather than putting them away. She seemed to flout the old order when she nonchalantly dropped things and told others who instinctively made to pick them up, 'Don't bother, it's all right.' Sometimes, when the mess got too much for her, she was aware of suffering from her own reaction to the rule imposed on her in the past, and then hated it all the more. Such a glimpse of the truth, that she still let the old order rule her, was not enough to free her from its tyranny.

When she had Melissa she recognised the necessity for a modicum of order. She could not just leave a baby's paraphernalia wherever she happened to use it since she found herself, as well as the baby, distraught the next time it was needed and not ready to use. Also, even she did not like nappies all over the place. With some effort she managed to prevent chaos and to maintain the level of disorder with which she was happy and which Freddie tolerated and shared.

He had tried to 'govern' her but now she was cornered by him. She had always thought of him as being on her side, but here he was standing over her, she felt quite menacingly. He had become one of the enemy; he was claiming a right to make her clear up a bit of a mess she would admit having got into. He insisted on her putting out into the open whatever she was hiding. The intrusion and the demand that became a command were horribly familiar.

This was worse than being cornered by a governess or teacher. It was more painful because she hated Freddie being in the position of the bully. What could she do about it? What bothered him so much wasn't anything terrible to her. As long as Melissa was there and was lovely, she couldn't get that worked up about the father. Of course it would be much neater and nicer for Freddie to be the proper father because he was the regular man and he cared for Melissa. It would obviously work so much better for practical purposes. Freddie seemed to have been waiting to act the father. She would feel beastly if she disappointed him. She felt so sorry for him, like for a child. But did she have to disappoint him?

'Hang it all, I don't know!' she exclaimed with more energy than she had yet shown through this night's encounter. She seemed to have completely woken up and sat up for the first time. 'I only said there was no good reason for doubt. The trouble is I am too damned honest. Perhaps it would have been better to have said nothing. I bet most people would have done that.' As she sat up, Freddie relaxed his physical and psychological hold on her and seemed to slump into depressed uncertainty. He lay back leaving Amanda somewhat relieved but uneasy. She decided that this was not the moment for discussing a paternity check. 'Sufficient unto the day is the evil thereof.'

Chapter 21

Therese had lain awake thinking about Amanda's visit that day, marvelling at what had happened to Amanda since she had last seen her. Here she was with this new person, hers, as much as anyone could ever 'have' another being. She and the baby were one in a wonderful way that she was happy to dwell on. Then a deep anxiety spoilt that happiness, like a black cloud taking the place of a previously pure, blue sky. It came with the conviction that something would happen to break that unity of the mother and child. Rather than a premonition, it told her of the monstrous fact of an accident that killed the parents who left their child. For a moment she wondered whether Amanda had left Melissa somewhere, but then she knew that this awful 'knowledge' Amanda and baby had aroused in her related to herself.

She knew of an accident that killed the parents who left their child: herself. She was puzzled by the inconsolable state she discovered in herself. From it came the desperate question 'Why did you leave me?' She felt a rush of emotion rising with the question that had apparently been waiting to emerge from the darkness. Yet the question implied some knowledge of the original unity that had been destroyed; as if through the agony of the accident, that blissful unity were still visible. She still knew it somewhere.

She was brought back to Amanda with her baby tucked up against her in its sling, next best to being inside her. She thought back to her impression of Amanda on her first visit. She was big and dressed voluminously enough to have been pregnant. She might even have been very pregnant. Her speculations made her drowsy. She had a vivid image of the shape of a woman in advanced pregnancy. As she was tempted to feel that big curve of the belly with her hand she realised it was her own body. That jolted her into being fully awake. She was shocked by the vividness of her experience and felt guilty as if she had been found seeing something that was not allowed.

It was not the unfulfilled wish to have her own child that Therese felt she must keep secret but the fact that she was carrying within her a developing person of her own. That, with the uncertainty of who was going to emerge, was cause enough for excitement and apprehension. She tried to return to the safety of thinking about Amanda and Melissa, whose unity she had been enjoying, but she could not recapture that. They were no longer close to her. She could only wonder, as she went to sleep again, who the baby's father was and where he was. Perhaps she could ask Amanda next time she saw her. She might not come again for a long time. She wondered about Daimeon, hoping he might come. . . .

When she finally woke and got up in the morning she felt still full of what had been going on in the night without being able to remember what it was. Strong mixed feelings were all that remained. She had to carry them into the day.

Therese was standing in a queue that was slowly moving alongside the table for the weekly hand-out of toiletries. Her eyes lit on a picture in a newspaper which was lying on the table. The picture was of a young couple in an embrace. She tried quickly to scan the story to enjoy all the more the wonderful feeling the picture gave her. It told of a couple united against all the odds: people and circumstances. She did not want to be separated from it. She did not realise how absorbed she was in the picture until she heard Doreen, next to her in the queue, exclaim, 'Anyone want a peep, girls? Here's what we are queuing for.'

Finding herself held up by the person in front of her, Doreen had looked at Therese, and followed her gaze down to the table on her left, where at once she saw the picture of the embrace. 'Don't miss it, girls!' she called out to the ones behind her as she pushed past Therese saying, 'You go on enjoying yourself!' The fully dressed couple in the picture could not excite her enough to delay getting her perks, as they called them. In passing she whispered something into Therese's ear and then, roaring with laughter, turned to the women in front of her. 'I was telling her, if that's what she wants, we can show her better . . .'

She was interrupted by a sharp voice. 'What I look at is my business and not yours. There's no censorship even in here and just as I don't tell you what I think of your pictures, I can do without your comments!' Therese was thinking of the page 3 nudes they pinned up as their role models.

There was laughter and remarks flying about, which Therese was too hot and bothered to take in. Other people's contributions aroused laughter, which took attention away from her, for which she felt grateful. She vaguely realised that her self-defence, as surprising to herself as them, had somehow worked. She had defended her feeling about the picture from their mockery. She had not let it be torn to shreds by them as she would have done in the past, and felt surprising satisfaction at what would usually have been devastating. Nor was she told off by the staff as she feared. They followed the rule of 'Don't interfere if you don't have to'.

Back in her little room she lay on her bed. It occurred to her that the picture at the centre of all the rumpus was somehow connected with some dream she must have had in the night that she could not remember but had been bothering her all day. There seemed to be the same feeling of something both good and painful. She felt embarrassed at being like a young teenager, captivated by a picture of a loving embrace. She wanted to say to that teenage-self, 'Don't be ridiculous! Be your age, woman!' She was supposed to have been a married woman. When she looked at this married woman in her mind, her heart sank. She was a lifeless, flat, grey figure. The deprivation of life she had experienced in being that shadow was terrible and frightening even in retrospect.

She became terrified apparently by an unforgivable crime, which was not that of killing Horace. Rather, she realised, it was the crime she shared with him in leading that grey non-life in which she saw herself locked with Horace. Had she come out of that by cutting Horace's hold on her, when she cut his life? Could she ever really come out of it? She was filled with fear as she seemed to be staring at that 'married woman' in her lifeless setting, now realising that she must rescue her. Only she could do so. It seemed a matter of life and death, not in the ordinary, physical sense but of ultimate or eternal life; as if her fate depended on this.

She was alone and felt in need of help. There was that picture that had caused trouble this afternoon. This had somehow led her to this painful state. For a moment she could not remember what the picture had been and could only think of the young girl in herself whom she had ridiculed for her reaction to it. Then she remembered: an embrace, of course; that was it! A wonderful embrace. She could now see that this picture was just a tiny illustration of something vital. Her reaction to it, apparently that of an adolescent, made her a laughing stock to the other women but at least that adolescent had colour and life unlike the flat, grey 'married woman'. She evoked horror, while the young one seemed to bring her an amazing assurance of something wonderful. The two were worlds apart. She seemed to be in a void between them, but there was that frightening imperative on her to save the grey one locked into lifelessness.

Daimeon had been looking forward to his visit to Therese so much that his high spirits had been noticeable to everyone. Hildegard feared an exceptional 'high' turning into an exceptional 'low' but reassured herself that before he had dived into the depths without any preceding 'high'. She realised that she had not got over his 'illness', as she only reluctantly referred to his recent state because that did not express her contempt for his weakness in cracking up like that.

Their good conversation on his last visit to Therese had remained so vivid to Daimeon that he did not doubt that they would simply continue in the same way this time. On arrival he said to Therese, 'It seems both a long time and no time since I last came. Long in that another meeting with you seemed overdue and no time because all we talked about last time is still vivid in my mind.' She smiled but he missed a more active response. Therese felt tongue-tied. He went on expecting to continue more or less where they had left off, but it didn't happen. He was reminded of coming home from school, expecting to tell someone of what he was feeling excited about and finding no response. No one wanted to know. He had learnt sadly to keep things to himself. He only knew how sadly when he had the surprise of his good conversations with Therese.

He was unsure whether she was preoccupied or troubled, or both. Or did she not want to see him today? He realised how foolish it was to expect her to be always ready to talk – in this place! It was a marvel that she ever could. He had given up expecting her to be depressed, as he had done at first, but now thought that was foolish. He became silent. It was better to be silent than go on chatting brightly to someone not in the mood for it. He then became aware of the breaks in other people's conversations; others' silence exposed their own talk or lack of it. Conversation ensured privacy, rather than the opposite. They both looked downcast to the officer on duty keeping an eye on them and three other sets of people. He thought, those two are having a sticky time. It made him shift uneasily from one foot to the other in sympathy. He was relieved when he saw Therese look up and start talking again to her visitor who, he had decided, looked a decent sort. His eyes left them to check on the others, moving regularly to and fro like a lighthouse beam.

Therese had been struggling. Why should she be tormenting herself, making herself do what she felt she couldn't do? Yet something in her seemed to be insisting that she must do the impossible. She looked up at Daimeon miserably. He feared she was going to say that he should leave because she could after all not see or speak to him. His fear was so great that he was preparing himself for it. Because of his frantic preparation he hardly heard what she was saying. Only when she was silent again did he realise that whatever she had said did not fit the dismissal he had expected. What had she said? It was about something she feared? He forgot his own fear.

'I said that I'm afraid you will think me mad, as well as bad.' He wanted to rebut the latter, first and foremost because he had hoped that she realised by now that he did not condemn her as a murderer. He insisted the word was unsuitable even though they had talked about this and agreed that they must not deny what she had done. When he reminded her of this, she said, 'I was thinking more of "the mad" than "the bad" just now. Perhaps it's being in this place. In one way it suits me, however awful, because I need time to think or just be on my own, but sometimes the things that come into my mind are more than I can cope with. I know they are real but they don't fit into what we call the real world. Their power can be frightening.'

She hesitated. 'When you came to see me the first time, you talked of things that had happened to you after you had heard of Horace's death.' She avoided 'murder'. 'I mean the sort of things you described then, that had happened to you, also didn't fit into what we call "the real world" but you knew they were real. That's what gave me the idea that perhaps I could speak about what's been troubling me. I hoped I might forget about these things but they won't let me, especially as I am left with the idea of having to do something about them; of someone waiting for me to do what apparently only I can do.' She gave him a pleading, troubled look.

'I may sound as if I were talking about a ghost. It reminds me of the college Hamlet I saw with Horace. Wasn't Hamlet plagued by the ghost of his father demanding action from him? I'd have liked to see more Shakespeare.'

She spoke as if her life in the world were finished; as if she were here for life, Daimeon thought. Was she determined not to think of a future outside prison, so as not to live on hope? She seemed to concentrate entirely on bearing life here and now. 'I expect you will see more,' he said tentatively, but neither of them dared speak of a distant future.

Disregarding his words, she continued, 'In one way it is like a ghost demanding something of me, but this ghost is of someone dead in life rather than someone still alive in death. It is not Horace's ghost haunting me.' She looked up at Daimeon firmly to make certain he did not make such an obvious mistake. 'That wouldn't seem as mad as the fact that I know it's the ghost of myself married to Horace. The woman who is still in a dreadful kind of marriage with Horace has given me the frightening idea that she depends on me to rescue her. Cutting myself off from Horace by the knife was not enough. It all sounds mad, I am sure, but it's true!' She hid her face in her hands.

Daimeon wished that the table were not between them, and he were not forbidden to go to her side of it; but then he was glad because her distress seemed too great for a little touch or a little word. He muttered, 'I don't think what you say is mad. I can't say that I understand, but I know these internal things are real and matter.' He remembered the intensity of his own experiences of a world that, it was troubling to know, had hardly any recognition in the outer world. Having it classified as sickness could itself make one ill.

He wished that something good in that inner world might come to Therese's rescue. She sobbed, largely with the relief of having been able to put into words, and so outside herself, what she had been carrying around inside for weeks. Even to feel distressed in the presence of someone sympathetic was a great help. Daimeon glanced fearfully in the officer's direction, afraid that he might come and take Therese away. To see the officer concentrating on a couple who, when Daimeon followed the direction of his gaze, he saw apparently quarrelling, was a relief.

Then, to Daimeon's surprise, Therese seemed to be on another track altogether. She said, 'I envy the women around me, you know,' and looked up, anticipating his surprise, 'however crude and foul-mouthed they are. I used to despise and shun them till lately I have had to admit my envy, because they are full-blooded and the very opposite of that grey living-yet-dead woman inside me.' She startled him by saying, 'I feel the grey woman is my real sin, rather than what I have done to Horace. That must sound terrible.'

She apparently looked at Daimeon intently but was intent on what her words to him were making her see. 'I feel guilty towards this grey, stony figure, even though it is me. Can you be guilty towards yourself? It seems you can,' she answered herself. 'You can deny what you know to be true and can deceive yourself. An outer part of yourself can say and do what is against a deeper, truer self. So the outer betrays the deeper.' She looked at Daimeon but was still looking beyond him in a searching way. Then, as if she had lost sight of what she had been straining to see, she gave up and looked bewildered.

They sat in silence. The clock in a nearby tower struck. It frightened Therese because she dreaded being left alone with that grey ghost-like woman who haunted her. As if she assumed her to be as real to Daimeon as to herself, she said, 'I seem to have persuaded her that that was marriage. She may well hate me – I hate myself – for that deception of being "a married woman". I don't know why this stupid phrase keeps coming up,' she said impatiently. 'Why is it so important? Who cares? People care less than ever whether they are married or not. Yet I feel almost condemned when I think of myself in that state; as if I might never be forgiven! I must have done something dreadful in cheating myself that I was a married woman.' She could not bear to say aloud, 'I was not a real woman and was not really married.'

However strange Therese's words appeared, her evident sincerity and intensity of feeling spoke for their truth. 'Against whom have I committed a dreadful sin? There is no doubt in my mind that I have done so. It's as if in persuading that grey woman that my/her way of living with Horace – with no light, no colour, no communion of living bodies or spirits – was marriage, I had not just lied, but had killed something! It's as enormous as that. It's strange that here I know unbearable guilt which I have never felt about Horace.

'I know people have been puzzled. The judge made a remark about something missing in an apparently pleasant, intelligent woman "who sadly fails to give any impression of guilt". Perhaps, he said, that missing factor was her undoing and her sickness of mind. I could tell that judge now that I've killed more, and know my guilt now. He wouldn't understand. He would think there were other victims to be found. I don't understand either, but I know. I can't help knowing the truth because it hurts.

'You see, to be a married woman was something to be; the married state was somewhere to be. But every time I use the word "married" it seems like the abuse of something even holy; an abuse of God. Is that because of "the holy state of matrimony" they speak of in church?

'I am still a flat, grey woman who envies the round, real bodies of the other women crying out for their men!' burst from her. What she had been too ashamed to say had come of its own. Now the pressure was spent and there was nothing more to be afraid of. After a little pause she could speak dispassionately. 'You could not have reckoned with all this when you came, and now you may be convinced that I am sick or mad.' Daimeon was too filled with what she had told him to have any prompt reply. She broke the silence that followed by saying, 'But I do know something different!' in so changed a voice that it made him look up questioningly.

She was thinking of the newspaper picture that had been so important to her. It had come to her mind several times while talking to Daimeon, as if it were relevant to what she was saying, but too embarrassing to be mentioned. This was private, she had said to herself. Now it seemed to demand recognition of its connection with what she had been talking about.

Why was it harder to acknowledge something good than something bad, though that had hardly been easy. Aware of Daimeon's questioning look, she realised that she had gone too far to withdraw. 'There is this picture,' she started, looking ahead of her, as if at the picture, 'I saw it in a paper lying on the table this morning. I couldn't take my eyes off it.' She hesitated before blurting out, 'It was of a wonderful embrace!' She felt as if a red-hot bloodstream were rushing through her whole body. It seemed to pour into her from some unknown source, to fill all the blood vessels she had never known she had. She felt as if they would burst. She looked at Daimeon as if expecting him to see what she felt.

'How extraordinary!' she said in amazement, as one observing an extraordinary phenomenon. 'Talking of that picture actually produces the opposite of that grey lifeless state I've been talking about! I regarded those two states as worlds apart, with me somewhere in a void between them, but now when I talk about that second one, of the picture, it seems to be inside me too.' She looked around her: the bare room with just a few people dotted about it who fortunately showed not the least interest in her. It was a public place in which to have so private and dramatic an experience, but the very impersonality of the place seemed to ensure her privacy.

Daimeon was glad of the new brightness, not only in her face but in her whole bearing. It was an astonishing change. He saw her eyes shining and the whole face intensely alive. He had had difficulty in appreciating the picture she had been talking about but he must now be seeing its reflection in her face. Perhaps that was more important than the original. Therese in front of him, more alive and happier than he had ever seen her, was all that mattered. She made him feel like saying, 'Come on, let's go and . . .' do something suitable for a lovely day, like go on a river, into a lovely garden or just for a walk. But of course they could not.

Therese was grateful that there was no need to describe the picture, or what had happened when she saw it. All that seemed unimportant now that an essence of it seemed to be alive in her. Anyway, their time was up, in keeping with her own good conclusion. When they had both got up and Daimeon held Therese's hand in a farewell handshake, on the spur of the moment he leant towards her to kiss her cheek.

Chapter 22

Daimeon woke from deep sleep and lay motionless in the power of a dream. To move might disturb it and separate him from it. Also he did not want to move because he had been very close to someone in the dream. Moving might end their unity in an embrace in which there was no more identification of separate parts of either body. They had become merged. But there flashed into his mind another, earlier image of the dream when he had struggled with another body in danger of drowning. He had struggled a long time, not only to keep this other person above water but somehow to infuse in her the energy and will to move of her own accord. He had never seen the other's face or the rest of her in any detail but she now made him think of Therese. That he might have shared an extraordinary embrace with Therese came as a shock. He had not thought of their relationship like this. Hildegard was lying near him in her bed. He had never been guilty of deceiving her or even thinking of doing so. Nor, he realised, had he done so now. He had experienced a simple, natural unity; he gave a sigh of satisfaction.

As he stirred, his separate, outer reality superseded the other. When he thought of the dream during the day, he could not help feeling that the other person in the dream must also know it. Then he realised that the embrace in his dream was neither with Therese nor any other particular woman but with someone greater than any individual and somehow encompassing Therese as well as others. He was relieved because he had no thought of an adulterous relationship and it was a relief to find the proper scale of the dream that otherwise felt inadequately treated. It was like taking it from a cramped into an appropriately spacious place.

Therese asked herself in exasperation why she always felt worse rather than better the day after Daimeon's visit. All day the darkness inside her had been growing while she had done her best to deny it. Yesterday Daimeon's visit, without any pressure on him to come and see her, had amazed her as usual. Even more amazing was finding herself repeatedly able to talk to him in a way she had never done with anyone. However embarrassed she might be at recalling what she had said, she did not really regret having talked as she had. The overriding impression of their meeting was feeling herself in strong colours, in a bright light, instead of feeling grey in a dim dreary light. But then this light had soon been overtaken by darkness.

'We're down in the dumps today, are we?' the duty officer not so much asked as stated.

'No!' Therese almost snapped defiantly. But even as she said it she felt the dark weight inside her that had been dragging her down. She had been resisting it all day, telling herself she was fine, when she felt as if she were in a dry desert where she could not even have the relief of tears. She was angry but could not tell with whom or what. Angry with being in the desert, rather than prison because hateful as that was in many ways she knew it was still the proper place for her to be. It was the dry dreariness inside that made her protest. A heartless part of her said that she might have got used to that by now, she'd had enough experience of it. This callous attitude in herself increased her anger.

This state led her attention to what appeared to be its source in her body, that had been dead during her life with Horace. Now there was a protesting life in it. She was dismayed by this new strange energy. She became filled with it to her fingertips, as if her whole body were seething with some power in protest. She felt helpless to deal with it. The energy seemed to demand to be let out, expecting some expression as an absolute necessity that was long overdue. What could she do? What would she do? What was her body asking? Dare she hear, see, take the message? She was afraid.

Her whole body, every particle of it, was crying out for something to which it belonged. She had cheated herself, or been cheated all her life into believing that she was a body by itself. It was screaming for that from which it had been separated. It would never stop screaming until it was fitted back into the whole. The scream was like a loud alarm that could not be turned off. It could only be stifled. But she could not see with what her own being was screaming to be reunited. All she knew was this fiery longing, flowing through her with no outlet. She felt its force pressing against every surface of her body and wanting to burst out even from fingertips and toes rather than through any particular opening because all of her had been painfully cut off. All needed rejoining in a huge embrace.

It seemed to be an already existing embrace. She did not know where, but the whole of her, to every fingertip, was reaching out to it. The force driving outwards from the centre of her being seemed to have an in-built knowledge of what and where it was meant for. It was a single force, of body and soul. She had always believed that she did not know what the soul was but here was no doubt about its reality. Then, this one urgent force made plain its destination and purpose. She saw in her mind the four letters 'LOVE'. Therese knew that that love was for all of life.

*

Therese stood stunned. She had not only forgotten what she was doing but was oblivious to her surroundings. She was on kitchen duty and supposed to be scrubbing carrots. Her hands had dropped; the brush in her right hand had fallen into the grubby water without her noticing. The kitchen supervisor passing by was struck by the limp figure with arms dropped, and for a moment thought this was someone about to collapse. When the posture was maintained her alarm changed to aggression. Her own posture became more upright and assertive as she faced the dazed-looking woman, like a puppet without anyone to pull the strings taut. 'Pull yourself together, woman!' gave Therese such a shock, it had the desired effect.

'Sorry! I'm sorry,' she muttered, brought back to here and now and starting to brush the carrots in the messy water. Of course she must get on with her job. She quite liked kitchen duty; it would be a pity to get taken off it.

It would have been utterly impossible for her to say that she had made a momentous discovery; that in the last 24 hours she had found out something earth-shaking which she could see transforming everything. The carrots were no exception. Nothing seemed too small or mundane to be transformed by the light which her new insight shed on everything. She then gave another, remarkably happy look at the supervisor, whose aggressive stance was rather lost in face of this odd sequence of shocked apology to inappropriate cheerfulness. All she could do was to mumble threateningly 'Get on with it then!' For once Therese did not hate the taped music; she even found some joy in it and then cut it out of her attention.

Chapter 23

'That's simple then,' Freddie said with bitter determination. 'As you say this was the odd encounter, you should be able to dispose of any doubt,' he said with such hurt and hardness that it could not help hurting Amanda too, 'by having Melissa and "the possibility" tested. If the answer is negative then I suppose I am assured of my position.'

The words were so charged with humiliation and the anger it aroused that Amanda could not help being affected. It was like an invisible electric charge that went through her. Nor was Freddie's proposal practical. It took all her sang-froid to say, 'I am afraid that is out of the question.' She could hear both the extreme nervousness and almost menacing sharpness in her voice. Freddie perceived something else behind the apparently obdurate refusal to co-operate.

He gave Amanda a quick, enquiring glance. Her flushed face confirmed his impression that there was something more than obstinacy or animosity in her refusal. He was shocked to see her so uneasy. He had not realised that the security he had long enjoyed had been largely based on Amanda's equanimity. He had enjoyed it without realising that it gave him a firm as well as resilient base to his life. It was like a good floor covering; only when it was removed did he realise how good it was.

Freddie did not want to know what was implied in her peculiar-sounding refusal, but it was his business to know. There was no turning back now. 'Perhaps you'd explain yourself.' They were both grimly aware of being where neither wanted to be, without the comfort of being able to share the predicament. She knew it was no good prevaricating. The sooner this was got over the better. 'No one in this world has any claim on Melissa. There is no one ... the person in question ... I mean the only one besides you,' she said impatiently, and angry with Freddie for making her spell it out, 'is not around any more.'

'Any more' should give the awful finality, if he'd only hear it. He did not and asked, 'What do you mean?' She groaned internally at his dumbness forcing her closer and closer to the sorest place. Her voice would not obey her, so she could not get out what she meant to say. The pause enabled Freddie to go floundering on where every step felt a trespass to her. She cried out involuntarily. He wasn't sure whether she said 'Oh don't!' Why did she sound as if he were cruelly hurting her when he was the injured party! It seemed a classic feminine ploy. He was not going to be confused by being made to feel guilty. The mere suggestion of this was so preposterous that the indignation it aroused gave him strength. 'I have a right to your explanation! To give it, is the very least you can do.'

They had renounced 'rights' in those distant unrealistic days. This right was of a different kind of which he had previously been unaware: a basic right to respect for his humanity by another human being, let alone one with whom he had a close relationship. 'I can't check on the dead!' came out as an anguished cry. Freddie looked at Amanda and felt himself go pale like her. Her words suggested something horrifying in the background that he had not yet seen.

He almost said 'I am sorry!' but resisted the impulse. He was puzzled but now also concerned for her. His eyes narrowed as if he were straining to see something. Finally he repeated slowly, 'Check on the dead?', as if he were turning over a stone in his hand, trying to see some significance in its marks. What do these words mean, for heaven's sake? was his unspoken question and appeal to her.

The thought crossed Amanda's mind that she might even want Horace to be Melissa's father. It was her way of standing up to the pressure Freddie had been putting on her during this long, testing night. The thought reaffirmed her independence when she had been feeling helpless against Freddie's assault. She had regretted a second meeting with Horace after a long time, because it marred the memory of the first brilliant one. Maybe the inheritance from Horace would be as good as, or better than, that from Freddie. He was an extremely clever chap. The fact that he was as innocent as a babe about love-making would hardly blight Melissa's life!

Though she quickly dismissed the thought, for its disloyalty to Freddie, even its brief appearance had given her new strength. It was as if she had been given one drop of a powerful potion that had the effect of making her feel herself again instead of being Freddie's victim. She felt able to stand up and breathe freely again when she had been laid low, powerless.

Once more Freddie found himself lying awake next to Amanda resuming her night's sleep in the early hours of the new day. After all, she had told him the facts of her brief encounters surprisingly simply. The one word 'Horace' had sunk deep into him. Its present power and potential for the future made him lie back speechless. At least he understood why there was now no rival claimant to Melissa. He agreed that Amanda needed to get all the sleep she could still have.

She had become cool and collected, as if another person had taken over from the distressed one who had troubled him. He thought sorely that if anyone had a right to be distressed, it was he. Rights again! The idea kept cropping up. Whether there was such a thing legitimately or not, it roused his feeling. But he must not get worked up again now. He too deserved some sleep after what he had been through. He had never had a harder night.

When he relaxed he realised how sore he was, like after a physical beating. You only realise how sore you are when you are past the shock of being injured, he thought. The later soreness was harder to cope with than what you felt in the middle of the battle; nor was there any medicament to deal with it. He was certainly not going to resort to tranquillisers, which he regarded as women's drugs.

For a moment he glanced resentfully at Amanda's peaceful face. She ought to know what she had done to him. She was responsible for his suffering. Did he still love her? Where was he, not only in relation to Melissa? He could not just roll over and go to sleep, with all these apparently unanswerable questions. Then he found a surprisingly simple answer. He could not walk out and leave Amanda and Melissa, either now or tomorrow, or the next day. He didn't know whether it was a good thing or not.

He still wanted Amanda; he would not let go of her. From lying on his back, he rolled over towards her, putting his arm round her. He felt intensely possessive and desirous of her. He had to restrain himself not to take her now but leave her to sleep. He too was tired and, his arm still firmly round her, he quickly went to sleep.

Chapter 24

Hildegard was restless nowadays. She realised that by rights she should be enjoying an easy time. She could not say that Daimeon was any problem. Both children were well and school problems had been resolved. Instead of enjoying calm waters she was restless, sometimes to the point of great irritability. It took her time to acknowledge that Daimeon was the main object of her irritability. She found herself repeatedly in the annoying position of showing intense irritation with him for no apparent, let alone legitimate, reason. His patient tolerance of her unwarranted criticism only increased her irritation. Had he defended himself or hit back, she would have had the chance to let out her irritation more fully. It would have been provided with a channel. Exasperated, she admitted to one of her friends that she had nothing really to complain of about Daimeon these days and yet sometimes felt 'she wanted to stick a knife into him'.

She was appalled by her own words; a manner of speaking, of course, that no one would dream of taking literally, she told herself. But it was less easy to use colloquially once the literal meaning had come within one's experience. The phrase would recur in her mind: '... stick a knife into him'. How could this ever have come into general usage? She did not wish to be reminded of her sister-in-law; of that aberration that did not belong to one's world. She felt satisfied that she had kept it out of the children's awareness. She managed this in spite of Daimeon's repeated prison visits. She ignored them. They were his business; like the office, no concern of hers.

'You need a holiday, dear,' her friend Ursula assured her. 'You may be having an easy time now but only after a whacking dose of the opposite. This irritability could be a delayed reaction, you know; a perfectly healthy one to the strain you've been under. Perhaps you are having to let Daimeon know how affected you have been. You may have been too self-sacrificing when he gave you such a terrible time.'

'What rubbish, dear!' Hildegard replied. 'None of this psycho-babble for me, thank you! You know that I made no secret of what I thought of his so-called illness, and that he had no business to be lying there when he ought to be at the office. I didn't actually force him out,' she admitted, 'just because I couldn't. That was hardly being "self-sacrificing".

'But now, confound him,' she went on, 'he seems to do as I've always urged him to do. He takes seriously his responsibilities at home and outside without any of the prodding needed in the past. It seems to have had a delayed effect! He's even been given more responsibility by the firm when I had expected them to have lost confidence in him. I ought to be pleased but I am not!' Hildegard walked from the phone wishing she had something to calm her nerves – could light a cigarette or pour herself a drink, as others did. To envy others' vices was normally the last thing she would do. To do so even remotely was undermining.

Another friend, Gillian, who prided herself on having shed ten years by starting a new 'post-family career' as she called it, told Hildegard to do the same. 'It's great,' she enthused, 'to come home with one's own business affairs instead of having to listen to one's husband's or put up with that preoccupied air of his; his mind on matters supposedly too important or complex to be discussed with you. Having to swallow that spoils any dinner.'

Hildegard was indispensable to several charities for which she did a thoroughly professional job and this, she firmly told her friend, was of as great, or greater, interest as anything she might find on the labour market. Gill really wanted a chance to preen her own new feathers, she decided, and went on doing so undismayed by Hildegard's lack of appreciation.

When Hildegard picked up the post because it had come unusually late – after rather than before breakfast, when Daimeon usually took it in – she recognised at once the small, cheap brown envelope with what was here the doubtful added value of OHMS on it; not from HM Inspector of Taxes but from HM Prison Dept. Daimeon had already left. She knew that he had to fill up an application form for each prison visit. If he picked up a form when he was there, he then sent it in about ten days before he wanted to visit, in order to have the pass sent to him in time. She had seen Daimeon pleased to recognise the envelope that always looked so depressing to her.

The small brown envelope stood out for her, even amongst the business ones, as a sordid little letter. She could not think why Daimeon had to visit his ex-sister-in-law. She applied the 'ex' also to her brother-in-law. They had disqualified themselves by nature of his death. For her they were both not 'as good as dead' but much worse than dead. There was never any problem for Daimeon of what he should tell Hildegard about his visits to Therese because she had made it clear from the beginning that she did not wish to hear about them.

She repeated to herself now that for her these visits did not exist and she would be deaf to any reference to them in her presence. Accordingly, as she picked up the little envelope, she tore it in half and dropped it into the wastepaper basket. It seemed the natural thing to do and she felt more light-hearted as she went on to do the morning chores. Once or twice in the course of the morning, like when her domestic help was telling her some rather boring tale about a shopping spree, she saw in her mind the torn-in-half letter and felt keen satisfaction. It never occurred to her to remove the envelope from the wastepaper basket but Doreen, the help, automatically emptied it into the waste-bin when she cleaned the room.

Hildegard and Daimeon had an amicable evening. It was a pleasant change for Daimeon not to feel the sharp edge of her tongue, which often made their conversation hard for him.

As usual, Daimeon felt impatient when he was due to see Therese. Each time it seemed especially important for him to see her. When there were only two days to go before his visit and he had not received the permit for which he had applied at the regular time of ten days before the visit, he was anxious. It usually came well before this. He told himself that considering the unreliability of the post, he was lucky that it had always come in good time. Such reasoning was no good the day before he was due to visit. He was not prepared to trust that the permit would arrive the next morning.

He phoned the appropriate prison department and was told they would check whether his application had been received and what had been done about it. He should ring again the next day. He protested that this was too late because his visit was to be the next day. They relented and said they would try to have an answer for him in the afternoon; the later he left it the better. When he rang they were pleased to be able to tell him that his application form had been received, duly dealt with and the requested permit been posted to him several days ago.

'But I have not received it!' he replied in an exasperated tone.

'There is nothing we can do about that, I'm afraid,' was a reply he could not challenge. 'It'll probably reach you in time.'

'To be in time it must come tomorrow morning!' Daimeon said impatiently. The prison official seemed not to have grasped the fact that since the permit would be dated for the next day, it would be out of date unless it arrived the next morning. When he pointed this out there was no real reply. The refrain was 'We've done our bit and the rest is not up to us.' Daimeon missed any understanding, let alone sympathy for his position. Later he chided himself for getting so exasperated by what was nothing compared to the frustrations Therese must be having to put up with every day; it must seem for ever.

After a restless night of anxious waiting for the morning post, he was not surprised that the one envelope he wanted to see was not amongst those dropped through the letter box. 'I knew it wouldn't come!' he said wretchedly to himself. As soon as he could, he phoned the prison again and made the point that they dismissed yesterday because he must wait and see if he got the permit the next day. 'If you've got a record of the permit you sent me for today's visit, it should be all right for me to come. You know that I have been granted permission, which is all that matters.'

'Oh no, sir,' was the shocked reply. He was very mistaken, the tone implied. He apparently did not understand that the permit had to be handed in on the visit. 'You would know this from previous visits, which I am told you have made,' the officer admonished him. 'You have to show the permit when you come.' Daimeon must understand that it was up to him to produce it.

How could he produce it when he had not received it! He felt helpless and exasperated. If the prison officials could not help and washed their hands of him, whoever could help? The post office was the only one to assail with his angry demand, but the thought of this little letter caught in that huge system was utterly dispiriting. Tracing that tiny item in the ever-moving stream of mail could take for ever. One read of letters received 50 years after they were posted. He was due to see Therese today. She had had to sign the application form and so would have the date fixed in her mind, as he had it in his.

He sat at his desk, his head in his hands. He could not let Therese down like this. It was inconceivable that he would just not turn up at the appointed time. He must get a message to her before then. He realised not only that there was not much time left to get a message through but also that only the briefest cancellation would get to her via the prison officer – the only means of communicating with her. That would hardly be the warning he wanted to give but just the disappointment he wanted to avoid. He had never felt her imprisonment as acutely. He felt that he was imprisoned too, unable to reach her; even unable to go and speak through locked doors.

The expression on his face struck Timson, his colleague, when he came into the room and Daimeon looked up at him. It made him recall that Daimeon had had some kind of mental breakdown, they reckoned, though his wife had never called it that. He was prompted to ask. 'Are you all right?' and at once regretted it. He wished the words hadn't slipped out.

They gave Daimeon the chance to say, 'I'm in a fix. I had an important appointment – private not business – this afternoon which it now appears I cannot keep ... circumstances beyond my control. I had the afternoon off for the purpose. The trouble is that it's impossible to get in touch with the other person.' After a moment's pause he added dejectedly, 'There seems to have been a spanner in the works.'

'I am sorry,' Timson said uneasily. He was glad that

after all he had not been quite off the mark when he suggested something was wrong but now did not know what more he could say.

As Daimeon seemed unready to collect himself to attend to what Timson had come to discuss with him, he said reluctantly, 'I suppose this can wait. Wish you luck with your problem.' He slightly resented having no choice because Daimeon's attention was evidently totally absorbed by his personal problem. Nothing else seemed to exist. Disconcerted, Timson decided that perhaps after all Carruthers was not as reliable as Saunderson believed.

Daimeon never gave a thought to Timson's reason for coming into his room. He must phone the prison. He hesitated, his hand on the phone, trying to think how to make the best of a miserable, minimal message. He hated to think that whatever he said, beyond the bare facts of his being unable to come, would probably make no difference. When he got through he tried to squeeze in some reassuring note, that he would write and be coming soon, but sensed the officer's disregard of everything beyond the simple fact of his not coming. It was hard to accept that not even a shadow of his concern would be perceptible to Therese. He remained in the office all afternoon but got nothing done. Saunderson looked up at him with surprise when he went through his office and said, 'I thought you were not here this afternoon.'

'You're right; I was not meant to be. An appointment I had was cancelled . . . rather, postponed.' He looked preoccupied but the preoccupation was clearly not with business, Saunderson thought.

He felt disconsolate going home and had to tell himself that this was not the end of the world. He realised that he was behaving as if he were not going to see Therese again. Thank God there was no reason to think any such thing. He was relieved for a moment but then the distress he imagined he was causing Therese, and his own disappointment, again filled him. He shared the evening meal with Hildegard in silence, unable to make conversation. She would only go as far as asking, 'Nothing out of the ordinary at the office?' to which his 'No' was the simple, true answer. She was slotting the cutlery into the dishwasher when the thought of the little brown envelope flashed through her mind. Was there a connection between that and his state of mind? She had not looked inside the envelope but assumed it concerned a prison visit. She didn't want to know. It was none of her business and she wasn't going to enquire now.

Daimeon went to his study and was still there when she went to bed. She vaguely registered that he went to bed late.

Chapter 25

The usual period of a ten days' wait for the prison visiting permit was bad enough, but now Daimeon had first to write for an application form, which normally he had from his last visit. He could hardly contain himself when this arrived with a note pointing out that, as a permit had been issued for a visit scheduled for two days ago, no further permit could be granted before the statutory period of two weeks had elapsed. They sent the application form but it would not be considered until the necessary interval between visits had passed. Hildegard could not help hearing his raised voice on the phone as he exploded with exasperation at the monstrous fact of having been prevented from having the recent scheduled visit for lack of a permit, and now being barred from another visit because a permit had been issued for the visit he had never had!

'Surely you know that I have not been! You know that I could not come on the day for which you issued a permit because I never received it. I repeatedly phoned about it and you undertook to pass on the message that I was unable to come, to Mrs Carruthers. How can you then reckon that I had this visit which you yourself were instrumental in cancelling?' It was like speaking to two different departments, one of which did not want to know about the other, when in fact he was speaking to the same department.

Hearing him shout down the phone, as she could not recall ever hearing him before, Hildegard wanted to tell him to control himself, and thought of mentioning that a prison letter had gone into the dustbin. She decided it was irrelevant. The information would not alter his position and so would not be helpful. When he finished speaking on the phone she deliberately did not look at him, behaving as if the extraordinary tone of his conversation had not aroused the least curiosity in her. She was busy.

At a climax of exasperation with the prison official, Daimeon had been driven to threaten that he would take his complaint to the Home Office, to whom it would be a matter of concern that apparently the prison kept no record of the visitors a prisoner had. This, he argued, was the implication of their refusal of a visitor's permit because he was supposed to have visited on a date when in fact he had not.

The officer did not follow the argument but had an idea that he might be caught in a trap, especially at the sound of the Home Office and mention of their records. Of course records were kept but it was not unusual to be too busy to fill in all the names on a visiting day. They did their best but if it hadn't been done on the spot and was done afterwards, it was difficult to be sure you got it right. Even if they had done nothing wrong in this case, problems might come to light incidentally. It was best to avoid trouble.

The officer said to Daimeon that in what appeared to be unusual circumstances, he would make an exception and deal with this application form on receipt. This meant that, after all, only the usual ten days had to be allowed till Daimeon could safely arrange a visit. Therese would get the form with the new date to sign and he would write to her even before. He would refrain from mentioning the difficulty with his visitor's permit as reason for the cancellation of his last visit. Apart from the need to avoid possible friction with the Prison Service, it might worry Therese.

The atmosphere in the Carruthers household was not

as good as of late. If one took a sunny view of things, Hildegard decided, one could describe Daimeon as preoccupied; otherwise one would say he was grim. There was no need to exaggerate, she told herself. She brushed aside any twinge of concern or crazy suggestion of her responsibility in the situation. Mood swings are a fact of life, she told Simon when he commented on Dad's lack of cheerfulness these days, adding, 'I hope he is not going to be ill again.' He had a shock when his mother snapped, 'Of course not!' and said no more. They don't forget, said an internal voice which she disliked. She had always maintained that, thanks to her good management, their father's mysterious long stay in bed had not affected the children.

When Daimeon received another Prison Service envelope only two days after sending in the application form, he was puzzled. The permit had never come back by return. Had they after all taken pity on him? He did not know whether to be disappointed or pleased when, tearing the envelope open, he saw not the permit but a note from Therese. His heart seemed to stop for a moment and then beat all the faster as he devoured the little letter for the essential message. In his already troubled state of the last week, it seemed to confirm the darkness in which he had been living since his failure to see her.

If it were not for the individual handwriting, which gave Daimeon a sense of Therese's presence, he felt that the brief letter could have been written by a prison officer. He had a moment's fantastic idea of the prison getting their own back for his threat of going to the Home Office. He knew that was nonsense but his dismay at the letter remained.

Therese wrote that he was under no compulsion to pay her any visit. She had never requested one. Far from ever expecting, let alone asking for a visit, she had never been other than surprised by his visits. In her peculiar and difficult position of having her life almost entirely regulated by others, she wished at least to make clear that she fully accepted being in prison and did not depend on outside contacts. She had to make her life in prison. It would be a mistake for an outsider to believe that she depended on a visit. She hoped he was well.

Daimeon was thrown into a confusion of feelings: personal hurt, concern for Therese, consternation at a misunderstanding that seemed to have been devilishly produced out of nothing and was, in their situation, devilishly difficult to resolve. There was the frustration he had already suffered during the past week that had impressed on him the gulf between the outside and the prison world. He hated the prison system but a calm voice told him that were it not for the prison in which he had been able to visit Therese regularly, he would not have had this friendship at all. He could not ignore this truth. Respecting it, meant being sensible and not being carried away by various emotions. If he remained steady, he would be more likely to respond sensibly to Therese. In the end he sent a card saying only, 'Hoping to see you next Wednesday'. He had torn up one saying, 'Looking forward to seeing you next Wednesday' as too definite since he had not yet received the permit; in case the devil, ready to exploit any weak spot, seized on the excessive confidence.

He was pleasantly surprised by the duration of his calm throughout the following week. It did not seem intolerably long and he was not distracted from his work. His relationship with Hildegard was strained. He felt as if she knew and kept reminding him of his uncertainty about Therese, which he longed to end at his next visit. He knew that this must be his imagination but found it hard not to hold it against Hildegard. Reason telling him that it had nothing to do with Hildegard was ineffective.

*

'No problem! You had anyway arranged not to be here this afternoon and it is past noon,' Saunderson replied to Daimeon's apologetic announcement that he had just had a phone call from his wife, in need of his help because of an apparently minor accident she had just had.

'There's a problem all right!' Daimeon muttered tensely.

Saunderson was not sure whether he was worried about his wife or whether this unexpected demand upset his plans for the afternoon he had taken off. One way or another, he decided, Daimeon was badly put out. 'Hope things work out,' he said more aptly than he could know. 'See you in the morning, but of course if you need to be late on your wife's account, don't worry.'

Daimeon muttered, 'Thanks; very good of you. But that'll be all right.' The stormy way he left made Saunderson uneasy. He hoped that there wasn't anything seriously wrong with his wife. He guessed that family could do without more trouble after Daimeon's illness.

Daimeon was troubled by the call itself but his overriding concern was that it put in jeopardy his prison visit that afternoon. That this might yet again be made impossible, he could not bear even to consider seriously. He would not accept that the immediate prospect, at last, of being with Therese could again be made unattainable. It was intolerable. He was blind to his surroundings and looked neither right nor left as he surged ahead in the direction of home. His usual way, whenever he had to get home from the office or vice versa at record speed, was to walk fast and hail any taxi in sight. In these fairly quiet streets that was a better bet than waiting for a taxi. He strode out with his head lowered as if he were struggling against driving rain or a gale that needed all his strength to counter it.

He meant to hail any cab in sight, but even if one had tried to hail him instead, he would not have seen it. He saw nothing. He was oblivious to the outer world, being absorbed by the inner, in which he was making his way against an invisible, inimical force threatening to blow him off his chosen course. Until now it had been the prison bureaucracy; now, alarmingly, it appeared to come from his wife. He felt both blocking his way to Therese. Having visited Therese in prison regularly without difficulty, he had come to take for granted a way clear of obstacles. Suddenly, as if the road were up, there was every kind of obstruction. Just when he had negotiated a series of diversions and was about to reach his destination long overdue, there was this unprecedented call from Hildegard taking him in another direction.

It was cruelly calculated! 'They' didn't know what they were doing: Hildegard and those vague figures he saw, in his imagination, surrounding her. They had all the authority of a respectable and honourable society for whom the absolute priority of one's wife's claim was unquestionable. He resented that overbearing authority, before whom he appeared as a weak and would-be-errant husband. Why should a minor accident take precedence over what was of major importance to him and, he presumed, to Therese in her specially vulnerable position? The impact of the phone call was like the shock of something crashing across his way to Therese, just when he was about to reach her.

It was like being in a road accident at the end of a long, strained journey and thinking only of being prevented from getting to one's destination, rather than being concerned about the facts of the crash. He could not see beyond his own and Therese's disappointment; the two were inseparable. He could not bear the thought of her anticipating his visit, waiting for the prison officer to take her to the visiting room – in vain. Whatever she said in her letter, he knew that his visit was important to her. He was always punctual at the start of visiting time so they had the freedom to choose whether they wanted the whole two-hour period or less.

This was the intolerable core of the situation. He felt like running away to the prison from his road home, before he could be further delayed or stopped. He would not even consider if there might still be time to get to the prison after going home. The idea of what Therese would make of his getting there late was also intolerable. If only he had already left the office before the phone call, he would have been safe. He couldn't have been called back. They would have had to manage without him.

Manage what? he asked himself. He was surprised to realise that he had no idea. He had a vague idea of people rallying round Hildegard. Doing what? he asked himself. What was he going to find? His lack of concern for her till now shocked him. She had sounded strained but cool and collected on the phone; but then she would be that. She would make sure of that before anything else. She had said something about having tripped on the stairs and done something to her hip. She had probably got badly bruised. Were he to be asked in a court what his wife had said to him on the phone, he would have to say that he could not remember anything clearly, which was shocking.

He forgot about the prison and his absolute need to get there, as he wondered anxiously what Hildegard had actually done and how she had hurt herself. Could she possibly be immobilised – got to the phone only with difficulty? He thought of her always as upright and imposing. Her figure emanated not only self-reliance but command, which made it unsuitable for one to worry about her. But now he was worried about her.

Chapter 26

Daimeon was surprised by Simon coming towards him as he approached the house, as if he expected him just then and was evidently relieved to see him. He said something about having come home early and finding mum unable to walk. Daimeon didn't listen to any more as he ran into the house. Simon, behind, gave a sigh of relief at not being in charge after all. He had had an idea that there were things a capable boy in his position should do, without being able to think what they were. He thought of calling an ambulance but dialling 999 seemed scarily drastic. He dared not ask his mother, who frightened him by having closed her eyes as she lay waiting for whatever attention she needed. He only knew her upright and in command and was terrified by her in this state.

Hildegard felt as if she were suspended in space though she was lying on the floor. Being unable to stand upright, let alone walk, and having no feeling of her body's usual relationship to her surroundings, she felt somehow above these. It was not altogether unpleasant but very strange. She had lost count of time, which seemed to be part of the rather light-headed state into which Simon had intruded. She found it a surprising effort to try and explain why and how she came to be here but muttered that dad knew. She had phoned him before she came to lie here. She did not want to remember the excruciating pain in her hip that had laid her low. It had gone when she lay there in an odd daze.

'Oh hello!' she said, opening her eyes enough to see

Daimeon before her. It was an effort to keep her eyes open and she mumbled, in response to his questions, that she had fallen down the stairs and it was the pain in her hip that was the trouble. Then it was delicious to let her eyes close again and allow herself to be taken by the stream which wanted to carry her away. Daimeon's arrival allowed her to go with it. He was there, so she could go. She felt that she should give him a wave as she went but was off before she knew whether she had done so or not.

Daimeon was shocked to realise that she had lost consciousness. Hardly a minor accident, he guessed. He phoned for an ambulance, which promptly took Hildegard and him to the nearest hospital accident and emergency department.

Standing in the reception room, with Hildegard on a stretcher, having regained consciousness in response to the paramedics' treatment, he was facing a clock on the opposite wall. '4.20' he saw, and winced, having to ignore the despairing call within that he should be at the prison. He was expected and knew what this meant in that place. He could not do this to Therese. He looked at Hildegard. If he left her here where she would get attention, and got a cab to take him to the prison . . . For a moment it seemed just possible. Could he explain to the nurse in charge? He saw himself telling her and running out. As soon as the running figure was outside, however, it lost its impetus and despondently turned back. No, his place was here, and whatever this meant to Therese and himself had to be borne.

It took several hours for Hildegard 'to be processed' and put on the rails to an operation to deal with a badly broken pelvis. Unfortunately that turned out to mean late that evening, after two emergencies before her. The nurse advised Daimeon to go away and phone after 9 pm, when there would be more information about the time of her operation and when he might come to see her after that. He accepted that suggestion with Hildegard's agreement. She had been given painkillers and, except when she was having active attention, had been mostly dozing during the hours they had spent here. 'Everyone will think I am an old woman having a hip replacement!' had been one of her few comments.

While Daimeon was giving belated attention to his children back at home, he was more and more preoccupied with having failed Therese and, he felt, also the prison after all the pressure he had put on them for his permit. Between being met by Simon and getting back from the hospital, the immediate situation had so dominated his view that it had banished his other concern into the background. As soon as the foreground was less demanding, all that had been pushed back burst to the fore. It was too late to go where the force of his feeling would drive him. If only one could arrive at the prison in an emergency, as at a hospital, at any hour of the night and day! It seemed the only humane arrangement; but a prison not only locked in those behind its door but locked out those outside. The prospect of the night ahead without a word with Therese or any communication with the prison felt impossible. He thought that he would be reduced to wandering the streets, which, he firmly told himself, he could not do because he must not leave his children.

Nor, however, could he leave Therese. She seemed to demand a rightful place in the foreground of his life. It came as a relief to realise that his commitment to her did not have to be kept in the background out of others' sight and he did not have to be untrue to his feelings. He saw, as if for the first time, that there was no need for him to be divided; even the terrible division he suffered today was not necessary. The acute conflict today had forced his attention to the surprisingly simple, now almost obvious fact that his relationship to Therese had equal status with every other vital part of his life and needed to be recognised as such. Far from having to be locked up within himself and their prison meetings, it needed to be free in his life and the world. He seemed to have corroborated the prison sentence by locking up his relationship with Therese. The realisation made him feel freed.

Daimeon told the children that he must make two phone calls. They knew that he had to ring the hospital. He explained that the second call was to do with someone else he was worried about, whom he had had to let down today through mum's accident; he had failed to turn up when he had arranged to visit this person. He hadn't been able to get in touch with her to let her know what had happened. He told them the person was Therese, their aunt, his brother Horace's wife. 'Your brother who is dead now?' Louise asked, and he nodded his head.

Simon remembered meeting this aunt at a party when he was quite young. 'It was Horace and Therese's wedding party,' Daimeon confirmed.

Daimeon explained that since this afternoon he had been worried about Therese feeling let down, without a word from him when he hadn't turned up as arranged. When Louise said, 'I don't expect she'll mind. She probably had other things to do or might have gone to see someone else,' he explained that Therese could not go out because she was in prison, where you can only have a visit occasionally, which made it an important occasion. Louise was sitting up in bed; her attention had been divided between her conversation with her father and a book she was looking at. She now gave him all her attention.

Simon too looked up from the map he was studying on the floor. 'In prison?' he asked for both of them.

'Yes, and for a long time.'

'Why? What for?' Louise appreciated Simon going straight to the point. She waited intently for the answer.

Daimeon had not reckoned with being so quickly faced with this question. He was unprepared. Hildegard had convinced him that talking about Therese and what she had done was out of the question. He regretted his passivity in accepting the prohibition unquestioningly. But he also now balked at having to tell the shocking truth.

'In a state of despair she was driven to end Horace's life. She killed him.' After a moment's awed silence he continued, 'She was as appalled as anyone by what she had done and was even glad to go to prison. She feels she needs to be there but of course it is also very hard.' The children looked at him intently. Perhaps the evident strength of his feelings accounted for their reticence in forgoing the question 'How did she do it?' They could not see into the depth but knew it was dreadful. Daimeon's profound compassion, pervading his words, communicated itself to them. It also made the children sympathetic with his present predicament.

Daimeon said he was going to try and get a message to Therese, if only the officer who answered the phone would co-operate. It was worth trying at least. Louise, settling down in bed, agreed emphatically. Simon, with unusual sympathy, said, 'I hope you can speak to someone useful.' He usually kept his distance from anything implying feeling. Daimeon felt grateful for the most unexpected blessing of family support. This, combined with an amazing response to his call to the prison, seemed to make a beneficent wave that lifted him from the consternation and confusion of the day to new hope and light.

A sympathetic voice – rather than the mechanical one he expected to tell him 'No messages for prisoners are accepted' – actually made him believe that his concern was understood and found an echo in the woman at the other end. When she said that it should be possible to get the duty officer on Therese's wing to give her a message, he was overcome by the simplicity and humanity of this response. He wanted to take the woman a bouquet of flowers and thanked her profusely. She felt uncomfortable with people who go over the top and answered, 'No problem.' She then phoned the duty officer, to say in the mechanical voice Daimeon had been relieved not to hear, 'A message for Carruthers: her relative couldn't visit her because his wife had an accident.' She never thought of mentioning what had no substance to her way of thinking, that he was sorry or that he would be in touch. Decent of him to bother about the prisoner at all under the circumstances, she thought, as she went back to the figures on her worksheet.

Since Therese had made prison history when her demand to have her light out earlier than anyone else was upheld against the prison officer who wanted to forbid it, she was known as the one who went to sleep early, although she only wanted her light out to feel safely on her own. It was all the more surprising therefore to have Glynis, the duty officer, come in with a message. Therese looked at her startled and tense, which made her say, 'It's all right; only a message that a visitor who didn't come today couldn't make it.' She hesitated because that hardly seemed a message since she supposed it would have been obvious anyway. She was relieved to remember, 'Because his wife had an accident. That was it: his wife had an accident,' she repeated with satisfaction. She wondered vaguely whether 'accident' made it a bad message but anyway Therese, who said, 'Oh, thanks,' seemed to make something of it all right.

Therese now had the experience she hated and always did her best to avoid: of having to pace up and down the tiny room, longing for proper space to walk in. Sometimes she tried to comfort herself by telling herself that she might well be frightened of open space nowadays.

But still body and mind, and particularly her legs, could suddenly demand so insistently the space to correspond to their need for movement, that it was hard for her to deal with it. She needed to run away from the thoughts she had been having here for the last hours. She wanted to get right away from them because she was ashamed of them and wished she had not had them. It was awful to be locked up with them in this cell. She only called her room a cell when she felt bad. She was not clear what it was she so badly wanted to disown but knew very well that it was something that had taken shape in this room, and she now desperately wanted to get away from it.

She stopped herself determinedly. Why not forget all about this unsatisfactory day and end it by going to sleep. She got ready to go to bed. Supposedly about to get in, she sat on the edge of the bed and forgot her resolve. Eventually she felt cold and thought she must have been sitting there rather a long time. She couldn't believe her watch; it was near midnight. She had travelled through a treacherous, rocky landscape with fearful chasms where she was totally cut off from human contact, corresponding to her inner experience of being twice let down by Daimeon. Then she had surveyed it in the new light of the message specially brought to her.

By its very length, the whole visiting procedure – from the application by a prospective visitor, which needed the prisoner's as well as the authorities' agreement, to the issue of the permit – seemed to give a false assurance that a visit was guaranteed once the process had been completed. The fact that it had failed for Therese a fortnight ago had seemed the exception that proved the rule. She had even felt that Daimeon had been unduly upset when he did not receive his permit as usual and so could not come. His postal message of concern for her then had effectively taken away her own disappointment, but not in the way intended. It had angered her. His concern for her had offended her pride. She saw herself put into the position of a child before a benevolent uncle who was saying he was ever so sorry but he had lost the bag of sweets he usually brought her, evidently fearing a tantrum.

She wrote Daimeon several letters before the one she finally posted. She had gone through many stages of humiliation, anger, and rejection of his friendship in the letters she did not post, before writing the one he received, which told him emphatically that she fully accepted her position in prison and did not depend on any visitor. She gave him to understand that his visits were almost irrelevant. At best they were a luxury she could do without; the essentials she had to find within the prison and herself.

When she had finished with this letter she almost felt glad of this breakdown of the visiting system, for having exposed what she saw as an awful deception, even a trap in which she was being caught unawares. Thank God she had seen it! She had kicked the trap away with all the force of her feelings. Only when she had made her final statement to Daimeon had she stopped smarting from her injured pride. After a week, she had a moment's remorse at the realisation that her letter might have offended a friend, and have been less than totally justified. She did not go as far as to regret it but was increasingly glad that she was soon going to see Daimeon again as she had signed his new application form. The fact that one permit had gone astray – which she had been told happened very rarely – seemed to make the next one all the safer.

She could hardly believe it when for a second time she was not being called to the visiting room. She had been surprised by her own keenness to see Daimeon again after her sharp rebuke to him. Her first reaction to not being fetched was disbelief. The obvious reason, she told herself, was transport delay, although it had never before made Daimeon unpunctual. She did not know that he always allowed about three-quarters of an hour extra for his journey, which he could do as he took the whole afternoon off and was always only too eager to start his journey. Nearly an hour after the start of visiting time the duty officer came to her with his list of prisoners and the visitors they expected. All he had to say was, 'Sorry, your visitor has not turned up.' There was nothing else to say. It was against the rules to get involved with prisoners.

Therese turned against herself. How could she not have anticipated this? Talk about falling into a trap! She had fallen into one that she had set herself! Of course she had asked for this. If you say to someone emphatically, 'I don't need you,' can you be surprised when he stays away? She need not have worried about possibly having hurt Daimeon by her letter. She couldn't hurt him, she told herself; she was not important enough for that. Moreover, since he had applied for the permit for today's visit, he must have decided to teach her a lesson. She saw him needled by her letter and saying to himself, 'All right, we'll prove that it doesn't matter if I don't come, or if it does, she'll learn a lesson.' Vindictive, that was evidently what he was.

The hardness of these thoughts, with which she attacked herself as much as Daimeon, served to protect her against the dreadful disappointment which they covered. The attack had been going on for several hours when the night duty officer had come so surprisingly with the late message from Daimeon.

Therese would not have been more affected by the news of Hildegard's accident if she had been her closest relative or friend. It struck her like an arrow in a deep central place. She wanted to crawl into a corner to hide herself in shame, not wanting to see all that she had been saying to herself in the light of the new facts. The view she had taken of Daimeon now turned out to be a reflection of something in herself of which she was ashamed. Her little prison room seemed to force her to see what she only wanted to avoid seeing. While at other times she had valued the concentration on herself that it gave her, it now felt intolerable. It made her pace up and down; the state of mind she dreaded.

Finally, after experiencing all the pitfalls of her isolated situation, her thoughts took her to a gentler landscape. When she woke from day-dreaming, amazed by how long she had been sitting there, she had admitted the wrong she had done Daimeon. Now she was concerned for him. She felt she could never admit to him her disloyalty and nastiness in believing that he could do what a devil inside her convinced her he had done. Even if he had found her letter nasty, would he have taken that sort of revenge? Could he go to the length of getting a visitor's permit in order to teach her a lesson by not turning up? What sort of person would do that? She was shocked by the depth to which she had sunk in her imagination. For a moment she was detached enough to feel sorry for the depraved person who thought such things.

Thank God she didn't have to say anything about all this to Daimeon. She was worried about his wife's accident. Would it stop him coming here for a long time? That didn't really worry her, she was so relieved that all she had imagined was not true. That was happiness. Her relationship with Daimeon after all was intact; nothing serious had happened to it. It was all right. That was wonderful. She now realised how desperately worried she had been when she had been convinced of the opposite. She went to sleep at last with a sigh of relief.

Daimeon had had to wait longer than anticipated for the hospital report on Hildegard's operation because it, and the one before hers, had both taken longer than expected. But all had gone well, he was assured. She had not had time to come round by nearly midnight but the nurse promised that as soon as she did, she would be told that Daimeon would be with her next morning.

At last he settled into bed with a sigh of satisfaction, even happiness. Should he feel happy with Hildegard left in hospital after a serious operation, and with Therese in prison having surely had a terrible day through being let down by him? How could he feel happy after such a day? He felt shocked and for a moment guilty. But Hildegard was in good hands and there was every reason to believe she would be all right. He had been close to her through the day's ordeal.

Strangely, now he could not help feeling happy also about Therese, in contrast to the agony he had suffered on her account much of the day. He felt happy because instead of letting her down he had let her into his life and into the world in some important sense. He was too tired to think about it but it was true.

Most obviously he felt happy about Louise and Simon. He felt closer to his children, and happier with them than for years; as if he had been kept away from them and had now been allowed in where they were. He had been able to bring Therese with him. In an internal world she had been let out of prison and was with him and the kids. They had been genuinely interested in all he said about her.

Chapter 27

Therese scolded herself for almost having forgotten Amanda's visit, fixed for two days after Daimeon's last scheduled one. Therese was always surprised when there was an application for a visit from Amanda; her visits were few and far between. She had regretted that the two visits were to be so close. As it happened Amanda's visit was well timed, since Daimeon had not turned up.

They greeted each other warmly. Each told the other she looked well. When Amanda said, 'You look much better than when I saw you last', there was a trace of curiosity mixed with her praise and pleasure. Amanda reckoned that anyone who didn't let prison get them down deserved praise. She wondered what had happened to Therese since she last saw her to make her look better. What sort of experiences could one have in prison, to make one look younger and more alive in these dreary surroundings? No men around; could Therese have a lesbian relationship? Prison proverbially drove people to homosexuality. She hoped it hadn't done that to Therese, though perhaps any relationship was better than none.

Aren't there any males around this section of the prison, she asked herself. Of course there are, she had been brought up here by a male prison officer. Goodness, you'd have to be pretty desperate to make a go for one of these! she said to herself. You'd have to go for the one rotten apple, as a decent one wouldn't be susceptible and ready to break his code of conduct. That would hardly be likely to make one feel and look good! What nonsense, anyway. Therese isn't like that.

Amanda said she hoped that Therese was not too disappointed by her coming without Melissa. Now Melissa was getting bigger she wanted to move around and investigate everything; it would be a pain to have her here. She herself would have spent all her time keeping Melissa out of mischief instead of having the time with Therese. She would much rather tell Therese all about Melissa; it would be much more peaceful. Therese noted that Amanda still laughed with almost everything she said. Amanda noted that Therese joined into her laughter more than before,

'Melissa is with her father,' Amanda said emphatically as if this were an announcement of import rather than a statement of fact.

'That's good,' Therese said, unsure of what Amanda's tone meant. It was in fact resonant of their trouble with 'the paternity business'; of her and Freddie's agreement to accept things as they were and let any question be buried.

Amanda said, not particularly joyfully, 'We're getting married, you know, Freddie and I; in two weeks' time. Then Melissa will have a proper mother and father, won't she?' She laughed at this but did not sound as genuinely amused by it as she was by most things she said.

She shifted about in her chair as if she felt uncomfortable, so Therese instinctively said, 'I'm afraid these chairs are hard. They don't believe in comfort even for visitors,' But as soon as she had said this, it struck her that Amanda's discomfort was probably not physical. She looked at her searchingly. She was at a loss for what to say. 'Is it good, your getting married?' she asked honestly, because she liked Amanda. Otherwise she would regret that she had not made the most of their meeting.

Amanda looked straight at her. She had caught the ball thrown to her unexpectedly. Her face relaxed as if she no longer needed to be on her guard. Therese had given her the chance to be honest. After a short, sharp laugh she said, 'I wouldn't choose to marry. I mean, I've always said I'd rather not. I'm sure it's jolly important that it goes on, for proper families; but I didn't ever see myself as one of those.' She laughed. 'I didn't want to be so serious about it all. You see, I'd have taken it more lightly if it had been left to me. Living together and having a child, you do make a family but a sort of free-flowing one, if you know what I mean; not one fixed by law. That doesn't seem to go with me and so I find it a bit worrying. I suppose it will be all right.' Her tone expressed doubt.

She turned from her own feelings to look at Therese with no particular expectation. She had talked as she might to anyone, with no special regard for Therese's experience. Had that been tactless, or foolish? she wondered. She hadn't time to work it out. What would a woman who killed her husband think about marriage? Heaven knows! Would she be against it for everyone?

To Amanda's surprise, Therese said, 'I've always thought it a good thing. Mine wasn't the real thing. I suppose I wasn't ready for it,' she added. She smiled rather unhappily, trying to be light about it and failing. 'It wasn't at all the real thing,' she repeated and then, turning to Amanda, said with a friendly smile, 'For you it's all right though, isn't it?', sounding so confident that it was more a statement than a question. 'You've got Melissa; that's lovely for a start. We . . . that was out of the question for us.' She thought of the awful barrenness of her life with Horace in a cold, harsh climate in which a child and family life were an impossibility. It was still terrible.

She saw Amanda living in a floral setting where there was natural life. There was just a flicker of recognition that this might be an idealised picture.

Amanda listened attentively to what Therese said. She

was interested to hear that Therese thought she and Horace could not have children. She remembered Therese looking at Melissa rather sadly. She now asked, 'You'd have liked children?'

'Oh, it was out of the question,' Therese answered almost vehemently. 'Impossible to fit in with Horace's work, apart from anything else . . .' and she thought of the shocking experience of their sex life. You could not have a child like that. Like Amanda, she thought of a child needing to be born of love, a wanted child to be cherished. That had been an impossibility. No, their relationship led to death not life.

She could not bear to think about it. She wanted to get up and go but knew she couldn't. She didn't know how to get out of the awful place in which this conversation had unexpectedly landed her. She gave Amanda a desperate look, pleading for rescue. Amanda had never seen such a look. It frightened her. 'Despair' was the true word here. 'I know I am very lucky,' she said almost guiltily, seeing her life as a bed of roses compared with Therese's. 'I am sorry,' she said remorsefully, 'you must have had a desperately hard time. It was thoughtless of me . . . I mean, I am spoilt, I suppose. It's so easy talking to you that I forget. I mean, I don't consider enough what you have suffered.' Feeling embarrassed by those words, she quickly added, 'I mean, your incredibly hard life,' and wondered whether the past could have been even worse than the present. She could not bear to look into that darkness. She stretched herself and wanted to laugh, to get away from it all.

'I'll tell you all about the wedding, after the event! Can you imagine me in a white dress and solemnly going up to the altar?' She had found a proper cause for laughter.

Therese looked at her, amazed. 'Are you going to?' Was Amanda's husband-to-be insisting on getting married like that?

Her expression gave Amanda even better cause for

laughter. 'Had I been born in another age, I expect I should have done. I love going to weddings but somehow I am always a bit surprised that I'm admitted into the church. No, we are having a party after registering the marriage. If it's fine we'll have a picnic by the river. I love being by the water, even though it's rather spoilt nowadays by having to make sure Melissa doesn't fall in. I wish you could be there.' She felt a real closeness to Therese and didn't like going on to tell her of the friends they were inviting. She felt she was giving cause for sadness when it was her business to cheer up Therese.

The incongruity of the pictures Amanda had conjured up made Therese wonder aloud, 'Wedding and marriage, of course they're different. You seem to me already married; I mean you've got the established relationship and a child, so you are there. It's something to celebrate.' Amanda was impressed by Therese's unusually passionate tone. Therese cared enough to dare continue, 'You must be fond of . . . Freddie?' She said the name shyly as if afraid of being too familiar. After all, she didn't know the man.

Amanda felt herself a very rich girl talking to a very poor one, and felt ashamed of still protesting. Here she was rather resenting that she was to be tied down to Freddie; thinking why shouldn't she be free to go to someone who might take her fancy one day. She had no hankering to go anywhere else these days but why be tied? She protested internally against this fixed arrangement, which she saw imposed on her by Freddie and the official who would marry them, as if it were a kind of insult to her dignity as a person. They seemed to be restricting and reducing her, which made her want to refuse to participate and declare that she was a free agent; that no one had the right to restrict her rights.

To her surprise she did not want another lover, but what right had Freddie or anyone to stop her? She wouldn't stop him if he wanted to go. People shouldn't want to possess each other. Thinking of Freddie demanding this fixed state, she wanted straightaway to join some women's lib protest and fight under their banner for women's freedom. Having agreed to marry Freddie now seemed madness. Wouldn't Therese be the first to agree? She had had to kill Horace to get free of him! Marriage had surely been disastrous for her. Wasn't she the most potent argument against it? Amanda saw this visit making her go home and say to Freddie, 'I can't get married after all; sorry.'

But then it occurred to her that Therese actually thought she had everything one could want, and which she herself longed to have. Didn't Therese think women ought to be free? Wouldn't she be all for women's rights and support their cause if she were out in the world? She looked at Therese and the expression on her face shamed her. Therese seemed to be looking intently at something that was invisible but was reflected in her surprisingly serene face. It led Amanda to think that maybe all she had been thinking about marriage missed the main point: a loving relationship one would never want to leave. Loving someone like that – which did not preclude hating them sometimes – was like a huge embrace that included everything. She could see and feel this all-embracing relationship that naturally implied commitment. Being married was giving recognition to it; also for others to know and respect it. It seemed simple.

She had never seen it like that but knew it to be true as soon as she saw it at all. She was grateful to Therese, who, she felt, had made her see it. She admired her for knowing it. 'I think I was being childish,' she said. 'It's my habit to be obstreperous and it nearly made me miss the point. I had missed it but you somehow made me see it,' she said with unusual seriousness. 'Thank you. Yes, you did! Oh dear!' she added, as the officer facing her pointed to the clock, to say that time was up. 'I didn't mean to talk all about myself. I suppose it wasn't really just myself we talked about, was it? One doesn't often get a chance to talk, specially with Melissa around. I must go and relieve Freddie!' she said, realising that time for her outing was up too.

She laughed in her good old way as Therese said, 'Thank you for coming.' Amanda gave Therese a quick kiss. She didn't care if it were against the rules. The officer firmly led Therese out of the room.

Poor old Horace, Amanda thought on her way home, if it weren't for him I might not be getting married. I might never have found out the sense of it. It needed Therese to lead me to that. How odd that she knows what she didn't have and led me to see it. A good thing I got there after all!

Chapter 28

Not only did Hildegard have to wait for her operation, so she did not come round from it till the early hours of the next day, but her recovery took much longer than she or the family had expected. It took them a long time to grasp that the break was an exceptionally nasty one – the pelvic bone having been splintered – because no doctor or nurse told either Hildegard or Daimeon. When Hildegard was getting increasingly depressed and impatient, the staff nurse one day said to her, 'I would have expected a woman like you, Mrs Carruthers, to appreciate that a multiple fracture like yours naturally takes a long time to mend and so you'll take longer to get on your feet than you would in the case of a straightforward break. I can assure you, Mrs Carruthers' – the repetition of her name jarred on Hildegard, who suspected that was its purpose – 'we have no wish to keep you here a day longer than necessary.' To herself she said, the sooner you go the better, as far as I am concerned, regarding Hildegard as a critical, haughty woman with whom her own breezy, dominating manner did not go down as well as with most patients. 'The very length of your operation shows what a tricky job it was and I'm sure you appreciate what an excellent job the surgeon has done.' She said the last almost threateningly, as if to say, 'If you don't . . .!'

Hildegard listened intently. She felt she was getting a dressing-down but found herself oddly amused and rather relieved. 'Well, thank you for telling me,' she said, 'why, I wonder, has it taken nearly two weeks for someone to say anything more than "Everything is fine, Mrs Carruthers, you'll be on your feet again in no time" or "Don't you worry, you'll be walking out of here before long", which becomes worrying when it doesn't tally with your snail's progress. I am horrified at my state every time I am helped on my feet, and I can see the same feelings on my husband's face when he sees me trying to get about. I don't believe anyone has told him any more than me. He tried in vain to see Mr Romney, who, we were told, had an assignment abroad immediately after my operation. His junior is a very nice man but has little of substance to say.' Relieved at getting down to brass tacks at last, she continued, 'He seems strong on bedside manner and weak on matter. I am no expert, but after what you say I should like to see the X-ray of my break when I came in,' and added, 'if that's possible.' She was suddenly aware that she might be going too far for future good relations that were in her own interest.

'I will see that you get them,' the nurse said curtly. She did not want any more discussion and the patient's case was reasonable. She too was irritated by the junior registrar.

At his regular evening visit Daimeon was happily surprised by Hildegard's livelier look. Perhaps she had had a good report, he thought, and said, 'You look better, dear; have you had a better day?'

'Only in so far as I know more where I stand – or rather where I don't stand!' she said, reaching for the large envelope with the X-ray which she had asked to keep till her husband's visit. 'It helps for the moment at least to see what's what. Don't suppose it'll make me any less impatient tomorrow.' Looking at the photographs together, they agreed that no wonder it had taken a long time to put all those pieces together again! 'Pity they didn't put a whole new hip joint in while they were about it,' Hildegard said, but Daimeon was glad that they had decided against that option.

The surgeon returned and Hildegard learnt from him

that she needed to reconcile herself to several more weeks in hospital, though she would be increasingly mobile. To become so was her work these days, particularly in the physiotherapy department. She found it so exhausting that she gratefully lay on her bed at intervals between strenuous exercise. She was lying down during Daimeon's visit one late afternoon when he told her that he had had an exceptionally busy day, not at the office as she would expect. 'I haven't been there this afternoon because I went to the prison for a long-overdue visit to Therese. The children knew I was going to be a bit late and all fitted in well because they were both going to be back late too, so we all arrived more or less at the same time.'

Hildegard often imagined the three of them carrying on at home on their own, though fortunately with the help of faithful Mrs Richards. She would hate to think what it would be like without her. She sometimes stopped herself thinking about it because, even so, the thought of the disorder, not to say chaos, they must be creating made her fear her blood pressure rising. She realised that the children were growing up during her absence, which had probably encouraged them to do so. Sometimes when the three of them came to see her together she sensed a new close bond between them. She felt a pang of envy and then sadness because she was outside this unity. She recognised that it had happened just because she was not there.

'Did they know where you had been?' Hildegard asked Daimeon bluntly. The question sounded challenging. Choosing to speak to Hildegard about his prison visit was a break with the past of silence because she had made it clear that that branch of Daimeon's family no longer existed for her. She had let down an iron curtain. 'Oh yes!' he said in a tone that implied 'of course!' but also with some trepidation. It was a step into what could be a minefield.

Hildegard was silent. She too knew it was a decisive and perhaps challenging move. For a moment she was going to take her habitual stand on this issue of the unacceptable side of the family that she saw as a kind of insult to herself; but she had an internal warning that this attitude was so out of date it was ludicrous for her to stick to it. She felt like saying 'How dare you . . .?' but saw that there was no real alternative to accepting that things had changed in her absence. There had been a break not only in her hip. It had been a multiple break. She had lost power; lost her position as ruler of the roost. The realisation aroused a fury in her which would make her fight to regain her position; but it was overtaken by a surprising sense of relief, which at first she was not ready to accept.

She seemed to be watching herself in disbelief. It appeared simpler, even rather good to lie back and let things be, instead of denying or trying to run them. She had a glimmer of independence: that here was a way of getting free of the others by whom she had been tied and prevented from getting on with her own life. Perhaps she had been freed rather than deposed by that fall. It seemed that something could be at work in one's life that was cleverer than oneself.

In the silence that followed their brief exchange she and Daimeon were both aware of change. Then Hildegard's question 'How was your visit?' made Daimeon look up at her with the look of a child being given what it had long wanted but thought it would never get. He was delighted to be allowed to talk about his visit to Therese. He would never speak about the content of his talks with her but wanted the visits not to be unmentionable.

'Oh, it went well. It was a real relief, at last to achieve this visit. The first for a long time because there seemed to have been a gremlin at work disrupting the tedious but normally reliable visiting procedure. I keep to the rules and have never had any trouble before, as long as I allowed enough time for all the to-ing and fro-ing.

'I mustn't go into all these boring details. What happened doesn't make sense anyway, except as the work of the devil who seemed determined that I should not turn up when Therese expected me. It was driving me distracted. You know it's bad enough to be in that position in ordinary life, but when you think of what it means in prison to expect a visitor who then doesn't turn up, and this happens a second time! Anyway, mercifully it didn't do any lasting damage. I shouldn't have been surprised, had it been considered unforgivable, even though it really was not my fault. Sometimes one has good surprises as well as shocking ones.'

Daimeon had come away from the prison astounded by the fact that when the break in his meetings with Therese might have been a hard-to-mend one in their relationship, it seemed actually to have produced something good. He had hardly sorted this out in his own mind during the journey home when he was fully occupied with the children. 'It was all right,' he continued. 'Therese was concerned to hear about you. I had sent a message about your accident, when I couldn't go for the second time. She hopes you'll get better soon.' It was the first time Hildegard knew of her own existence in Daimeon's prison life; it was the first time she had permitted any mention of it.

'How is she bearing up?' Hildegard asked. She might as well know something more interesting than a polite enquiry about herself.

'Remarkably well . . . I have great respect for her. I doubt there are many prisoners who take their lot as she does, making something of prison life. It's an achievement to make a life beyond just surviving in that bare existence.'

'I'm glad to hear it,' Hildegard said as from a great distance, 'there are many more facilities now than there used to be. I expect she has to do a certain amount of work, doesn't she? Perhaps they are encouraged to learn something?' She never waited for an answer to her question and went straight on, 'Of course she was quite an educated girl when your brother married her, wasn't she? I mean he had' – she stopped herself saying 'picked her up' to – 'met her at university, hadn't he? Education evidently is no guard against crime.'

Hildegard tried to recall the girl to whom she had been introduced at Horace's so-called wedding party. She was disdainful of people who claim to have a wedding party when there was no wedding because they chose to be married in a sordid registry office. This had hardly predisposed her in favour of the new sister-in-law, who was unlikely to make any difference to relations with the brother-in-law whom she had always found impossible. He was one of the most awkward people she had ever met; he had none of Daimeon's charm, and his brain, which everyone praised so highly, far from helping him to get on with people, seemed more like an impediment. She remembered Therese as a very slight and very nervous girl. Not much of a sister-in-law, not much of anything, she had concluded coldly.

'I suppose she has changed since we met,' she said to Daimeon, yawning.

'You're tired,' Daimeon said. 'I won't stay long. I'm tired myself with the extra travelling.' The prison visit had buoyed him up but he had rushed back to be home before the kids. Then rushing out again to the hospital was a bit much.

Hildegard said, 'If you *will* make these visits!', her emphasis on the 'will' making it sound like wilfulness. There was no question as to which visit Hildegard was referring to; she was looking as sharp as her words. They cut the previously friendly atmosphere. 'Visits are your forte, aren't they?' was reinforced by a rather mocking look. It was contemptuous but dressed up in amusement.

Daimeon was shocked by Hildegard but grateful to feel stronger than in the past to take her jabs. He realised he had become so through his breakdown that seemed also to have been a kind of re-formation.

He laughed in answer to Hildegard's remark. He was pleased that he could be amused by his 'forte' at visiting. 'Yes, I suppose so,' he said. 'It fits my limitations . . . a visit . . . doesn't it? You've got something there.' He thought of being able to communicate with people well for a relatively short time in a concentrated way, but then being glad to be on his own. If he had to be with people all day he came to feel isolated because he could not remain in active contact, as others did, with ease.

Hildegard was taken aback by his light response to her remarks. It seemed almost insensitive of him not to have been struck by them. She wondered again how she would arrange her life when she got back. She would not admit her apprehension but talked to Daimeon about making practical arrangements for the first week or two after her return when she would still be learning to get about.

'You'll have extra help anyway,' he reassured her. 'If Mrs Richards can give us extra help now, she will surely go on doing so when you get back and need it.'

'I may look into having more, and a different kind of help, in the longer term,' Hildegard said and, to Daimeon's surprise, went on, 'because it will be a good time for me to take up other work.' She had made up her mind not to go back to her previous existence and to start a new career, not home-based. 'I suppose I shall have to do something profitable for us to afford more help beyond the emergency period. That may serve as an incentive and give me a lead to what I should do . . . so I won't do anything like flower-arranging!' She laughed because Daimeon knew that women studying flower-arranging were a stock object of derision for her.

Daimeon had also not been able to envisage Hildegard's return to where and what she was before. He did not see how any of them could go back into their old positions and was apprehensive of what would happen. Her tentative suggestion seemed to offer a way out of an old family pattern that no longer fitted. 'Good idea,' he said encouragingly. 'I must go now because it's time that I released Mrs Richards sitting in with the kids. The programme she was going to see will be over any minute and she won't like it if she has to stay beyond that.' He bent down to kiss Hildegard's cheek to say goodbye.

It wasn't a bad visit, he said to himself on his way home. He was glad that he had told Hildegard about seeing Therese, so confirming that she was no longer in 'solitary'. He would keep her here in the world, as by a strong rope by which he would pull her out of the prison rather than being drawn in when he visited her. That had made him of less use to her and had divided his life, so both parts tended to seem unreal. The change was good.

PART 2

Chapter 29

Sometimes Amanda looked at Melissa with puzzlement. She was only seven but read avidly, and was what Amanda called serious and studious beyond other bright children either at school or among their friends. Amanda was embarrassed when she had to persuade Melissa, sitting absorbed in a book, to come and play with the children of visiting friends. Sometimes she was disappointed that her daughter was not more like her. Then she told herself that it was selfish to want your offspring to be an extension of yourself. Good to have an opposite; that's what fathers are for. But Melissa was no more like Freddie than her.

The paternity question that had loomed large nearly seven years ago and had given the impetus to Freddie's wish for marriage had been lost sight of. Amanda was glad for it to have been laid to rest. Just on the odd occasion like today, when she wondered at Melissa's absorption in an encylopaedia and rejection of any suggestion to go out, there came the thought of Horace, who was otherwise forgotten. But a freak intelligence could crop up anywhere, she told herself; it just made her the odd black sheep in the white flock that one enjoyed. Positive thinking, not negative worrying! she insisted. Amanda did her best to interest Melissa in her clothes and pretty things around her and tried not to be disappointed when Melissa didn't care about them. Her only preference was for comfortable clothes she did not have to think about.

Freddie was such an established father that his position

was never in doubt. He had qualified through all Melissa's phases: comforting her as a crying baby, crawling alongside her unselfconsciously when she was at the crawling stage, walking her out, however painfully slow her progress when she insisted on walking, even in bad weather, rather than being pushed. He enjoyed reading to her but she treated that as an opportunity to learn words in order to read for herself. Freddie enjoyed others' admiration of his bright little girl but was often also a little dismayed. Was Melissa always going to want to do without them and leave Amanda and him far behind? Freddie's devotion to Melissa pleased and suited Amanda but sometimes she wondered if he did not go too far and neglected his own career.

Amanda decided it was time to apply for the permit to visit Therese. Sometimes she forgot about her for weeks on end but she seemed to have an internal mechanism that was set, like an alarm clock, to go off after several weeks, making her ask, 'It is time, isn't it?' When she then looked up the date of her last visit, she was always impressed by the reliability of that internal system in preventing her from exceeding her regular interval. It was time she sent in her visitor's application form. When she received a prison envelope the next day she felt something must have gone wrong. In all the years she had been going to the prison she had not once had a letter from them other than in response to her application for her permit, which this could not be.

'Wait a moment!' she called out to Melissa, who was calling her to help get a book from an inaccessible top shelf. She must just see what this letter said. When she opened the envelope there was nothing to get hold of quickly. She scanned through several paragraphs without getting a clear message. She couldn't make out what they were getting at. She went to sit down on the couch as if it would help the letter to sink in. But as Melissa called again, she put it down and went to her.

It was not a simple matter of getting down a book because whatever Amanda got down was not the right one. She had an idea of a particular book she said daddy had put up there, and which she wanted to look at now. She was sure it had been on that shelf. She felt that it was Amanda's fault that she was not giving her the right book; especially when her mother said, 'You'll have to ask daddy when he comes home.' That, meaning the end of the day, was ages away.

Then the idea that only daddy could give her what she wanted made her anxious. She wanted her mummy to give it to her. Sometimes she felt bad when she enjoyed sitting on her father's lap with a book and saw mummy on her own. She wanted her mother to be able to give her the book that she wanted. She got very agitated and became more and more unreasonable in Amanda's eyes.

Was she becoming a spoilt child, having a tantrum at the least provocation? Amanda wondered. Should she clamp down on this kind of insistent, almost frantic demand Melissa frequently made? Amanda tried to distract her with alternatives to what she had set her mind on. They were rejected. Melissa got more and more extreme and troubled. Amanda's patience gave out and she became the strict mother who was going to put a stop to this. That ended in both of them being more upset than ever until Amanda sank into the couch, utterly frayed. On the one hand she was accusing herself for not managing better and on the other she was angry with Melissa both for being so trying and making her, by implication, a failure as a mother.

She tried to persuade Melissa to come out for some shopping by promising to go also to the library. That bait failed when Melissa asked whether she could get the book there. As neither of them knew its title, that was impossible. Not till after lunch, which put an end to the exhausting, unsatisfactory morning, when Melissa was playing a computer game, did Amanda sit down. She was looking forward to putting her feet up and reading the paper when she found on the couch the letter from the prison. She had forgotten all about it. It seemed to require the mental energy she now lacked more than ever. The paper the prison service used was off-putting. It was so different from a personal letter on coloured paper. She always wrote on coloured paper, often so strong a colour that it was difficult for the writing to show on it. When Freddie said it was unsuitable for the business letters that she occasionally wrote, she said that was just what business needed and she hoped that whoever she wrote to would appreciate the personal touch.

She had to make an effort to find something alive in this off-putting letter which would mean something to her. She caught sight of the words 'The Parole Board', which aroused her interest and made her less weary. The gist of the letter appeared to be that a decision was to be made in the foreseeable future about parole for Therese Carruthers. That sounded great. She had difficulty in getting to whatever else was hidden in a mass of dense words. It turned out to be that she and one relative who had visited Mrs Carruthers over the years appeared to be her only connections with the world outside prison to which she would need to be re-introduced in due course.

The prisoner's wishes or intentions were always the main guide but in cases where a prisoner had no particular place to go to on leaving prison, the rehabilitation department tried to find an appropriate environment in which the prisoner could initially spend short periods. In the majority of cases there was of course the prisoner's family or a friend's home, though that often had its own problems. In some cases, particularly of long-term prisoners like that under consideration, there was no place for him or her to return to. For such people the Prison

Service provided hostel accommodation both for parole and eventually for release at the end of their sentence. At this stage they sought the co-operation of anyone who had maintained a regular personal contact with the prisoner while serving his or her sentence.

Amanda had eventually extricated from all the verbiage that Therese might before long be let out for a day or a weekend, and they wrote to her as one of the two people who had taken an interest in Therese while she was inside. They were asking her whether she would be prepared to do something for her on her way out. Take her out? Have her in her home? For a meal? Amanda wondered. Or even for a weekend? The question seemed exciting, considering the years Therese had not set foot outside that prison, so it was hard to imagine her out of it. The thought was wonderful and rather terrifying as well. What would Freddie say? She could not wait to tell him. For a moment she thought of phoning him but dismissed the phone as unsuitable for such good news.

'You don't sound very thrilled!' was her disappointed comment on Freddie's lack of reaction to her news in the evening. 'I thought it was brilliant. Just imagine, after all these years! Whatever does Therese feel at the prospect? I am dying to see her. Do you think they've told her? Perhaps they don't until they've made sure it's safe. I mean safe for her, not others. No one could be safer than Therese. We are every bit as much of a danger to society as she is, I can tell you! Can she be safely let out into the wilderness of the outside world? God! I don't like to think of being released into this world. I know prison is no nice nursery or convent but whatever the motley crowd inside, life is so damned ordered and generally predictable – unless there is some riot!'

Freddie made some confirming noise of understanding and mumbled something about pretty rough characters making sure that there was no confusion with a convent, however single-sex the institution. 'I bet your "gentle friend" has learnt things from her prison mates that she didn't know before, to fit her for the rough world awaiting her! I bet it's a good education.' Amanda didn't care for his stress on 'gentle' that verged on the sarcastic. She knew what it meant. Freddie objected to her fondness and respect for Therese, gained through the years of infrequent but regular visits. He had often pointed out that Amanda seemed to have a short memory.

He had said more than once, 'You seem to forget what she's there for! I remember, if you don't, your shock at the newspaper cutting I brought home. You're always praising the way she copes with being there, forgetting what got her there in the first place! You go on about what she makes of it, even her wisdom that's apparently greater than anything we manage. It's going a bit far, isn't it?' He sounded hard and mean to her. Once he had burst out: 'Oddly enough I'd prefer someone less wise whom you can rely on not murdering their nearest and dearest!' It sounded light-hearted enough but Amanda heard a serious note and caught sight of a dark shadow.

Freddie now said, 'You may be able to forget what she's done but you can't expect others to do so when she comes out.'

Amanda looked at him in astonishment. 'Fred!' she exclaimed, as she sometimes called him rather as a joke when he was not the familiar Freddie; and then 'Freddie!' as if urgently recalling him to be the person she expected him to be. She had been thrilled at the prospect of sharing a fantastic experience: the gradual release of a friend from years of prison life. She had been enthusing at the prospect but was stopped in her tracks by Freddie's reaction. Her exclamations seemed to say, 'You can't mean it! Surely you will see what I see!' He could not, or would not see what she saw, and she could not see what he saw.

Now, more than ever, Freddie wished Amanda had never got mixed up with this whole murky business. Ages ago he should have said, 'Don't go there. I wish you wouldn't get involved', but Amanda would probably still have gone. He still could not help thinking of Therese and Horace together. Visiting Therese could not be separated from Horace for him, but the word 'Horace' had for Freddie a particular, frightening ring. It had once threatened the security of his whole personal world. It appeared still to be charged with frightening power. Horace was gone and his wife had been safely incarcerated but 'safely' meant so little. In his mind Horace and the horrifying murder were merged into one threat. He felt as if he were facing a door with the zig-zag sign warning of a deadly electric current.

'What shall we say when I write back?' Amanda asked but didn't wait for an answer as her thoughts carried her on like an unstoppable stream. 'Just imagine coming out of that fortress for the first time, having all those doors opened for you after all those years! I feel I should be there to hold her hand.' However wonderful, it seemed to her also a terrifying prospect for Therese. She laughed at herself and the whole peculiar business. Freddie was used to her capacity for laughter even when he was shrinking with fear. 'Don't look so grim, Freddie! We are not talking about going into prison but coming out! The first step of coming out.'

To Freddie the first step meant danger. Horace's wife would be able to step further into their world, into which till now she had only intruded through Amanda's concern. He felt strong sympathy for victims of violence or their relatives who protest when their attacker is released back into their neighbourhood. Just knowing indirectly a murderer about to come out was enough for him to share their feelings. He had been disappointed that Melissa did not stop Amanda going to the prison. He had only given up trying to dissuade her from going when she made fun of his nervousness about going near anyone who had got on the wrong side of the law – or the wrong side of life, as she saw it. She pointed out that he didn't even care for visiting people in hospital and asked him if she could hope for a visit from him if she found herself in one of these places.

'Eh Freddie, would you come?' she pressed him when he refused to take her seriously.

'I wouldn't if you were in for murdering your husband!'

She laughed. 'You'd be excused.'

When she tried to get a practical suggestion for her reply to the prison department's letter, she not only got no help but could see that the subject was making him ill-tempered. If she went on talking about it, it would only lead to trouble. She must go ahead without him. When the time came for Therese actually to come and visit them, she told herself, with luck Freddie would get over his peculiar feelings and get on with Therese as he did with most of her friends.

Amanda eventually wrote to the Prison Service saying she was delighted to hear that Therese Carruthers would be due for parole soon. She would be very pleased to come and fetch her for a visit to her home whenever that would be a good idea. She said that she thought that a visit for one meal would probably be best initially and assumed that that would not be the first time Therese came out.

On reflection she had decided that she was not the best person to cope with that. Perhaps it would not really be as she imagined but it seemed to her like a birth. She didn't feel up to coping with a birth by herself. She would get too excited and a calmer person would be better. She hoped the other faithful visitor was a steady, strong character fit for the job.

Chapter 30

Hildegard had not anticipated her return home to be bliss. While she was longing to leave the hospital, she told herself that returning home would not mean sinking back into a cushioned place ready waiting for her. She must expect things to be different and not all to her liking. Her warnings were ineffective. They did nothing to protect her against the cutting edges, sharp corners and rough surfaces she found when she got home. After a week her physical and mental states were such that her GP advised her to go for a couple of weeks to a special hotel that advertised itself as ideal for recuperation after operations or other prolonged hospital treatment. In the past it would have been called a convalescent home. It had qualified nurses on its staff.

'You can sort the sheep from the goats, the hypochondriacs from the real convalescents even before you have talked to them,' Dr Boswell told her with amusement. 'But it's very good,' he said with conviction. 'They go along with the imaginary, or perhaps more psychological than physical cases, and give specialised help to those with particular needs of rehabilitation. You'll be able to have your daily walks in lovely grounds that will encourage you to go a bit further every day so you'll get your stamina back.'

Hildegard accepted gratefully the belated chance of an intermediary stage between hospital and home. Daimeon blamed himself for not having had the foresight to arrange for a more gradual transition which would have saved everyone a difficult time. Though Hildegard didn't know which was worse, the first week in hospital or this first week at home, in retrospect she was glad to have had that shocking experience of her return. She later thought of it as a kind of watershed.

She had known that she would not be returning to her previous life at home and that this was a chance to find a new direction in her life. In hospital she had toyed with various ideas but thought she must wait till she had regained her normal mobility and strength before thinking of doing anything new. When she left home again after a week, she felt more incapacitated than when she arrived. Her outrage at the exposure of an extremely vulnerable long-stay hospital patient like herself to a home that is totally unprepared to care for such a person, of whose needs the family has no understanding, fired her into her normal active position from the passive one of the victim.

This was the challenge she had been waiting for. She felt herself ready to spearhead a movement for the protection of patients released from hospital, yet unfit for ordinary everyday life. There must be a suitable halfway house. The greater the pressure on hospitals to increase their turnover, the more acute the problem. The idea of meeting that need excited her. She saw herself making a start in pioneering a service that initially would have to be private. It would evidently need a lot of building up, but with support from the right people she believed money could be raised for an effective service. She thought she would be able to rally a team of volunteer helpers as a start. She was now raring to get investigating and organising. Her new impatience to regain full health and normal energy gave impetus to her recovery, which the staff called 'brilliant'. When she left they decided Mrs Carruthers would make an excellent advertisement for their hotel.

Her problems of readjustment within the family became absorbed in the wider problems with which she was now preoccupied. She must give Daimeon his due. He was not only supportive but eventually encouraged her in campaigning and training to get her service going and recognised. She realised that it was better for the kids to have to look after themselves more than she had intended when she came out of hospital. They had got used to coping during her absence, even though it was not always in ways of which she approved, and had no wish to go back to how things were before. They thought of that as 'when they were very young'.

The tensions from which she escaped, thanks to her doctor, after that harassing week at home made clear to her that at best she might modify the ways the family had adopted during her absence but there was no question of 'getting things back to normal'. She no longer wanted that anyway. She even decided before long that, after all, she had rather nice children who had not been ruined by several weeks in their father's care. 'If you call it care!' she nevertheless added to her friends. Though she complained that her home, if not the children, was showing signs of serious neglect, her friends assured her it was still impressively well organised by their standards.

Hildegard again accepted the periodic appearance of those shoddy Prison Service envelopes as a familiar irritant. Had it been weekly instead of monthly or more, she would have protested. One day she wondered for however many years these things had been coming; she had lost count. She suggested to Daimeon that there should be something like a season ticket to save the prison service and himself the time and money of all the forms and permits they completed and posted to each other over the years. She refrained from asking how many more years Therese had inside, but once repeated the question she had asked in hospital, 'How is she getting on after all this time?' After her experience of being hospitalised she wondered what on earth this woman would be like after years in prison, but she would rather not know, and so got no real answer to her question.

Once the arrival of the familiar envelope reminded Hildegard of the one she had torn up and thrown away. It had neither done good nor harm, she thought, considering how many more were to come and how faithfully Daimeon went on visiting this sister-in-law who, she insisted, ought to be taken out of the family, as well as society, by law. She supposed prison visiting had become a habit for Daimeon and he would miss it when one day she came out. She did not believe that he would want to visit someone else. She could not think what he and a woman prisoner found to talk about but that was not her business. Fortunately she had better things to do.

It was unprecedented for Daimeon, opening what Hildegard called his sordid little envelope, to speak about the contents, let alone exclaim at it as he did now. Hildegard could not help showing interest in something unexpected coming out of that dreary envelope. She saw Daimeon's face lit up as she would expect it to be had he hit a lucky lottery number. 'Good news?' she asked casually as she watched him turn over the letter from one side to the other to confirm the contents.

He had not misunderstood. Still staring at the paper in his hand he said in an incredulous, delighted tone, 'She is shortly coming out on parole!' He had not let himself believe the moment would ever come. He had been trained by Therese to live in the present even though privately she sometimes got lost in what she called irresponsible day-dreaming either of being out and free or being hopelessly lost in a strange outside world. She thought the latter more realistic than the former.

Hildegard felt herself hit as by a missile. She was amazed that she could be struck like this. She would not be surprised if her face were white as she looked at Daimeon, absorbed in his happiness. How ridiculous to care so much! she protested internally. What does it matter to me? implying 'not at all'. Yet all day the news acted like a threatening cloud over her. Daimeon did not notice his wife's reaction. Had he been asked what his wife thought of the news, he would have said, 'I have no idea,' and might have added, 'she wouldn't be interested.'

Hildegard had got up from the breakfast table, saying she needed to get on with her own business, which was meant to encourage Daimeon to do the same. Just before leaving for the office he re-read the rather obtuse, indirect message from which he had extracted the kernel of Therese's imminent parole. He understood that they were asking his co-operation in the transition period, which especially in the case of the long-term prisoner could be a testing time. He was delighted. There was not a cloud in the sunny-morning expression on his face. He was eager to ask them what he could do. He put the envelope in his pocket because he must go to the office but would get in touch with the prison officials as soon as he could. He and they had become friends, he felt, which was great. He was longing to rejoice with Therese, whom he was not due to see for a while.

When Daimeon came to look at the letter in the evening, without the excitement of the first impact, he understood that a specific enquiry was addressed to him. In what seemed their customary way of communicating by forms, they were apparently suggesting he chose one of a few specific options offered. At last Daimeon came to the hard reality. Was he willing to offer Therese Carruthers hospitality, and to what extent? They did not actually print the choice 'for a day', 'for a weekend' etc. and ask him to tick or delete, but he suddenly felt cornered.

For a crazy moment he felt as if his relationship to

Therese was going to be prescribed and confined by others, after having been free from interference. The limitation of prison visits now seemed to have given a precious freedom that they were about to lose. He was being asked to think about bringing Therese into this house as a visitor. Were they suggesting that he might eventually ask her to stay here for a weekend? His heart sank and he wondered at himself being jubilant at the best possible news this morning. He still agreed that it was cause for joy but to answer the letter he had to make a practical proposition, which was another matter.

Hildegard was a vital part of the picture. He imagined the cold, oppressive atmosphere into which he would have to bring Therese. The relative neutrality of the prison visiting room was a haven by comparison. There one could produce one's own warmth; each prisoner and visitor could light their own little fire. He believed the kids would be interested and welcoming were he to bring Therese home. He would so like to think that Hildegard might rise to the occasion. She had changed a lot and might have left behind her old prejudices. He might be misjudging her. He imagined her coming towards Therese, receiving her with friendliness. But then another realistic side of him would not let him indulge in this wish dream. He had to admit that his wife would make any visit by Therese impossible. There was nothing to be gained by discussing the question. It would only create, or release much ill feeling. He felt utterly dejected.

Though Hildegard was in the habit of carrying on regardless of moods, she found it almost impossible to ignore the weight of depression spoiling their evening meal. Remembering the complete opposite, Daimeon bursting with delight in the morning, made this particularly irritating. Such mood swings in an adolescent were bad enough but at a supposedly mature age! She felt his behaviour a personal insult. Was he totally unaware of her? One look at him made her condemn him as totally self-absorbed. This judgement incensed her more, confirming the insult to herself.

Her indignation burst out. 'Unless you are ill,' said in a contemptuous rather than concerned tone, 'your behaviour is inexcusable!' She was ashamed not only of him but of letting herself be treated like this. 'Who does he think I am?' was the stock phrase that came to mind. She felt herself standing up for a standard that any woman must defend, fighting against the disregard for her in a man's world. She saw the situation as a throwback to when women were figures in the background, quietly bustling about to see to the domestic necessities of life, after meeting their husbands' desires and producing families. They were more or less agreeable necessities in the world which was man's possession. Daimeon needed to be brought back to this day and age!

The present perception linked with a state of bitter isolation in which she had found herself as a child. The cold in that state had reached her heart, where it left a hurt for ever. It made its mark on everything that followed. As she now faced Daimeon, apparently impervious, she wished that same hard cold to penetrate his inaccessible person, like a sword. She wanted him to feel the pain. It would reach him, as she could not.

He felt it. Her words did not make sense to him but the spirit was unmistakable. It linked with the bad news he had received from within – in contrast to the good news from outside this morning – that Hildegard's coldness would make it impossible to bring Therese here.

Daimeon looked at Hildegard miserably. His crumpled look suggested that she had already defeated him, and gave her satisfaction mixed with a trace of unease. He appeared as a creature on whom she had expended more strength than was needed to overcome him.

He felt hopeless, all the more depleted for having been so full of joy. He did not know what to say, and would have stayed in his darkness if the expression of intense demand on Hildegard's face had not conveyed to him that he must respond. He wanted to say 'What can I say to you?' but knew that he must answer the question himself. The answer came of its own. 'I dare say Therese won't mind as much as I that we cannot have her here. Perhaps it's just as well for her to know before she leaves prison that people can be imprisoned out here, where they're supposed to be free; that it isn't blessed freedom outside and imprisonment behind bars inside. She has borne prison as well as she has because she has known some freedom there that she never had outside.

'I was looking forward to welcoming her here, as a first stop, after her first steps outside . . . but we are not free to do it. There's no more getting out from behind our bars than there has been from hers.' He looked sad but less crumpled than before. The words seemed to have unfolded him.

Therese! Was that all he cared about? Did he hold her up like a red rag to a bull? Hildegard was incensed for a moment but could not muster the strength needed for an attack. Daimeon's curious speech seemed to have distracted, even dispelled her arguments and accusations. She was curiously crestfallen. What was all that talk about imprisonment? Though she muttered, 'I don't know what you're talking about,' his words had penetrated and been more effective than any she could have answered.

They managed to say a few words on unimportant, factual matters of the moment while finishing their meal. Both feeling hurt, they seemed to be surprisingly at one. Before the end of the evening Hildegard said, 'Talking of prison letters, I've been meaning to tell you for quite a time that long ago, before my accident, I had thrown away one of those regular prison letters.' She saw herself tearing the letter in half but it was not necessary to tell him that. Nor did she say that she was sorry. The fact was enough. He accepted it as simply as she said it.

Chapter 31

In the event Daimeon was able to be at Therese's side and share the experience of her first steps from prison into the outside world. The first short exit was followed by gradually increasing walks and ventures. Eventually a 24-hour stay was planned at the hostel for prisoners who had no relatives or friends with whom they could stay. Daimeon happily accepted the suggestion that he could take Therese to the hostel. He assured the deputy governor, who had asked to see him as Therese's only known relative and consistent visitor, that he would readily both take Therese to the hostel and collect her to accompany her back to prison.

The deputy gave Daimeon a searching glance across his desk, and after a brief silence said, 'That is a kind offer. It will be important for Therese to make new contacts with the people she meets at the hostel and to learn to adapt to a new environment in which she will eventually be living for a time. I am sure that if you were to take her and collect her from there it would ease the transition.' He looked down at the paper in front of him and saw again 'brother-in-law' next to Daimeon's name. Rather unusual for 'nearest relative' and most unusual in a case like this, he thought. And he has kept the connection all these years. Probably unique.

'You have your own family?' he said, more confirming than asking Daimeon. 'They are behind you in this help you are giving?' He noted that they had never visited their relation in prison and that Daimeon, in his written reply to the prison enquiry, had spoken of his regret at being unable to invite Therese to his home in the foreseeable future. These facts raised possibly important questions, to which, for his limited purpose now, it was not necessary to find answers. He had better not ignore them, though. The man he was facing showed no particular signs of stress which conflict in the family might produce. His attitude seemed entirely positive. A suspicion that in the context of the family situation he was perhaps unusually eager to help was the only cause of unease.

'I am only undertaking what I shall be able to do,' Daimeon said, wanting to assure the deputy that even if he could not invite Therese to his home he could be relied upon to play his part. 'I've been a pretty reliable visitor,' he said with modest self-esteem, and added, 'with the odd exception of unavoidable emergencies.' He thought of Hildegard's fall down the stairs and of the thrown-away envelope. Perhaps they were potential answers to the official's barely articulated questions about the family's attitude. Neither side was keen to go into that. He thought of his daughter Louise's continuing interest in Therese. She had said that she would like one day to go with Daimeon to see Therese in prison. He had been reluctant to cause any difficulty with Hildegard and answered that he had better discuss it first, and then forgot. Now he would be able to say that they would soon be able to meet out of prison. Louise might not be too pleased because she was curious to see inside a prison and looked forward to being able to say she had been in one. He hoped she would not want to boast of an aunt inside.

After Therese had got over the initial shock of the interview with the governor at which he discussed parole with her, she felt beset by a legion of worries; they were only occasionally dispelled by a thrill, like lightning illuminating a black sky. She wanted the interview with his deputy at which definite proposals were to be discussed to be put off as long as possible. Yet when the ordinary routine went on with no hint of impending change, she felt let down as if the governor had spoken of momentous things without knowing what he was doing. She then became indignant at what she called the psychological torture.

After she had finally had the second interview nothing was the same, and sometimes she wished she could be back in the previous, undisturbed monotony. She felt as if she had been helplessly lifted by a great crane from inhospitable ground in which she had nevertheless become rooted during the last seven years. She felt herself put down at a closed gate and when it opened she would be put outside, where anything or nothing awaited her. It seemed to her an unbelievably cruel process against which there was no appeal. Everyone seemed to accept it.

It was no good discussing this with Daimeon on his visit. He was worse than the others. The first time she saw him after being warned of parole, he was full of ideas that were for her hollow words, floating about in a void. He told her how wonderful it had been to receive the letter from the deputy governor. Therese felt furious and told him that she could see no reason for this letter to have been sent to him. Daimeon was cut to the quick. Therese seemed to object strongly to his part in the parole procedure about which he had felt so happy. She apparently did not want him to act as an aide in her reintroduction to the outside world.

He felt as though he had usurped someone else's position and ought to yield to the person with a rightful claim to it. For the moment he assumed that he had overlooked some closer relative or friend who would obviously have priority. He was undeniably a distant relative with no prerogative to accompany her in her venture back into the unfamiliar world. Others would be better qualified. He felt rejected and angry. He looked at Therese enquiringly. Surely she would not have kept another person secret. He must not lose the sense of their relationship, grown over the years. It was real and he must not lose confidence in it.

Looking at Therese, absorbed in her own feelings and thoughts, he realised with a shock that he did not know the person whom he had promised to help find her feet in the outer world. She would not be the person he had been visiting here and certainly not the woman he had met out there before, newly married to his brother. There was no knowing what Therese would be like in the unpredictable, insecure world outside. What would she be like in a totally strange setting? For a moment he saw being turned out of prison as cruel as being put in, and understood to some extent Therese's behaviour this afternoon.

'I see what you mean, a bit,' he said hesitantly. 'I wish there were an easier way of coming out of here.' He longed to be able to give her a welcoming family setting that would enclose and protect her. Again he wished his own home could at least be supporting but knew it was no good trying to persuade Hildegard to have Therese. It would not work and that would be intolerable.

'You know, hard as it seems, to come from here into a strange hostel probably has advantages. It's foolish to imagine other people going back to loving families or the equivalent. Much more likely they are going back to all their old problems and new ones, through appearing as intruders in the set-up that has grown up in their absence.' Daimeon shuddered at the thought but laughed as he said, 'It could make one want to run back to prison. You'd give anything for neutral ground. That's exactly what you are being offered. We may be the lucky ones after all!'

Therese had listened attentively but only now her face

and posture relaxed. She saw the good sense of Daimeon's conclusion and looked at him more happily. 'I see what you mean. To be an intruder in your home would be dreadful, and being trapped in terrible tensions would make you long for the sort of place that I am to go to. Anyway, yours is an alternative view to mine of the supposed transit camp for people with nowhere to go. I'll remind myself of it when I feel lost wherever I find myself.'

Daimeon felt encouraged. 'It's only for one night and a day in the first instance, then a couple of nights at a time for you gradually to get acclimatised; rather like putting your toes into the cold sea and then moving in gradually. Perhaps the turning point will be when you don't want to come back here. With luck it'll coincide with your being finally turfed out.'

She muttered something about very likely feeling awful in both places; about a choice between the devil and the deep blue sea, but then added as an afterthought, 'Perhaps the deep blue sea is the place to be. I might have a real bathe next summer. What a thought!' She seemed to have caught sight of an amazing view that gave her hope.

Daimeon responded eagerly, 'Louise and I will take you to the seaside in the summer. We'll do that!'

'I know, I must be positive,' Therese said doubtfully, but as she said it her heart sank. ' "Positive". What a thing to try to be! Positive,' she repeated almost contemptuously. 'No one can live on that.' Then as if rejecting the nonsense enabled her to see sense, she said firmly, 'No. I've got to have faith in what I've found while in here. I've found what feeds one; if only one will turn to an inner source and be ready to take whatever is given. You have to keep going to it even when you cannot believe it exists.' After a little silence she repeated, as much to herself as Daimeon, 'I must draw on what I've gained through the years here. I'll take it out with me, as in a rucksack! I'm still terrified at the thought but I can see what I've got to do.'

'That's a great thing,' Daimeon said.

'It's all I can do,' she said fearfully and faithfully.

The supplies in Therese's rucksack did not run out. They were replenished by a guiding spirit that maintained and strengthened her. They seemed to come with unhappiness or suffering as much as with happiness. She had found in prison that one could turn into the other, so you no longer thought much in those terms. That saved trouble, not having to seek exclusive happiness that did not seem real to her but was something other people had or believed in. It now seemed narrow and far more precarious than something combining pain and joy that related to all of you and sustained you.

She had been given life rather than existence; wine made out of water. It was perhaps always to be made, with one's co-operation, from the fruit of one's true experience. The cup could be sour or delectable. It was always life-giving.

Chapter 32

Therese was given sedatives on the Thursday before the weekend when she was to go and stay at the hostel. She was not able to eat and felt more and more ill. She was unable to answer anything said to her. She could not distinguish between snide remarks prompted by jealousy and encouraging ones by generous spirits able to share another's imminent release. It seemed to her that she was about to be born into an unknown world, like an infant with no mother to receive it. On Friday she only wished that she could vanish somewhere; even wished to be obliterated because she could not bear to go out the next day, when to stay inside had also become impossible. She felt that forbidden by an inner authority more than an outer.

There had been a momentary feeling of relief when she woke on Saturday morning; the relief of escaping a very troubled, dark night. But as soon as she remembered the day to which she was waking, the relief disappeared and she sat on the edge of the bed with her face hidden in her hands; delaying the moment of actually putting her feet on the ground on which she must walk into the day and out of the prison. The thought of that made the ground tilt so she had to hold on to things around her to stay upright. She got herself to breakfast in time with difficulty but then could neither eat nor talk.

'Anyone would think she was about to put her head into the noose, or that the next chair she was going to sit in was the electric one,' was heard but not registered by her. 'I suppose it's got to be scaring but – God – how I'd like to change places with you! Good thing I can't because you'd soon regret it.'

Another's advice: 'You lucky b......, get out of here as fast as you can!' made Therese look up and stare at the person sitting opposite her with such a blank look, it made the woman uneasy and wonder whether Therese wasn't ill. As Therese seemed not even to consider answering them, the others gave her up as a bad job.

After breakfast that she could not eat, when she could not bear to take the next step, the idea of Daimeon coming to accompany her seemed inspired. Yet when she saw him in the office block with the officer responsible for her temporary discharge, she hated the sight of him because she was overcome with shame at being seen by him in her helpless state. Barely acknowledging him, she went through the formalities and finally had the prison door inside the gate opened for her. Daimeon had asked to take her bag, which she let him do reluctantly, feeling too confused to decide whether she wanted him to take it or to hold on to it herself. Sensing Therese's weak state, Daimeon instinctively put out his free arm to steady her. He had never dared do this on previous occasions, even the first time she had stepped out after more than seven years. He could not understand what made Therese so extraordinarily troubled, when this exit seemed to him not so different from the other times she had gone out with him before. He tried to understand that going to stay in another place made all the difference to her.

Therese could not speak during the quarter of an hour's walk to the hostel. She looked so pale and weak that Daimeon thought of hailing a taxi if there were one to be seen, but when he muttered something about it Therese shook her head. Anything extra that was new must be avoided. Better just to keep walking, step by step, even though she dreaded arriving at the hostel. She felt bitterly cold though the sun was shining on a fine autumn day. It was almost as difficult to stand outside the hostel door, waiting to be let in, as it had been waiting at the prison door to be let out.

When Daimeon left her before lunch she knew what a child feels like, left at boarding school for the first time. She felt utterly deserted. The woman co-ordinator came to suggest she saw her little bedroom. Therese was relieved that she was not going to have to share a room or even sleep in a dormitory as she had feared. Her room was barer than her prison one, but then that, she told herself, had become her home. She wondered whether she would have the same room when she finally came here from prison. 'It's very small and simple but of course you will hardly be here. During the day we are together downstairs, where we are lucky to have plenty of space,' the woman, who had introduced herself as Marion, said firmly.

When Daimeon came to collect Therese on Monday, he was relieved to find her very different from how he had left her. He had thought of her anxiously throughout the weekend, trying not to let the family think that he was counting the hours till he was due to go to the hostel where, he had admitted to Hildegard, he had left Therese in a worrying state. Hildegard wondered if Therese had made a scene and just hoped she would not get into a state that would trigger off Daimeon's instability. However, remembering her own post-institutional experience after six weeks, not more than six years, she said with a note of compassion, 'It's bound to be difficult. I suppose at the hostel they know what to expect and how to deal with the acute post-institutional stage.'

Daimeon found that Therese had been roped into the hostel household much as she would be as a longer-term resident. That had not only given her a place and function in the community but, by demanding her attention for the tasks allotted to her, left her little chance to think about her situation. She complained about this on her way back to prison, saying she would be glad to get back to time on her own in her prison room. Daimeon, who would normally be sympathetic with the need for solitude, felt grateful that she had been occupied. She mentioned that she had had a little conversation with one man that was better than any she had with people in prison. Daimeon wondered what crime he had committed. Although his view of people in prison had changed through the years of his visits there, he wished Therese could be meeting people other than ex-prisoners.

The relief of returning to familiar surroundings was a shallow one. Therese found herself unable to enjoy more than momentarily her own company in her little room, and realised with surprise that her stay outside had made this finally impossible. It had become difficult before, after only a few hours outside. Now, whether she liked it or not, she had been turned, like a ship, in the opposite direction. She must move into the outside world. Although she was threatened with panic when she looked towards that outside world, a featureless unknown, the time for being inside was over.

This last period in prison was almost as difficult as the first. It felt impossible to be inside and impossible to be outside. Anger at what or who put her into this cruel predicament was preferable to the biting fear that attacked her at other times. She readily accepted medication, and was glad to be told that this was regularly given to prisoners during this last phase. It was a comfort to know that she was not the only one to take the process of release so badly.

'You're like a cat on hot bricks!' Freddie said accusingly. 'And not just tonight either. One would let it pass as "just one of those days" if it were, but you manage to make one regularly uncomfortable in one's own home! What is the matter?' Amanda felt that Freddie was complaining, not asking. He was aggrieved and sorry for himself;

annoyed with her rather than concerned or really interested in what troubled her. She therefore refused to answer. It was beneath her dignity to pander to such feelings. How could she possibly explain her feelings to someone so enclosed in his narrow self-interest? She would not be able to get through, nor would she want to get inside those confining walls. Talk about prison!

She got up in disgust from the sofa where Freddie had joined her and, she felt, assaulted her like this. She went to the bathroom on her way to bed but there the anger that rose up in her made it impossible to go to bed. She picked up her jacket from the chair in the hall and left the flat.

Freddie sat on the sofa dumbfounded. He was left not only speechless but motionless. He guessed she must have got out of the front door by the time he thought of going after her, and he could not leave Melissa alone in the flat. Good thing too, he admitted to himself, as he did not want to go after Amanda. He felt more stubborn than guilty at realising it. No, he was not sorry for what he had said and did not want to catch up with her to hold her in his arms and just make peace with a kiss. If she couldn't take his criticism and, damn it, it wasn't even criticism but a reasonable observation, too bad! Such over-reaction rather suggested she needed a jolt.

He got up and emptied the dishwasher before returning to his place on the sofa. Feeling fully justified, as he did, was not satisfying. It left her out there and him in here, fully in the right. Being right was no help at all. What was the matter? Why were things so difficult these days? Amanda and he seemed to be no longer like a pair of horses happily running in harness together. He had come to assume this over the years, even if there were the odd jerk or jolt. They had carried Melissa along with them like this quite nicely, though sometimes he felt her upsetting their balance and unity. They always managed to readjust and keep on their way.

Why was there now this upset? Instead of the sense of moving along together, there was an unnerving suspicion that Amanda was pulling in another direction. Minutes ago he had self-righteously decided that Amanda seemed to need a jolt to make her aware of what she was like these days. Now *he* felt jolted, to ask what was going on. He groaned and kicked a toy on the floor out of the way. He had thought these troubles were a thing of the past.

He did not want to remember that time when Melissa was very young and they nearly came apart completely. He shuddered and thought, but there's nothing like that now. He could see nothing on the horizon that meant trouble. Then the thought of what was 'on the horizon' brought into view a dark troublespot. That woman! Horace's wife. He still always called her 'Horace's wife' and had to make an effort to think of her name. He knew this rattled Amanda. She felt that he did it on purpose and it made her furious. 'She is someone in her own right! You don't have to be a raving feminist, do you, to demand that a woman be called by her name? Good God! What year is this?' she had burst out.

He conceded that there was some special reason why he could not call this woman by her name. It wasn't that he had been so close to Horace that he could only think of her as his wife. He objected strongly to saying 'Therese', as if the name were repugnant. It was like shaking hands with her, and that was the last thing he wanted to do. That was the trouble, he now saw plainly. It was this woman who was drawing Amanda off their joint course. What the hell had this woman to do with them! What right had she to interfere with their lives! He wanted to shout at her, 'Get out and mind your own business! You've done your damnedest to ruin your own life. At least don't go messing up others'!' The idea of her doing that was so outrageous that he was ready to shout about it from the housetops.

If Amanda's feminine feelings misled her into this

woman's orbit, his masculinity was needed to stop the rot and protect them all from an obvious threat. He was ready to play his part. Why had Amanda walked out? What did her being like a cat on hot bricks have to do with that woman? He would never have made that remark had he suspected that it led to her. He would do anything to keep her out of their lives. Now he seemed to have let her in inadvertently, it was no good just saying 'Get out!' He must look at Amanda's connection with her.

The trouble, he saw, was plain enough: Amanda wanted to say 'Come in!' to her when he wanted to say 'Get out!' He recognised with dismay that Amanda seemed to feel every bit as strongly as he did. He could see neither of them giving way. He felt himself gritting his teeth and digging in his heels and saw Amanda determined to stand by her friend, as she called her, which Freddie hated her doing. Was their marriage going to founder on that rock? What the hell did this woman mean to Amanda, or to him for that matter?

Freddie longed for a cigarette to light as he went back to sit on the sofa to try and sort this out. He had never smoked much but Amanda had persuaded him to finish with it altogether for Melissa's sake. 'Don't pollute the air in her own home, Freddie; it's bad enough having to take her out into that awful pollution. I'm sure it's worse than what they used to call the smog. They bothered to get rid of that, for much worse to come.'

Freddie felt himself getting hot with angry protest at recalling a great scene Amanda had made when he said he would not have this woman here. Even in her absence now, he corrected himself to say a reluctant 'Therese' as if to avoid giving further offence. Amanda, already deeply disappointed by Freddie's lack of co-operation when she received the letter from the prison about her friend's parole, had been outraged. She felt Freddie's attitude utterly stupid and degrading to him and herself.

It made her hate him when she wanted to love him.

When he made himself a prejudiced blockhead, he deprived her of being able to love him, which she felt a terrible thing to have done to her. At the time she could only look at him with contempt and bitter anger. She felt that had he been unfaithful to her with another woman, the betrayal would be no worse.

All right, if that's what he chose to be like, he must take the consequences. No way was she going to submit to his prejudice. Even if she had not cared about bringing Therese into her home, this would have made her insist on doing so to make clear her utter rejection of his prejudice. She finally told him that she would not subject Therese to the shame of meeting a man with his attitude, and therefore asked him to absent himself from the flat when she brought her friend here. She would certainly bring her to her home. While Freddie objected to her, he must stay away while she was here. For a moment Amanda had been scared that she could find herself faced by Freddie's 'OK then you must choose between her and me.' Surely he would not stoop to such melodrama!

Talk about pollution! Freddie said to himself. The memory of this scene, combined with his lack of a cigarette, made him say to himself indignantly, to have a murderer in your home is to pollute it far more seriously than you could do by smoking. 'Think of Melissa' indeed! The harm of the odd cigarette, even a lot of cigarettes, seemed utterly trivial compared with that of having a woman who had murdered her husband, here with Melissa. He found Amanda's insensitivity, even irresponsibility, extremely worrying. How could she be so blind and uncaring for their child? Was she wanting to shock or provoke him? Sometimes she seemed to flaunt her sympathy with adolescent rebels, but surely not in this case? Here something more important seemed involved.

Did she never think of Horace? Even now it made his flesh creep to think of this man they had both known being murdered with a knife. They had known him. That they hadn't cared for him was neither here nor there. Amanda, going out of her way to make a friend of the murderer, was unbelievable. He saw it now as a kind of betrayal. He had no strong views about the dead or their afterlife but could not help feeling that they did not simply disappear and that one still had some obligations towards them.

But then he felt confused because he saw with surprise that he objected to Amanda befriending this woman, more because she recalled Horace than because she had murdered him. Horace spelt danger for him. Why? Oh God! Must that come up again? It seemed of another age: that dreadful night, on account of Melissa, that put his whole life with Amanda in jeopardy. But with a sigh of relief he then smiled at the past worry that had been disproved by all the subsequent years of his fatherhood. It would surely be more appropriate to object to fraternising with his murderous wife on Horace's behalf than on his own.

Cold reason questioned his view of fatherhood; was it proved by faithful service or established at the source? Was he to be prey to doubt all over again? This was absurd. Where was all this leading? He got up abruptly. At that moment the door opened and Amanda walked in. Freddie exclaimed, 'Oh good, it's you!' as if she were the last person he expected, and her arrival was the happiest surprise.

Amanda looked at him, also surprised by this quite unexpected welcome. 'Didn't you expect me? It's time we went to bed. I am tired.'

Freddie had lost count of time but was ready to agree 'It is.'

They made love. It was good. They went to sleep in each other's arms.

Chapter 33

Daimeon internally rejoiced at a change that he had thought impossible. Louise was to go with him to see Therese at the hostel, with her mother's knowledge. He felt it a watershed though he warned himself that it might not imply as great a change of Hildegard's mind as it seemed. Louise was surprised that her coming with him seemed to mean a lot to her father. She was disappointed not to be going to see her aunt in prison because she was more curious about prison than about her aunt. Even though her father had told her that one never saw the prisoners' quarters – certainly no cells with iron bars and clanging metal doors – but simply sat in a large, bare room facing the person one visited across a little table, she had hoped to get some interesting glimpse of life 'inside'.

Much to her mother's irritation, she had made quite a fuss when Daimeon said he had forgotten to discuss it with Hildegard, and by now it was too late because Therese was coming out on parole. When Daimeon persuaded her that it might be even more interesting to visit the hostel because she would be able to see more of the other people, he gave an anxious glance at Hildegard. She was sitting at her desk concentrating on some papers so she appeared not to hear what was going on. He was sure that she was in fact hearing everything but refrained from protesting. He was right. Although she was ostensibly going through a series of documents relating to her work, more than her curiosity was aroused by the discussion of the next-best to a prison visit.

She had long become used to the changes that had taken place while she was 'out of the way', but the idea that Daimeon had intended, even promised, to take Louise to see his sister-in-law in prison aroused hot anger in her. It seemed a betrayal. He must know that while she tolerated his prison visits, the person he visited did not exist for her and, she claimed, for her children. For him even to consider taking Louise to this woman was like breaching a frontier agreement.

Yet here she was, having to acknowledge that Louise was going with Daimeon to see the person she had decided did not exist for them! The papers she had in front of her seemed to persuade her that they were more important than these family matters. They demanded her attention. Her work generally held her and kept her energies from other things. She occasionally complained of it but basically knew it was a good thing.

Looking up for a moment, she had caught sight of her daughter looking at her father, ostensibly reproachfully but transparently enthralled. She felt a moment's protest, wanting to expose and so break this special connection. Louise's adolescent love for her father embarrassed her, tempting her to make fun of it. When Daimeon got up to answer a doorbell, she felt like making some mocking remark; but to take advantage of the moment she and Louise were alone seemed low and she desisted. Nor did she want to drive her daughter further away from her. Facing her own work, she said to Louise, 'Don't you think it's time to get down to that essay waiting to be written? All that material you've been collecting, waiting to come into its own!' She herself started typing as if leading the way and expecting her daughter to follow.

'I suppose so,' Louise said reluctantly as she got up from the couch, 'but I must get a drink first.' Hildegard thought of the old days when there was a fixed routine: home from school, change from uniforms into home clothes, a light tea straightaway to interfere as little as possible with supper, homework after a little play, etc. All that structured life was now gone. They had done as they felt like when she was not here and seemed too old to be put back into her harness on her return. Fortunately Daimeon did not let them have things just as they wanted, and as early adolescents they were still fairly amenable. Better to have Louise in Daimeon's pocket, unpleasant though she found it, than have her out with a boyfriend.

Hildegard maintained her detachment after Daimeon and Louise had been to the hostel on a Saturday. They were having guests that evening, which helped because it meant she was too busy in the kitchen to be able to take any interest, let alone ask questions. Yet even with blinkered eyes and stopped ears, she could not help registering Louise's lively state and that she had evidently enjoyed herself. Fortunately she could be confident that Louise would not talk about her afternoon experience at dinner, and would choose to spend the rest of the evening listening to music in her room.

But Louise came to stand by Hildegard and, looking at what her mother was making, said, 'We had a smashing time. There were some really nice and interesting people.' As she said it, she realised that her mother might not agree if she saw the people she was talking abut. They were not her sort. She knew that her mother and father liked different sorts of people, that they were more different from each other than many parents. This had troubled her more before she actually realised it a short time ago. 'They were interesting,' she repeated more thoughtfully. Hildegard did not like to think what that might mean.

Louise avoided thinking of some people whom she had been rather afraid to look at; troubled-looking ones who sat alone, and one rather scary, powerful-looking man who made her want to forget that these people were ex-criminals, or speculate what their crimes had been. She would not want her mother to know of those; but her aunt, she was great. 'Aunt Therese is really nice. You'd like her,' she said, without thinking. 'We got on very well.'

Louise had been struck by how easy her father and aunt were together. She was not used to seeing him so easy with anybody, and cheerful. Therese had made her feel good too, which made her wish she could do something good for her. She said enthusiastically, 'I'd like to invite her here soon. It would be a nice change for her. Dad wouldn't arrange anything but I think she would be free to come when she likes. The hostel won't mind, will they? After all, she's not in prison any more. She did say they have to do quite a lot of jobs but it isn't like being in a job either, is it?' She snicked a scrap of smoked salmon that her mother was distributing over the hors d'oeuvre plates. 'Let's have a bit of cucumber to go with it, mum.' She held out her hand to her mother, who had the cucumber in one hand and a knife in the other.

Hildegard felt an urge to cut something more resistant than a cucumber. This woman should be cut out of their lives. 'Go to your room, be a dear! I must concentrate on what I am doing.' It took considerable self-control not to follow her inclination to slap Louise's face for what she perceived as an insult casually flung at her. She could see and feel herself doing it, so near had she been; even imagined her hand smarting as it would have done, so sharp was the intended slap. Part of her regretted that the natural response had been forbidden, but another knew that she would bitterly regret doing what she felt like.

Louise had gone and Hildegard was left shaking with the impact of the inner forces she had just experienced, especially an almost brutal strength she had not known she had, which had restrained her own violence. She felt as much its victim as its source. She picked up the knife that had fallen on the floor. She felt a shudder at the fleeting recognition of what might have been a temptation for some people, in some circumstances.

Had Louise got the message? Nothing much had actually been said. While firmly telling herself that now was not the moment to get worked up about it, Hildegard repeated to herself, it must be made clear beyond any doubt that this woman is never going to cross the threshold of this house. If her daughter wished to befriend her . . . she gasped at the torrent ready to follow. It made her check herself again. For God's sake, woman, get on with the job . . . this dinner!

Hildegard had more to drink that night than usual. Daimeon looked questioningly at her when she asked him not to pass her by, as was their rule when he refilled glasses. What was making her break it? She seemed to be taking more trouble about these guests than he would have expected. They were not people she cared about. They needed to be invited occasionally to repay their hospitality. They were an undemanding couple not wanting more than a good meal and casual chatter. Hildegard's bright state and challenging, sharp-witted conversation left the mild and moderate-minded couple at a loss. They tried to laugh off some of her provocative statements and opinions that were beyond their grasp. She seemed unaware of the inappropriateness of serving such strong stuff, rather as if she were plying them with spirit, which they did not drink.

After their guests had gone, they cleared up in silence. Daimeon felt it an uneasy silence. The contrast with the fireworks Hildegard had provided earlier made him uncomfortable. 'You must be tired,' he said, as much to give an explanation for the silence as to express sympathy. 'You provided a splendid meal. I'm sorry Louise didn't help as I hoped she might.' Hildegard looked up from what she was doing and gave him a searing look. It told him at least that it was not tiredness that was the cause of her silence.

In a flash Daimeon saw in that troubling look the source of the excessive brightness that had made him uncomfortable all evening. Getting to bed, the welcome end of the day that had seemed so near, seemed to move out of sight. 'Have you had trouble with Louise?' he asked hesitantly. He gave consistent support to Hildegard in what seemed a regular adolescent stage of mother-daughter difficulties, while father was given preferential treatment. It was a pity that Simon was away, so Hildegard missed the compensation of the son who could not stop criticising his father while his mother was treated well.

Hildegard's look at him in response to what had been meant as an innocent and rather friendly question, reminded him of a flash of lightning that is followed immediately by a clap of thunder indicating that a storm was very near. Hildegard was lost for words. 'Trouble with Louise?' She wanted to spit out the remark rather than repeat it. 'You know perfectly well this is not Louise's responsibility.' She found his evident unawareness unbelievable and inexcusable since he was not an idiot. It was his business to be aware of what he was doing. She was choking with all that there was to be said, but to have to start telling him now the elementary facts of this long story that she had lived with since that fateful phone call years ago, was an indignity to which she was not going to submit. Looking at Daimeon with amazed exasperation, she could only ask, 'Where have you been all these years?'

He felt like a foolish schoolboy made to realise that he was missing a point that ought to be obvious. It occurred to him that their visit to Therese had something to do with Hildegard's extraordinary behaviour. He stared at her with an anxious, troubled expression. Putting down the tea towel with which he had been rubbing up the glasses as Hildegard liked them to be done, he said timidly, 'I am not sure what you mean.'

There was no ill will in his whole stance; it might have been easier for her if there had been. Only bafflement came through to her. She was not disarmed but was made to see that she must not be so carried away by her outraged feelings that she saw only the monster in her mind and not the man before her. But the unspeakable facts remained: Louise talking about 'her aunt' in a way that seemed to put her back into the family circle, against all that she had vowed. She took a long breath. 'What do I mean? I mean that you are breaking up the family wilfully. You have chosen', and the words were so hurting and explosive to herself that she felt afraid of all their destructive potential, 'to take your daughter, on whom you have great influence, to see a murderer who by killing your brother has also killed her connection by marriage with our family. The mind boggles at your wishing to bring your daughter into the relationship you cultivate with the murderer. You chose to do this when for years the woman has already blighted our marriage. This new initiative suggests to me that you wish to destroy our family.'

She turned to leave the room, surprised by her own words that had said more than she had thought she could say. They seemed to have presented herself as much as Daimeon with a summary of the situation, whose implications were alarming to them both. She went to bed chastened rather than enraged.

Daimeon was shocked. He was tired. That dinner party was a mistake, coming after the long-promised visit with Louise to Therese, leaving no chance for communication with Hildegard till it was too late, at midnight. Had he tried to speak to her earlier, she would certainly have protested that when she was busy preparing for a dinner party was hardly the moment. Anyway, neither of them normally expected to talk about his visits to Therese so it had not really occurred to him. Yet, hearing again Hildegard's words '. . . chosen to take your daughter . . . to become a friend of the murderer', he saw that obviously

Louise made all the difference. Because the protracted discussions about her accompanying him had gone on in Hildegard's presence he had been under the impression that she had accepted it. He had failed to see. . . .

Chapter 34

Daimeon was on the threshold of sleep. The phrases came and went. 'You are breaking up the family wilfully.' Surely he was not going to have to defend himself against such an obviously absurd charge. He turned in bed, away from it, to go to sleep. It was the kind of exaggerated thing that is said in the heat of the moment, perhaps to provoke a reaction. Surely she did not want a protestation of love which, he believed, she would have laughed at? She would regard it as ridiculous at their stage, and probably at any stage. He would not feel easy assuring her of his love, though he felt uneasy at that admission. However, that was a long way from wanting to destroy the family, he defended himself, and evaded what he had hit upon inadvertently. As if this were the end of the matter, he rolled on his side again, deciding it was time to go to sleep.

'You are breaking up the family wilfully. You have chosen to take your daughter, on whom you have great influence, to see a murderer who by killing your brother has also killed her connection by marriage with our family. The mind boggles at your wishing to bring your daughter into the relationship you cultivate with the murderer. You chose to do this when for years the woman has already blighted our marriage. This new initiative suggests to me that you wish to destroy our family.' Daimeon heard the accusation in full as if it were read out to him. After the initial bewilderment, he faced it with some detachment. He sat up to be readier to meet the charge.

He felt himself both prosecutor and accused. The defence admitted that what he had done was probably thoughtless but was certainly not deliberately destructive. The prosecution said that such thoughtlessness would suggest a deliberate blindness or disregard of his wife's feelings since these had been made very clear to him. Well, yes, he admitted; he had been disregarding Hildegard's feelings.

At first there had been a command he felt compelled to obey, to go Therese. It arose from the whole experience of his illness, which linked him with her. Over the years, the friendship that grew from his visits had become the mainstream of his life. There was then a different kind of compulsion. He needed the visits. Each one gave substance to his life and so to himself, from which he thought others also benefited. When he had doubts he told himself that Hildegard too would suffer were he to give up his prison visits.

The prosecution suggested that the phrase 'prison visits' could be a cover-up for his relationship with Therese; not just with 'another woman' but with a murderer; and not just in Hildegard's eyes, as he liked to think.

He had refused all the time to call Therese 'a murderer' and wished Hildegard would stop doing so. When he spoke to the children about Therese, he had had to mention painfully why Therese was in prison but then expressed his disdain for the view of her as 'a murderer', as if that were an ignorant, almost barbaric view. Was he corrupting his children? Was he one of those soft-brained rather than soft-hearted people who would not call a spade a spade? Who by their so-called superior understanding blurred all distinctions of right and wrong? Thereby leading their children into a jungle without guidelines; giving them no moral compass? He seemed to hear a verdict of 'guilty on that count' and was shocked.

He realised that he had never considered Hildegard's

feelings seriously. He had treated them like baggage that he accepted always having to carry. Every so often, when it dragged him down, he had to haul it back up on his shoulder. He had put up with Hildegard's feelings passively; they were something that one could do nothing about. He was starting to break out in a cold sweat at the implication that they presented a valid demand that he was guilty of having persistently ignored.

He wanted to plead that the judge did not understand that things become like that in a marriage in the long run. Stumbling blocks seem curiously to become pillars of the marriage. Through one's skirting around them the marriage becomes distorted, which gives rise to chronic pain, but then this also makes itself accepted as an apparent necessity of life. The original difficulty has then so spread into the marriage that it has become part of its fabric. Dealing with it would mean a serious operation which might be dangerous. It is avoided on the principle of 'Better the devil one knows. . . .'

Daimeon balked at the idea of attending seriously to Hildegard's feelings and views. There was every kind of objection. There was no point, he wanted to shout at the judge, who did not appreciate the complexity of the situation. He wanted to say that Hildegard would not really want her feelings to be examined. The judge would say, 'They need to be known.' Daimeon wanted to leave the court but was not allowed.

Did he really not know Hildegard's feelings in the present situation? Had she not told him plainly? Did he ever listen to what she said? What would she say? He need not go and wake her to tell him. She would explode, 'How can you ask, after all these years!'

Of course he knew that Hildegard had cut Therese out of her family, or rather maintained that Therese had cut herself out once and for all by what she had done. She saw Daimeon, instead of accepting the fact, going out of his way to pick up the cut-off branch, cherish it and do everything possible to reconnect it to the family tree. He had confirmed the connection by taking Louise with him to see Therese. Was that not asking for a violent reaction? Daimeon lay down again, as if defeated.

He had reached the core of Hildegard's allegation. 'This . . . suggests that you wish to destroy our family.' He could say that he had no such intention. He had never thought of doing such a thing.

This prompted, 'You should have thought! Should have known what you are doing.' He could hear Hildegard's scornful voice adding, 'How could an intelligent man like you not know?'

'I did not want to know' was the honest answer. 'I suppose I disregarded what I ought to have seen. I was going my way, doing what felt right to me.' He seemed to say to Hildegard, 'I suppose I hoped that I could be joined to the bit of the tree with which you made a break, while remaining joined to you and the rest.'

Did he dare ask himself, let alone answer, whether he wanted, or at least did not mind, splitting from Hildegard? If he could not be joined to both Hildegard and Therese, he could not doubt that he must keep his connection with Therese. His assumption seemed to have been that he was attached to Hildegard in any case, so she need not be considered. He had dismissed her feelings as a narrow-minded, intolerant attitude he had to endure, while her suffering had not been real to him. When asked what she suffered, he felt like a schoolboy asked a question on a subject he had never troubled to look up, so he could not begin to answer. Why should she suffer? he might even ask. He was sure she did not miss him the few hours he spent on his prison visits. Their marriage had never been that close. She did not want him with her much of the time. But, he told himself, that wasn't the point, and finally judged that he had taken Hildegard for granted in an unthinking and uncaring way.

Daimeon got out of bed, put on his dressing gown and went into the living room to work out, in a clearer light, what he should do. When he went back to bed more than an hour later, he had decided that next morning, Sunday, was a good time to talk to Louise, with Hildegard around or even present.

He and Hildegard had an uneasy breakfast. He hoped that Louise might not get up too late so he would not be waiting all morning. He needed to get his talk with her over as soon as possible. He wondered whether he might knock at her door and say he wanted to talk to her but saw that was out of the question. He must control his impatience and anxiety. It seemed a godsend to see Louise appearing when he was about to leave the breakfast table. 'You are early!' he said happily, and Hildegard looked up at her daughter enquiringly. It was almost unheard of for her to be up at nine o'clock at the weekend. Louise said she could not sleep. Both her parents wondered whether the previous day's visit had something to do with it.

Hildegard was startled by Daimeon saying at once, 'I want to talk to you, Louise . . . about our visit yesterday.'

'Now?' Louise asked, as if this were surely the most unsuitable moment. Quite apart from her own disinclination, dad surely knew better than to talk about this with mother at the breakfast table. She looked up at him dismayed and even disapprovingly.

'Yes, the sooner the better,' was the surprisingly determined reply. 'I want to correct my one-sided and probably misleading attitude to Therese, particularly in taking you to see her yesterday.'

Daimeon concentrated so intently on what he had to say that he had no awareness of anything else. He was oblivious of Hildegard's stunned look. For a moment she wondered whether she was meant to be a witness or was expected tactfully to leave the room. She sat awaiting what was to follow, more alerted by Daimeon's introduction than Louise, who still looked not completely awake.

Daimeon looked down in front of him. 'Not just yesterday,' he went on awkwardly, 'but since mum was in hospital when I first told you of my visiting Therese in prison. I remember telling you because I had to phone the prison that night as well as the hospital.' Hildegard did not know which night he was talking about and looked up at Daimeon attentively, trying to think of a specific occasion. 'Anyway, to cut a long story short . . .' Daimeon was afraid he might never get to the point, it was so hard. He must forcibly put himself there. 'I have always given you my view of Therese and of course now you have had your own view, but influenced by me. Yet many people would share your mother's view, which you probably realise is very different from mine.'

He felt as if he had to move a great load of large stones singlehandedly. He could not bear the words he had to use. '"Murder", I suppose I am lily-livered. I've hardly used the word when I've talked to you about Therese because I believe I've understood, as far as one can, how she came to kill my brother, and feel for her. In some ways I've even felt myself sharing in her crime.' Seeing Louise's look of amazement, he said quickly, 'Never mind about that now; I know it sounds strange. No, of course I wasn't there nor was there any question of planning it!' He himself was horrified at the false trails to which his remark might lead. He said impatiently, 'I want to get away from my view; that's the whole point.' He needed to put Hildegard in the picture. 'Your mother's view is indisputable: that this woman has committed the most horrendous crime and thereby excluded herself from society and from her family; particularly ours, to which she was of course only linked by marriage. You must respect that view. Murder must always be condemned, whatever the circumstances. I believe I have never made that point clear. For many people this makes any contact with the murderer impossible. I should have shown more respect for such feelings even if I don't share them. I should have paid more respect to your mother's feelings and then, I suppose, the question of your coming to visit Therese would not have arisen.' He sounded contrite.

'Maybe you are puzzled by Therese, a gentle-seeming person you seemed to like. She obviously liked you.' Daimeon could sense Hildegard bristling. 'She is not a monster but she had done something monstrous. I can see that I have brushed this aside and so have given you a one-sided picture. That was wrong and I needed to correct it.'

He had no idea if what he said made sense and what had got through to Louise. He had had to concentrate on speaking to her, rather than to Hildegard as well because that would have confused him utterly; but he hoped that Hildegard had got something from what he said. He thought he had finished. They thought he had. Everyone seemed to wonder who would make the first move, either saying something or getting up from the table, to clear away the breakfast perhaps.

Unexpectedly Daimeon found himself talking again. 'This had to be said now,' he said more confidently for having unburdened himself of his main message. 'It is urgent because all our lives may be changed by Therese coming out of prison. While she was in prison, banished from society, my visits to her were kept apart. Society now is about to take the ex-murderer back.' Calling Therese 'ex-murderer' felt like a betrayal, which made him hate Hildegard for forcing it on him. He imagined her objecting to the 'ex'. 'I am ready to have her in the family. I have come to respect the opposite attitude but I cannot take or act on it myself. It would be impossible for me not to remain related to Therese, because I am related to her as indisputably as to anyone else. Since this is in contradiction to your mother's feelings and beliefs, we may not be able to carry on as before. I see that now.'

He seemed to have come into a clearing from a thicket and was surprised by what he saw. 'The situation forces a decision on us. Therese is nearly out of prison. She will be for good, in a week or so. I need to help her. She cannot come here, so it may be necessary for me to live elsewhere. It may be necessary for us to separate,' he added, amazed at where he had landed.

Louise was waiting for her mother's reaction. Hildegard looked at Daimeon astounded. She marvelled at him. Daimeon, as she thought of him, could not have said this; would not do what apparently he was ready to do. Had she led him to this by what she had said to him last night? That had come as a surprise to herself. He must have gone a long way during the night.

Hildegard said, 'I appreciate your openness and clarity.' He was pleased that what had felt such a tortuous business could be praised for clarity. She went on gravely, 'A plan of action will be needed.' In shock, she added weakly, 'It'll have to be worked out.' Maybe, she thought, the last months' experience of organising a 'recuperation service' would stand her in good stead.

Daimeon put a hand on Louise, who was the first to get up from the table. She was thinking of telling Simon. Daimeon hoped that making the outer situation somehow correspond more to the inner one of their lives might be of benefit to everyone. But he too was stunned.

Chapter 35

It was hard to say goodbye to the other girls, as Doreen insisted on calling them. At school or college you left together. When Therese came to her final leave-taking it was like a postage stamp being torn from all the rest on a sheet by the series of perforations, till finally it is loose and apart. The process had begun with her first weekend at the hostel. That first tear was the most drastic and hardest to take for all of them. After the initial tear felt by everyone, however unwilling companions they were, all were prepared for the subsequent moves. Yet on the last day most of them were subdued at breakfast. The atmosphere would have been oppressive but for Doreen, who could be trusted to cut any tension by an idiotic, preferably coarse remark that dispersed troubling feelings. 'She can't wait to get to that dark, handsome stranger that's waiting for her at the hostel,' she fantasised, 'and for him, any newcomer is welcome. "A change is as good as a...."' The obscenity was drowned in laughter so Therese could not hear it. She felt relieved by the laughter, but the cause of it, like countless such remarks, emphasised her separateness, which made the leave-taking easier.

She still could not help feeling guilty at leaving them, especially as she had the idea that it was harder for them to be here than it had been for her. In the end, after clearing away her breakfast things and on her way out, she turned back, gave a quick final wave, seeing nothing and nobody, and walked fast to her room. She picked up her ready-packed possessions and went to the office where she was expected to go through the final formalities.

She went through these and through the prison gates with eyes lowered, raised only for seconds when she responded to something said to her. She did this more impassively than on any of the trial runs for leaving the place where she had been imprisoned for so many years. She gave the least possible acknowledgment of Daimeon, waiting to accompany her out for the last time.

Therese was very cold when she sat over a mug of coffee at the hostel during that morning and she went about shivering for the rest of the day. She made apparently automatic, polite responses but seemed neither to hear nor understand even simple remarks or questions, which consequently got no answer. Marion, the hostel co-ordinator, recognised the state of shock as a fairly common phenomenon. She gave Therese a pill before she went to bed and offered her an extra blanket if she were cold, which evoked the first, live response from Therese. She looked up with grateful surprise at this sign of someone in touch with her. It warmed her as much as the blanket.

The hostel routine, the elements of which she already knew from her previous weekends there, included outings with one or other hostel inmate on small errands so she became familiar with the main routes of life: shopping, transport and communications, which had all changed during her absence. The experience reminded her of being a tourist in a foreign country but this now was subtly more unnerving. She was misled by apparently familiar things making her feel on sure ground, only to be tripped up because they had unexpectedly changed. She was often exhausted and baffled at the end of her outings without having achieved anything, as she complained to Daimeon.

Although such basic rehabilitation took all her energy and the hostel made sure that her life was structured, she felt that structure imposed and unrelated to her, and therefore irksome. It might have been a help at the beginning, she conceded, but by the end of the second week she was inwardly protesting against it. She was supposed to be out of prison, to have ended her sentence, yet her life was ruled by others as much as ever. The thought of that made her feel claustrophobic and want to get violently out of all these systems in which she felt enmeshed. She did not want to do their chores any more, or be grateful for their care and protection. She was not a juvenile in need of that, and wanted to tell them that she must get on with her own life, which was her, and not their, business. She was mature enough to see that it was all very well to feel like that but to put it into practice needed thought and action.

She must ask Daimeon, the only person to help her find a place out there, in any sense; but the thought of that also rattled her. She was angry with Daimeon for being the one person she could always turn to, hating her dependence on him. She had fought against this in prison, making sure he knew that she was not dependent on his visits. When Daimeon arrived at the hostel late one afternoon, impatient to see her and apologetic for his lateness due to traffic hold-ups, he felt rebuffed by the very opposite of impatience for his arrival that Therese conveyed. She made all his urgency to get to her, his assumption that she would be waiting for him, seem out of place. Her behaviour suggested rather that it did not matter whether he came or not.

The experienced side of him reminded the other, which was taken aback and disappointed, that this situation was not new and was not to be taken at its face value. He had been rejected before and had come to understand that it was not ill feeling towards him but something else important in Therese that accounted for her off-putting attitude. 'I was looking forward to our going to the British Museum ... wondered whether you would like the idea . . .' The sentence started with keenness and fizzled out in doubt. He felt as if he were trying to light a sparkler in a drizzle.

More than ever, he felt this way of coming to take Therese out unsatisfactory. He too was fed up with it. She showed no sign of wanting to come out, yet it was no good staying here, where there was neither privacy nor any particular social activity. Daimeon did not realise that he was walking up and down as she had done at bad times in prison, which was particularly irritating to her. She looked at him exasperatedly. He said apologetically, 'Sorry, it's the reaction . . . after rushing here,' but felt sorry for himself. She might have just a little consideration for him. He looked at her tensely, waiting for some suggestion from her.

She felt trapped. She must get out of here but where was she to go? The idea of the British Museum horrified her. Trailing round the huge galleries and marvelling at the treasures of the past would make her feel the lack of a living present more acutely. She would again be in a vast institution when she urgently needed four walls around a little space that was her own. She must have that little space outside of prison so she could be both secluded and more open to the world; could come and go as she liked, be neither Horace's nor anyone else's prisoner.

She realised that she had never lived in the outside world without Horace or the aunts imprisoning her, or being in some institution, even if a loose kind. 'I must get somewhere to live, on my own,' she said to Daimeon with urgency both in her voice and face as she turned to him.

'Is it so bad here?' he asked; foolishly, he felt as soon as he had said it. After a moment's thought he said, 'I see; I can see you want . . . I was just taken by surprise because you hadn't mentioned it before but of course we always knew that this place was temporary.' Someone came into the room and went to turn on the TV so

Daimeon said rather desperately, 'Shall we go out for a bit? Just a walk. It's not raining that much.'

'You know I don't mind the rain,' she interrupted impatiently. 'I like it if we can walk and not hang around shops.' They were both irritable.

They walked in silence. Looking sideways at Therese in her blue raincoat that she had belted tightly around her, Daimeon thought she looked younger and more delicate than in prison. But then he had mostly seen her across a table and only for moments standing or walking. She looked as if she were shivering. It was damp but mild and he wondered if she were not well. 'Are you all right?' he asked anxiously.

She felt herself shaking but not with cold. She experienced some power within affecting her whole being with increasing pressure so that it felt dangerously as if it must burst out in some way. She felt her heart beat and her whole body vibrate so that she wondered what to do or what might happen. She could not explain to Daimeon. Even her teeth seemed to chatter through the pressure inside her. Was she going to explode? With what?

'We were going to talk about a place of your own,' Daimeon started hesitantly.

'Oh Daimeon, there's a church over there,' was an exclamation rather than a reply. Therese pointed across the road, where she had noticed a small Victorian church. 'Perhaps I can go in there. Perhaps . . . I feel so peculiar!' She saw herself just able to get in there and get on her knees when she no longer felt able to stand up, let alone walk.

Surprised and concerned, Daimeon took her elbow as they crossed the road to the church, where mercifully the door was not locked. He opened it and Therese walked in as if she were a pilgrim who had walked a hundred miles and only had the strength left to drop to her knees, almost helplessly, in one of the pews.

Oh God! God! God! she pleaded internally. The

immense, uncontrollable pressure inside her that filled her chest to bursting and made her feel the muscles on her neck stand out with intense strain went into this one appeal by her body and soul. She pleaded Oh God! with her whole being. As after an earthquake or hurricane when all the regular structure of houses and whole streets lie flattened on the ground, when the usual paraphernalia of life is so much rubble, she felt there was nothing left of her so-called life. She wondered if there had even been anything of substance when all she could see or feel was meaningless debris. She had seen pictures of people after a bomb attack salvaging odd things from the rubble. She had nothing to save or recover. She felt empty and helpless, as if totally deflated and flattened. But there was a potentially dangerous, flickering fire in the wreckage within.

All the unbearable pressure inside her went into that single call. God! It was all that needed saying with all her might, soul and mind. In the prison chapel services she always wondered why the first and foremost commandment to love God with all your heart, soul and mind left the body out. It was her whole being that now needed God desperately and cried out for Him, and was nothing without God; was like the dead bones to which Ezekiel was taken and which needed God's will to bring them together, and His breath to give them new life. 'Please God! Please God! Please God!' She felt that she could say just these words for ever, like monks who endlessly repeat one simple chant. Have me in life not death! Give me a body and a way! was her silent prayer.

She had been propped up by outside constraints; the prison, the hostel. What was she? She would have said 'nothing' were it not for the overpowering pressure within her, the very strength of which had reduced her to utter weakness so she collapsed on this church stone floor. Only in directing that overpowering force within to God, the source of all power, was it to be prevented from causing havoc. Only from that source could come purposeful direction of this energy. Only in turning towards God all that was within her could she ever become whatever she might be, and have anywhere to go. She was frightened of having to get up and leave this church where she could address God with all of herself. It felt impossible to manage unless she submitted to Him at every point and all the time.

That submission to God was real. The terrible pressure within ceased to course through her threateningly. She had not disposed of it but it was a power that must find its particular way in life by the will of God, to which she must be attentive and alert. She would need to wait in faith. She was convinced that there was no other way. It was not a question of thought but a fact of life and death. All discussions about God, even questioning the existence of God as there had been at college, seemed now ridiculous; like arguing whether there was such a thing as fire when you were about to be engulfed in flames.

Therese came up from her knees to sit on the pew and saw Daimeon at the front of the church, absorbed in reading the inscription on an old tombstone on the floor. She sat quietly watching him when suddenly there came into her mind, like an announcement made by someone else, that she loved Daimeon. It struck her as incredible. She had found peace in looking at him in a moment of indeterminate being, having risen from the turmoil below to the threshold of the world that had as yet no shape or form for her. She felt as if she had been caught unawares; as if something or someone had taken advantage of her vulnerable state to pronounce this extraordinary fact.

It seemed too close for her to be able to push it away, but she did not know how to accommodate it. Oh no! she wanted to say firmly. No, no! That couldn't be right. Absolutely not. She was not that sort of person. That was not for her; others, yes. She? Daimeon? The frightening thing was that she could not help seeing it as shockingly obvious, at the same time as being sure that it was out of the question. She looked anxiously to her side and behind her, as if to make sure that no one had seen what she had seen. Daimeon, ahead of her, was reassuringly absorbed in the tombstone, so he would not know. Even so, she felt that she must hide what had come to her, when he rejoined her.

Then to her much greater alarm she felt the same terrifying great force, from which she had only been saved by falling on her knees before God, rising up in her again. It was like an angry being roused again. What had she done to provoke it? Could she assuage this terrible force that in a second reduced her again to utter weakness, even helplessness? My God help me! She must try to understand the meaning of this extraordinary, painful power within.

She could then feel and dimly see someone far down within her who, after the initial angry rising up against her, had fallen back in dreadful distress and inconsolable weeping. She could only wish to bring some comfort to one so deeply distressed that she seemed beyond comfort. She could only mentally put a hand on the hunched body of which she had an image, crouched in a heap within her. The familiar distress of this person seemed something in her that was beyond time and place. Her sympathy flowed to what she thought of as an ageless woman. But this was not enough; more was demanded of her. She was responsible for this distress here and now. Everlasting though it might be, she had now unwittingly aroused and enflamed it.

What had she done? She had learnt that she loved Daimeon; a fact she could only regard as shameful. To hide it seemed the only possible course, as if she had no choice in the matter. But now there was a disturbing awareness of a link between this attitude and the utterly distressed, permanently sobbing person within her. It was borne in on her that what she thought and did intensified the distress within. She realised with astonishment that her rejection of any idea of loving Daimeon violated a vital part of herself, and aroused violent protest at the suffering caused.

Therese came to see that, however strange it might seem, she took for granted that she could not and must not love; that she treated love as something shameful, never to be admitted. This had been an unquestioned axiom all her life. She felt she would die of shame if she were known to love Daimeon. It seemed no more admissible to her than if she were wanting to kill him.

It seemed that the admission of love would in some sense kill her. Not only could she not summon the strength to stand up and state the apparently dreadful secret, that would surely mean her being laughed to scorn, but she would even feel she had committed an unforgivable wrong that would bring death on her. It sounded like madness but felt an undeniable fact that made her sweat and shake with fear and pain.

A dispassionate, observing part of her saw that this was a reversal of the truth. Some profound personal experience must have convinced her of this falsehood, imbued with enormous emotional power. However mad it might sound, there was no doubt in her that to admit that she loved Daimeon would somehow kill her. That she truly loved someone must not be considered for one second. It was felt as something so terrible that it was apparently like the Gorgon's head: to look at it would kill her. She could only turn away and hide her face from it. Only in trying to shut it out of her view could she feel safe.

That was how she had lived all her life and how, it seemed, she must go on. Just as she was feeling calmer, she was reminded of where this 'only possible way' of keeping her loving out of sight and life, of hiding it as something utterly shameful, led. She had been shown that this 'only possible way' caused the never-ending weeping and 'gnashing of teeth' deep within herself.

Daimeon, who had looked up from the tombstone inscriptions and started walking towards her, saw her looking at him with an extraordinary, desperate look that he had never seen on anyone's face. He wanted to shake himself free of such horror, as of a terrifying dream. It gave him the fearful idea that she might kill herself. Was that to be the end, just when she was well on the way out, to a new life?

Therese was sitting still in a terrified huddle when Daimeon came back to her pew and quietly sat down next to her. Although it was afternoon, they seemed to sit in darkness, in total uncertainty and suspense. When Therese found herself keeling over towards Daimeon so her head rested on his shoulder, she departed from the way to which she had always kept as the only one that would not bring disaster on her.

Now she had left that path. Leaning over towards Daimeon, she felt as if she were stepping into an abyss. As if she might be throwing herself into the outer darkness, she dared take the first step on the way of love. She did it in compassion for the one within, in eternal-seeming distress. It was as if she were giving her life for that other. This was the end of her prison sentence. Perhaps it was the beginning of her salvation.